THE
FANG
GANG

Kevin S. Hendrick

Prologue

They all proclaimed, "The west is the best!" It was a place where many ventured; many without any clues as to what might await them in this unknown and unforgiving wilderness. Most from town to town, or settlement to settlement, lived day by day. Prayer after prayer, and meal after meal. They all hoped for a chance of survival here, and a chance to prosper. However, then there came this unholy, and unknowingly powerful force. A force of more than disease; a curse if you would? The dreaded curse that brought the dead back to life. Many thought it to be European folklore. No, it was very real for this one town of Canden, Texas. The curse of the undead, Vampirism.

Though this is obviously a supernatural tale; it in some ways is a reflection upon the unknown. The type of situations that no mere mortal can explain for him or herself. It quite honestly reflects upon the history of western expansion, and a great mystery that was indeed "the true unknown" and that is the western frontier. Think of this as satirical, intense, and unbelievable. A tale woven around the fun of the horror and westerns that some grew up with. To that notion, this novel is dedicated to you. The year is 1880, the place is Texas, and the season is winter.

Chapter 1

Here I was, Terence Edwin Hill, hidden deep in the brush, on the side of a river, and it's so cold I can barely feel my hands at the moment. Though I have my gloves on and the interior of my wool coat covers me, I'm still miserable as hell. At this exact moment, I have to take a piss. But trust me, I'm not about to stick my pecker out in this weather. It's below average for temperatures, and the winds aren't helping. There's a river in front of my view; it's frozen in some spots. Most of everything around me is dead. There's barren trees, a few bushes, and there's not much wildlife prowling about either.

Though I must say, being a bounty hunter has its perks. For one, I get to stay out in the wilderness to myself, and I get wonderful views of the mountains of North Texas and Indian Territory. Though honestly the most stimulating part about my job is I get to kill, and I get paid for doing so. It's a job not meant for the faint of heart. I'm currently waiting on two bounties at the moment. The first is Roger Lee Allen, a man wanted for killing two men in a saloon in Fort Worth, Texas. The other is his partner in crime

Patrick Dickerson, he robbed a train that was inbound to Lubbock, and he also robbed a Wells Fargo carriage in Clay County last August and he shot both drivers. Each one of their bounties come in at $200 each.

I sit here, still as the trees that surround me. I had seen both of the men earlier, around a half an hour ago to be exact. They had both set up camp in a ravine, about five-hundred yards away from me. Both of them I watched from a distance; they were passing around a bottle of whiskey and they were eating what looked to be deer. I figured they'd be making their way over to get some water at the river soon, considering all the whiskey they had. Though I've been in my place for a few minutes; it feels like the cold is getting colder. My breath that I see seems to get denser as well. In a moment of boredom, I pulled out my pipe, which was in the interior pocket of my coat. I then whipped out a match, lit it, and then slowly lit my pipe. My eyes continued to keep a gaze on the adjacent riverbank; there I knew any minute one of them scoundrels would appear. The pipe tasted like honey, but it was quite bland as it had been in my pocket for a long time. Regardless, I still smoked it without one care. It was the only thing keeping me warm in this unearthly cold weather.

My head though, started to throb with every puff of smoke, and my heart pounded. The anxiousness began to set in. It was always a constant worry, believe me, every bounty hunter had it. We always questioned if we'd miss, what would we do? Thankfully that was a rare situation but considering most of us took our work quite seriously, it was a question that plagued every single one of our minds. Hopefully, I can kill them where they stand, round up their bodies, and then make my way further into Indian territory afterward. This is where I would capture my third bounty, Fredrick Boothe. Boothe is worth $500; he shot a state representative in the back of the head which paralyzed the representative from the neck down. Either way, by the end of this week, once I get back to Austin, I'm hoping to be taking sacks full of money back home with me, no doubt.

Something that plagues my mind also, are the eerie sounds of a pack of coyotes; they're howling off in the distance. Thankfully, these wild dogs are miles from me, so hopefully I will not encounter them later. After a few weary moments, I look up and see the sun in the sky. It's about to settle over an adjacent mountain side. I must say, the sky looks as if God himself dropped a beautiful trough of colors upon it. The western sky has pink, orange, and blues in it. It's marvelous, and honestly it's a sight that I never get tired of. Unfortunately, I know the night will soon consume the beauty, and I'm just hoping my bounties will come along any minute now. I still had my pipe dangling in my mouth, and it still tasted stale. But I still smoked it regardless as the warmth of it feels good in my throat. I know later, I'm going to have the nastiest cough imaginable. It will be a prolonged misery for certain.

As my thoughts ramble, I hear my horse about a hundred yards away from me snort loudly. With that sound, I'm hoping my two desperados didn't hear the stead. The last thing I need is to give myself away. It's pretty quiet; I can hear for miles. I can hear the rustling of the grass; I also hear a few deer off in a field, and I still hear the cries of the coyotes. There's always other sounds that sprinkle in as well.

Despite this dead, but lively world, I continued to stay still and silent in my place. I hear the beautiful majestic sounds of the water flowing downstream. It's the type of sound that could almost put any man to sleep, and much to my surprise it started to. I began to slowly drift away, but the sudden sound of footsteps awakened me. I quickly gazed through the brush, and there they were. Those two sons of guns, walking through the brush on the adjacent riverbank. They were sort of stumbling it seemed, and with that I thought, these two must be drunk. I thought to myself, with them two drunks like that, their coordination should be miles off. This should be two easy kills, no problem.

I quietly grabbed my shotgun; it was resting on a large rock behind me. I then slowly cradled it carefully, and then I swiftly shifted my position which was cross legged, to a shrug-like kneel. I still remained hidden out of sight. The two looked to be laughing and pissing around. They both bent down with their water flasks and filled them with flowing water. I remained calm, but my blood soon began to boil, I was absolutely nervous. I concentrated carefully on the two men; I was the predator and they were the prey. I then slowly rested my index finger on the trigger, not pressing it though. The reason for this was because both men were moving quite frequently, and I was waiting for the perfect opportunity to make the perfect two kills.

Everything around me seemed to pester me for some odd reason. I felt like everything that ever existed, every living creature, every little sound, and everything that was in motion around me in the natural world was locking in on me. Everything depended on this, and I began to sweat as I locked my focus on the two ever so moving men.

Roger was tall; he had blonde hair and blue eyes. He was wearing old ragged clothes and he had on an old ten-gallon hat. Patrick had black hair and brown eyes. He had a curled mustache and he too was wearing ragged clothes, but he was not wearing a hat unlike Roger. Patrick was also holding a whiskey bottle. Both men looked as if they hadn't bathed in God knows how long. I swear, I could smell them all the way over here in the brush, God it was awful. My gun was moving slightly left and slightly to the right; I remained affixed to the men. Then, perfection was in my sights. The perfect shot, Patrick had stopped for a moment in front of Roger, and I knew there was no better time to fire than now. It was a risk, but I took it. I pulled the trigger. *BANG*! I got Patrick directly in the backside. The first shot I fired hit Patrick in the shoulder to be exact; I then noticed the whiskey bottle in Patrick's hand. Old Pat was stumbling towards Roger who started frantically looking around. The bottle was obstructing though; as it was right near Roger's face. In regards to the movement, I had underestimated Roger's stagger. He swayed left, that's when I quickly fired another shot, hitting the whiskey bottle instead of Roger. I missed, but it still injured Roger for sure. The bottle instantly exploded, and the shards of glass flew right into Roger's face, who instantly reacted in pain. I took the pipe out of my mouth, shook it, and then put it back in my pocket. I then slowly stood to my feet, hearing Roger's agonizing groans and swearing. "Ah, dang flabbit!" He exclaimed. I started slowly walking towards Roger who had fallen onto his back. Patrick was deader than the wintertime air I was breathing. Roger, though, was holding his face; blood was in his hands. Patrick fell face first into the water, hitting his head on a rock where he had busted it wide open. I soon got right up on Roger, he was swearing everything in the book, "Ah, screw you bounty hunter! You yellow belly dog! You piece of dog vomit!" He cried. "Ah, damn you to hell!" Roger kept groaning; I then pointed my gun right at Roger's head.

I then remarked before I pulled the trigger. "Sorry I had to shatter your plans, old Rog," I sarcastically stated. I then fired my gun; Roger finally was silenced. The bullet instantly hit the top of Roger's head, causing it to literally explode. Blood and brain matter went everywhere. I then whispered to myself, inhaling the gun smoke and holding the barrel up to my nose, "Ah, yellow belly…that insult never gets old," I remarked. I grinned and began the long tedious process of rounding up my two bounties.

I swiftly drug Roger's tall body back over to the riverbank, and then quickly carried Patrick's back over as well. Both men had an unbearable smell, and both of them smelt like straight Old Forester. I laid them on the cold dirt riverbank, it was quite moist. The sun was starting to sink low over the mountains. I then walked back over to my horse and grabbed two large sheets. These sheets were going to be used to wrap the dead bodies in. I also grabbed a bundle of twine to tie them. The wind was still blowing gently, and the cold was still biting my face as I made my way back over to the bodies. I worked diligently, scooting both bodies onto the flat laid sheets. I folded the sheets over each body, and then finally I tied them tightly with the twine. One at a time I carried each body with me; Roger was the hardest to transport since he weighed the most and was tall. However, Patrick was short, and I carried his body in my arms with ease. I then placed both men on a sled that my horse had been pulling. This custom-made sled was made from some rope for the bottom. The sled was also being used to pull along my food and other essential remedies. For the time being though, it would be my personal dead body cradle.

I was surprised everything could fit together on the sled like it did. Mainly because my sled was loaded down from all of the essentials that I had brought. Realizing that possibly the two's fire might still be going in their camping area, I climbed up on my horse and rode off back into the gorge where the two men had been laying low. The sled pulled along quite nicely, despite going over the river on a rock slab, the bodies stayed exactly in their positions. To be safe, I had tied both to the sled with extra rope, assuring that both would withstand the long treacherous journey into the mountains. I noticed as I was going slightly down hill towards the ravine, that the large adjacent mountain side before me was now covered with a large white cloud. I was hoping this wasn't a bad snowstorm. The mountain was quite large and was located in Indian Territory, and it was right in the general direction of my next bounty too.

I eventually reached the bottom of the ravine where the men had been camping. The two had pitched up a tent, a rough looking one I might add. There were whiskey bottles on the ground, and it looked like the two had been playing cards. Their fire was still going. But as a last resort, I still needed a little bit of tobacco buzz for my long trip. I noticed a pack of Figurado cigars by the fire. I figured there'd be no harm done if I stole this pack. Also, I stole a flask of water. Though more importantly, I needed a cigar at this point, a celebration was to be in order for my killing. I whipped out one from the pack; then I used the two's fire as my light. I took a puff of the cigar, man, it tasted so good. It had a way better taste than my pipe had earlier no question. It almost had a sweet fruity taste to it, like blueberry or something? I opened up the flask that I stole and tilted it over the fire. However, nothing came out. I went over and grabbed my flask and finally put the fire out that way. I took a few glances around the ravine. I then freed both men's horses, made a quick grin, then I jumped back on my horse and proceeded onward into Indian Territory where my third bounty awaited me.

Was I stubborn? Of course I was. Was I hell bent? Well, most of the time. Was I cunning though? To be honest, I can not answer that question for once. Being a bounty hunter is tough, but I'm a man of my duty, and what has to be done, has to be done!

Chapter 2

       The night was hastily approaching as my stead was pressing onward through the cold. Soon, a light snow shower began to accompany my horse and I. The sled was still pulling and it stayed perfectly in line with my trail. I trucked over some rocks, hills, and even small creeks. My supplies and the bodies still stayed intact. The sun was now over the mountain ridge, the night time sky had started to consume the last remnants of the day. I could still hear that pack of coyotes I heard earlier, in fact, the sounds were getting closer. The horse was strutting along perfectly, nothing could stop it. The stead took me through a small ravine, then I found myself out in the middle of a wide-open valley. Mountains surrounded me all around and it seemed to get lighter. I was out in the middle of an open prairie, with not one sign of life except for me, my horse, and the coyotes far behind on a ridge. There were a few trees here and there, but mainly the prairie was covered with grass, bushes, and a few small creeks. The snow started to taper off a bit, but it soon picked up again as my horse got closer and closer to Clay Mountain.

Clay Mountain was essentially the border line that separated the state of Texas from Indian Territory. Either way, I was hoping to cross over it before twilight. The sounds of the coyotes began to pick up again once more as the cold wind brushed against my face. This though, must've been another pack, because these howls and barking were coming from an adjacent hillside ahead of me. I then motioned for the horse to move faster, hoping to maybe outrun the pack, and get out of their territory. However, the barking and carrying on started to pick up more, despite the fact I was moving away. The worst fear had come to mind, this pack may be stalking me and my horse. I motioned again for the horse to pick up speed. The horse went faster, hoofing itself strongly through the brisk cold. The howls and barking continued, they crept into my ears and made the hairs rise on the back of my neck. My stead still pressed on; this horse was not about to let anything on the face of this Earth spook it. God, I thought to myself, please lead me through this in one piece, I prayed in my mind.

Eventually, I noticed that Clay Mountain was getting closer and getting much bigger in my sight. The pack of the wild dogs' unearthly sounds started to get further and further away from me. I was breathing heavily and my lungs were tightening. However, I soon became calm, and I began to rest my weary thoughts. My horse was trotting along hard, every single step felt heavier and heavier by the second. Soon, more and more trees started to come into view; we hit a massive wave of snow. Snow, and nothing but it, began falling heavily on us creating a whiteout. Now I needed to find a good spot to camp for the night. My breath got denser; I could feel that the temperature had definitely started to drop significantly. The cold was starting to make my whole body numb, from my head to my toes, but there I sat still pressing onward. The snow picked up more, I began to truck up a large hill, the trees became more predominant. Soon, I found myself in a forest, and eventually I was on what looked to be a dirt road in the middle of a tree grove.

The trees were oak, some trees were apples and peaches. However, none of those trees bore any fruit. Either one of these trees wouldn't bloom until Spring or Summer. My horse still trotted fast, but I soon signaled for the horse to walk steadily as I wanted to observe my various surroundings. The snow was now falling steadily, but I soon felt something watching me. I felt a presence, in particular I felt that something was up the path ahead of me. I gazed my eyes forward; the grove I was in was located on a flat piece of land at the bottom of Clay Mountain. Through the grove, I started to notice a faint light, almost what looked like a lantern hanging from the front of a stagecoach. I then noticed the silhouette of four horses. My horse walked further and further, we started getting closer, and now I could clearly see that there was a driver at the front on this stagecoach. However, the driver seemed to be hiding himself under a bearskin, presumably the driver was keeping him or herself warm. My horse finally got within twenty feet or so of the stagecoach; that's when I stopped the stead in its tracks. The stagecoach, a few seconds later, stopped as well. The horses, both mine and the stagecoach, snorted, as my curiosity began to rise. I wanted to know the true identity of this mysterious looking driver. I climbed down off my horse and grabbed my Winchester rifle just in case. Just in case maybe, it was old Fredrick Boothe himself.

I cautiously walked forward towards the coach; it had those four horses pulling it. The ground in the grove was covered with newly fallen snow. I could hear the snow *crunch*, in every step I took. I'm pretty sure there was some ice in this snow. I took a few cautious steps towards the side of the coach and stopped at the driver. I observed him; the bearskin he had on was quite large. This bear had been gutted well, even the head was still there on top, the arms looked floppy. It was the only thing I'm sure that was keeping the driver warm. Wanting another hit of tobacco, I whipped out one of the stolen cigars and lit it. I stood there for a few seconds, slowly gaining the urge to speak. I found it odd that this guy didn't want to give me any word, he was silent. "Well, it would appear that you're the shy one in this here conversation, so allow me to break the silence," I took a puff and grinned. "So, Where's your wind taking you stranger?" I asked.

The driver turned and looked in my direction, "I'm heading eastward," it was a man's voice in reply; he then pointed his index finger in the direction east. "I plan on finding a good spot to camp there for the night," the man added; his voice sounded muffled.

"Well," I replied, pausing and staring at the ground. "You better push yourself, this snow's starting to pick up my friend."

"Are you a lawman?" The rider asked.

"I'm not, I'm a bounty hunter, why do you ask?" I inquired.

"Just curious, my friend," the rider replied; I began to pick up on a foreign accent, it sounded German.

"Who or what you got in the back of that coach?" I inquired.

"Well, more than likely, I'm carrying along a log right now," the rider giddily added. I was then confused by the driver's statement. I quickly became blunter and sterner.

"Could you please take off that bearskin? Also, what do you mean by log?" I asked politely.

"Well, a sleeping person, that's what I was referring to, and personally I'm quite cold thank you," the man replied; moving his hands freely.

"You got somebody else in there?" I then pointed my gun over towards the coach door. At this, the driver put up his hands and then took off his bearskin, and at this I clearly knew that this man wasn't Fredrick. It was a slim looking man; he looked no more than a day over fifty-five.

"Listen," the driver anxiously stated, "I'm not looking for any trouble, my name is Doctor Dietrich Von Branson," the driver, now a doctor, then put out his hand for me to shake it, to which I did. The doctor gave me a firm shake, he smiled.

"I'm Terence Hill," I introduced myself to the doctor.

"Nice to meet you Mister Hill, but just to let you know, bounty hunter, I'm currently on a very elaborate journey," Dietrich said.

I smiled at Dietrich's remark, "Well, what do you mean by elaborate? And again who exactly is in there?" I asked, tilting my head towards the carriage.

"Well, it's a long story my good man, but I'm carrying the sheriff with me right now, and I'm sure he would be delighted to meet you," Dietrich replied.

"A sheriff is with you?" I asked.

"Yes, in fact, let me wake up the sleeping beauty while I'm pondering on that thought," Dietrich replied; he then banged on the carriage door behind him. "Sheriff!" Dietrich shouted.

"Yeah! Son of a!" I heard a muffled voice in the carriage exclaim and curse about.

"We have an unexpected visitor, sir," Dietrich said with a smirk.

"Alright doc, just give me a second to get my two cents together!" The muffled voice in the carriage shouted.

"Give him a minute, he's been like this ever since we left Kessler's Ridge," Dietrich said jokingly.

"Give me a damn minute here," The voice inside continually spoke; then the door opened, and within the flickering of my dim lantern I saw an old friend come into view.

"Well, tickle my fancy and put me in a dress! Florence?" I inquired, noticing it was indeed Florence Potter, my old-time friend and former deputy, now sheriff from Canden, Texas. It was unbelievable.

"Well if I ain't one of the chosen few?" Florence asked himself. He then projected a huge smile of relief. "Well if ain't the best damn boss I ever had, Sheriff, oh I'm sorry, Bounty Hunter!" Florence brought me close and gave me a huge grasping hug.

I patted the top of Florence's right shoulder, "Good to see you again Florence!" I exclaimed.

"The same goes for me, double that statement!" Florence replied; his cold breath was fogging up my focal points.

"You two know each other?" Dietrich inquired.

"Since we was no more than little tiny kiddos!" Florence replied.

"Yes indeed, and have you been alright?" I asked Florence.

"Oh you know, same piece of shit I was when you left me!" Florence jokingly replied.

"Well, that doesn't surprise me at the least," I responded, smiling big as I did. "Now, don't mind me asking, but why in Sam's hill nation, are you

20

two out here?" I curiously asked. I then noticed Florence was getting nervous.

"Well, doc?" Florence nervously turned his head away from me, directing all of his nervous ques towards Dietrich. "It's your little bloody expedition," Florence said.

"I guess with the way you put it like that, it might as well be, Sheriff," Dietrich responded. He then straightened himself on top of the carriage. "Mister Hill, I must confess, we are hunting, but not for wild game," Dietrich began explaining.

"You two ain't bounty hunting too? Are you?" I asked, laughing under my question.

"You tell him, because I sure as hell ain't," Florence stated; I then noticed Florence had a small, rolled cigarette dangling from the corner of his mouth.

I turned and looked towards Dietrich, "To an extent Mister Hill, we are bounty hunting, but not for financial stakes, thrills, or for the sake of finding our people alive," Dietrich said.

"I'm confused?" I inquired; I was feeling quite anxious as a cold chill traveled up my back. I heard Florence from behind me light a match and ignite his cigarette. Now he was furthering his silence I could tell. "You see I'm looking for a man named Fredrick Boothe, he's got a high price on his forehead," I stated. I quickly noticed Dietrich's face; the name Fredrick had caught his attention.

"Did you say Fredrick Boothe?" Dietrich inquired.

"Yeah, hunting him dead or alive doctor, what's it to you?" I asked.

Dietrich was silent for a few seconds; he then cleared his throat. "Well, he, along with our other suspects, are neither dead nor alive, I'm afraid," Dietrich nervously responded.

"What do you mean by that doctor?" I inquired.

"Mister Hill we are hunting vampires… Six to be exact…Mister Boothe is one of them, and I'm afraid the matter will only further churn your mind in confusion… So on that, would you like to camp here for the night? I have some explaining to do?" Dietrich asked with a smile. His tone and delivery though, had a very awkward sound to it now.

Then within a dead silence of about ten seconds, I responded subtly with, "Sure."

The rest of my journey, had certainly become interesting. Both Florence and the Doctor Dietrich Branson, were both looking for the same man, as I was. There was though, but one question that crossed my mind, and that was within regards to this vampire hunt and statement. The doctor and Florence were tracking down criminals; though there was something very otherworldly about them. What the hell did it all mean? I wasn't for certain in all honesty? My trip had only now grown stranger I'm afraid.

Chapter 3

Let's get one thing straight here, I'm a bounty hunter, and a man of logic and reason. However, hearing some claim that the man I was hunting, had now become some blood-sucking demon from the bowels of hell, had certainly become an interesting affair for sure. But it also baffled and flabbergasted me. One thing that kept with me though, was the horrible stench of my clothes. Good God, it's been three days since I last bathed. I was hoping to find a good hot spring somewhere in Indian Territory, but for right now, I've got to sit here with this stench. There's nothing worse though, than sitting around this fire and grinning like an asshole, I tell you. However, I needed to talk some matters over with Dietrich and Florence. Honestly, it ain't too bad, though I don't smell too good, I'm at least able to eat up a quick bite. Florence had brought along with him a loaf of bread and some soup. However, the soup had no flavor, despite the fact that it had sliced potatoes in it. However, it felt warm, and the bread at least had some flavor. Though there wasn't much flavor to the bread, it at least was something digestible, and it wasn't too bad. I couldn't explain myself in this situation though. I ate like the horseman of famine was coming through tomorrow. The food wasn't anything to write home about, but I consumed it with much delight. Son of a bitch, I was hungry!

Dietrich had settled the carriage directly behind our camp. The horses had begun to settle down, as Dietrich and Florence ate vigorously, as none of us talked. We sat there, on uncomfortable stones, freezing our asses off. The snow had let up, and we ended up camping in a ravine about five hundred yards from the grove where we had met earlier. My eyes wandered throughout the camp; there were many trees surrounding us. Mainly the trees were cedars and oaks. We had pitched up two tents, one was originally supposed to be for the doctor, while the other for the Sheriff. But I guess a compromise was to soon be in order. Either I would sleep with Florence, or I would sleep with Dietrich in the same tent? However, that was the least of my concerns.

I took a good stern look at Dietrich and Florence. Florence had that same old curled dark-blonde mustache I remember him having a few years back. I had noticed however, that he had shed off a few pounds it seemed. Florence was wearing a large white ten-gallon hat, a beige colored coat, which had many tassels hanging from under the sleeves, and he was wearing the same color for his pants. He also wore a pair of heavy-duty boots which had spurs on them. Dietrich seemed to be a much simpler man; he wore a black button up coat. Under the coat, I noticed what looked like a nice white button up shirt, he wore black pants, and he also had on black boots.

I continued to *slurp* on my soup, the warmth of it was probably the greatest feeling in the world at this point. I then began to speak. "So, Dietrich, a doctor huh?" Dietrich nodded at my inquiry. "How long have you been in Canden?" I then asked.

"Well," Dietrich started to speak, while he finished chewing. "I've been in Canden for, let's see, this Thursday would make," Dietrich began counting on his fingers. "One, two, three, four, five months...Five months now that I've been the town's doctor, and all I can say is I wish I knew where the time went," Dietrich said with a smile. He then took another bite of his bread.

"Did you become a doctor in Germany?" I asked.

"Yes, I did, I went to a school in Munich," Dietrich replied.

"Why did you get yourself in such an elaborate profession?" I asked, slurping on my soup.

"Well," Dietrich replied, he then took a hanky from his breast pocket and wiped off some soup from his chin, "Honestly Mister Hill, the reason is quite complicated I'm afraid...You see, my beloved, Vera...She past ten years ago this very week actually...Cholera found her, very bad case too," Dietrich started to knot up in the throat, he looked as if he was about to shed a small tear, but he held it back. "She was the world to me...So naturally, I took that as profound strive...I then dedicated my life to medicine after that, registering myself at the Munich School of Medicine, you see I was thirty five then, can you believe that...God, the time has flown...Anyways, now I'm here, and it's a move I do not regret that's for sure," Dietrich concluded.

"Sorry to hear about your wife, I'm sure that was a very difficult time for you?" I inquired; feeling sympathy now for the doctor.

"Indeed it was," Dietrich replied, he then smiled lightly and added more to his talk. "But, the Lord pushed me through, I got my education, practiced in Germany for a bit, then I immigrated over to America where I practiced in New Orleans for five years, and needless to say all bad omens sank to the bottom of the most endless sea after I came here," Dietrich concluded once more.

"Well, that's nice to hear doc, but why did you make the big trip out here into this God forsaken pit that we call home?" I asked.

"In all honesty," Dietrich began, smiling as he did. His face then switched to a stern look. "I guess you could say I wanted a little bit of peace and serenity," He then admirably said.

"Well, I believe you got neither of them things out here my friend," I replied with sarcasm.

"Yes, yes, most certainly," Dietrich responded, laughing at himself.

"Yeah, you missed that shit, by a country mile," Florence chimed in with laughter, Dietrich and I then joined in laughter with Florence.

I then caught my breath, and got serious "So, vampires?" I inquired, with much disbelief.

"That is the verdict my friend...You see," Dietrich then placed down his bowl and straightened his posture. "I was in Canden for nearly twenty weeks, then out of nowhere, folks there began dying without any explanation...Then matters got even more strange...Long story short, those folks had become undead, we had mainly prostitutes who had fallen prey... We even had a kid we had to stake...It was the dark times for sure," Dietrich explained in pity.

"Stake?" I inquired.

"Yes," Dietrich replied, "We had to stake their hearts with a sharp piece of wood...We pierced it right through their chests, then we had to bless their bodies with sacrament...We must've staked more than ten folks, before we drove some of them out of Canden," Dietrich stated in affirmative words.

"You said six of 'em?" I inquired; slurping my soup as I did.

"Yes, there are six, but mainly there's three we're after," Dietrich responded, crossing his arms.

Confused, I asked, "I thought y'all were after six?"

"Well, we are, but them three, Thomas Oswald, Julius Verna, and Fredrick Boothe…Them's the ones who caused the most hell," Florence stated, grinning on his face.

"Mister Hill," Dietrich began, stroking his chin, "I understand that this is a lot to process…Shoot, the Sheriff couldn't hardly comprehend it himself when it all started…But rest assured, I will find all of them, and I shall do, what I have to do," He spoke; pounding his fists into each other in subtle rage.

"So, you're going to perform these here rituals you speak of, staking and blessing the bodies?" I asked.

"Yes, what other way have I?" Dietrich inquired.

"Well, doc, it just seems shit like that…Is a little sacrilegious to me, also I'm not one to believe in tales of ghouls and goblins," I snickered, I then whipped out a cigar and lit it using an old match from my coat pocket.

"Mister Hill, these are not just tales we tell, your Sheriff is a witness to that," Dietrich then nodded his head towards Florence.

Florence nodded and added to Dietrich's word. "Ter, as one to testify, I've seen some crazy stuff! God I swear on the book of life itself I have," I could read a worrying look upon Florence's face.

"Well, gentlemen, you see I'm a man who sees before he believes," I then took a puff of my cigar.

"Well, I assure you Mister Hill, you will believe, we're edging closer to one of them now," Dietrich stated giddily.

"One of them three?" I inquired.

"Well, one of the town's folk, three other people escaped after we blessed Canden, a prostitute named Elizabeth Wilkens, bordello owner Marcy Greene, and a traveler whom we've identified as Peter Shepard...We later found out he was from Austin," Dietrich replied.

I then collected my breath, knowing all that mattered was Fredrick. "What about Fredrick and the other two?" I asked.

"They've formed a possy, an alliance I'm afraid, but we're hot on their trail too," Florence responded.

"I see," I stated, taking a smoke once more, then I continued. "Well, I could give a rat's puckered up asshole, about them other two, Fredrick is mine!" I explained with affirmative intentions.

"That may be easier said than done, Mister Hill...But you must understand that vampires are cunning, smart, ruthless, and above all, they will never give in," Dietrich stated with sternness.

"That may be doctor, but you see, I've got this here bounty I've got to collect, we're talking five hundred here, and it's on the line! I've frozen my nut sack off out here, and dang it I'm gonna get him!" I stated sternly.

"Ter, we understand, but all we're asking for is a little assistance here now...You know this land

30

better than any other man I've ever known," Florence said, while he ate his bread.

"Mister Hill, Florence and I were discussing some matters over by the bushes when you weren't around, and we believe you could provide for us some guidance…I mean, we are looking for the same man, Fredrick…Be at that you are comfortable with this—"

I then interrupted Dietrich, "Now listen!" I stated with aggression, "I'm not about to perform some kind of a…Half ass ritual on some…thing! Or things for that matter! I came out here for my bounties, and I assure you that Mister Boothe is coming with me…Whether he's what you say he is or not," I then lowered my tone.

"Terence, listen," Florence caught my attention, "You can take him, no questions asked…But please help us…For Canden…It don't kill to have a third hand, and you know that better than any other Sheriff," Florence said with confidence.

"I ain't law no more Florence, I do what I want to do, when I want to do it…I'm my own boss now," I stated with pride. "I ain't going on some crazy ass expedition—"

"It's not crazy Mister Hill," Dietrich chimed in politely. "This is serious, now you know it yourself, where most criminals hide out here, and I think that the undead will do exactly as the living do…Where do people hide out around here?" Dietrich inquired.

Not wanting to be a part of their journey, I sarcastically responded, "They got places, I don't know?" I inquired in annoyance.

"Terence, come on! You know we're going to give you Boothe, and you know these lands best! The least you can do is give us directions here," Florence responded in anger.

At this point, I pondered with disbelief, but if the doctor and Florence would lead me to Fredrick, I guess I couldn't help myself but join their expedition. The part that bothered me though, was the absurdity of this here predicament. I had never dealt with such outrageous claims in my life, but Florence was an honest to God truthful man. Florence was also trustworthy, and I guess I couldn't have asked for a better deputy than what he was with me. Although times had changed, the doctor and Florence had been through so much with Canden. I guess, in the grand scheme of things, I couldn't argue with them. My two dead bounties that I had, laying on the back of my makeshift sled, would more than likely just freeze over the course of the next couple of days, but that was fine. I ain't got no due date for them bounties, and besides, this expedition did intrigue me in some way. However, I still had trouble accepting this. "Alright," I calmly started, "I'll help y'all...But I will collect my bounty, and in return I will provide you with accurate navigation," I said.

"Do most outlaws hide out in these lands?" Dietrich inquired.

"Not so much in Texas, but in Indian Territory... You see, Mister Boothe was suspected in those areas more recently, and that's why I'm out here you see," I stated. "Whether he was spotted as a human or not? I couldn't tell you," I then calmly delivered.

"You possibly think them others are with him too?" Florence asked.

"Possibly, usually gangs move around together, but um...You're the expert on these vampires, maybe you might know a thing or two?" I nodded my head over towards Dietrich, while I took a puff of my cigar again.

"Well, I'm just very knowledgeable In folklore...Growing up in Germany, much of my family would share stories of these undead creatures," Dietrich spoke with a straight forward grin. "However, those stories are now reality my friend, and I'm sure it will take a lot of persuasion, but you will see," Dietrich said.

"I'm sure I will," I responded, knowing that I still was in a state of disbelief. "Again though," I then added with a tremble beneath my voice. "I've gotta see it first doc, oh and by the way, how the hell do we protect ourselves from such cunning creatures?" I inquired, sarcastically.

"Well my friend," Dietrich began as he stood up, smiling as he did. "I'm glad you asked."

"Yeah," Florence chimed in, "Terence you ain't gotta worry about protection, I think the doctor's got us covered...He brought a shit ton of shit, in that there poke," Florence nodded his head over towards Dietrich's handbag; which was lying on the ground.

Dietrich then unbuttoned the bag, "Yes, I have all the essential instruments needed, my friend," Dietrich then pulled out what looked to be garlic cloves. "These will do their job I assure you," Dietrich stated with glee.

He handed me the garlic cloves, as I examined them, I became bewildered, "Only thing I thought these damn things were good for, was giving you the shits," I said with sarcasm.

Dietrich laughed at my statement, "Oh, no my friend, these definitely will serve a much, much different purpose, I can assure you that."

Florence then spoke, as I continued to process what I had learned, "Yeah, the doc has been showing me the whole time what these here creatures fear, and let me tell you, these methods aren't just as easy as shooting them right dead center in the face," Florence then got close to me, he then took out his pipe, he was going to smoke it. "This here clove, if you can believe it," Florence began, as he took out a match to light his pipe. "This thing sends them running like hell, can you believe that? Something like that, so small, sends them running like a bunch of yellow bellies in Dodge City!" He exclaimed.

"That's not the only thing we will be using here," Dietrich chimed in, he then reached back into his bag, and pulled out more, multiple religious looking items. He withdrew a crucifix and wafers, holy water, and mustard seeds. I really became puzzled by this point.

"A Crucifix huh?" I examined the cross, as Dietrich gave it to me, "I guess that makes a whole lot of sense, but can they be killed?" I inquired in fear.

"Very particularly," Dietrich responded, "It's more than just killing, it has to be all of the methods that I mentioned earlier, like staking the heart...However, we did try sacred bullets back in Canden...They seemed to have worked out well."

"A sacred bullet?" I asked.

"Yes," Dietrich replied, shaking his head, and before he could finish, I figured it out on my own.

"You're talking about bullets...That has been blessed?" I then inquired about the second part.

"Blessed by holy water," Dietrich stated, whipping out a small containment of it from his bag. "We simply just take a bullet, and dip it in the water, subtly dry it...very simple actually," He concluded.

"You see Ter," Florence began, as he took a puff of his pipe, then he exhaled and continued. "Simple, you still get to bring your guns along, and you still get to do what you said you do."

"Kill Fredrick where he stands?" I inquired.

"Precisely," Dietrich replied, "We have the protection needed, we have you as a great navigator, and now we have a chance to rid the world of this evil," Dietrich said, smiling as he did.

By this point, it was quite plain to see that my own journey had turned into another journey. However, this journey was all about facing pure evil itself, and though I still couldn't believe it until I saw it, I was beyond intrigued by this whole matter. Were there really vampires out here? Or, have the doctor and Florence lost their damn minds? Either way, I guess this journey would only reveal that for me, and as these few thoughts bumped about in my head, I then added to the doctor's statements, "You said, rid the world of evil?" I curiously asked. Then I asked, "Thought we were fighting for Canden? Now we have the whole world in this?" I wondered.

Dietrich then calmly, but nervously commented on my questions, "Yes, we are hunting them down, but just like any other disease, this spreads...All it needs is a small little sleepy town like Canden...Then before you know it, they're in Fort Worth, maybe New Orleans...Who knows? Maybe New York City eventually? Vampires will find their way to spread their dreaded, undead curse upon the world, by sucking the blood of the living, no doubts there...That is why you must help us." The look upon Dietrich's face seemed desperate for sure, but nervous all the same.

"Remember, my bounty, I'm getting him," I firmly stated, pointing my index finger at Dietrich's face, I then added, "No bullshit or anything either, as long as this here trip leads me to Boothe, then consider me one of your hunters!"

"You have my word, bounty hunter," Dietrich then reached out his hand for me to shake it. For a moment I hesitated, but eventually I shook it strongly.

"Hey, and boss," Florence began, as he got my attention, "You have my word too," Florence then stuck out his hand for me to shake it, to which I did as well. Now I had dug myself into a shithole, I knew it, but I guess at this point there was no turning back. I had agreed to help out both of these men, time to do what I needed to do. As long as this journey led me to Fredrick, and as long as it got me that five hundred dollars. Though more importantly, as long as it would make the doctor and Florence be happy and satisfied that's all that mattered at this point. Needless to say, the rest of the evening was quite strange, not in the sense that Dietrich and Florence were weird, but that I still had a lot to process at the moment. I didn't know what the hell I would find, and I didn't know what the hell awaited me out there? All I knew was that Fredrick was out there, dumbass as ever, and he was just waiting for that bullet right now I knew it.

However, as for other worries in the night; that was a whole different story. The one thing that was the worst to process was just pure and simple, and that was the cold. My Lord in heaven, it must've dropped significantly below freezing, as the winds around us began to pick up in speed. Thankfully, we were in the bottom of a ravine, so we didn't get too much cold air, but it still bit the hell out of us. All night, we laid in our tents, frozen like a couple of icicles. I eventually slept in Florence's tent, and surprisingly, it wasn't as awkward as I thought it would be. Florence had brought along many cowhides, they made the best blankets, especially for a night like this. Florence's head was on one side of the tent, while my head was on the opposite side of his. I hated that Florence had to smell my disgusting, corn-invested feet, but that son of a gun, I'm sure didn't mind. His feet weren't any better either, I swear he must've walked right through a pig's sty. That whole entire tent smelt horrible, but I guess if this was for five hundred dollars, then so be it. Every time the wind violently hit our tent, the more nervous I got. I thought for sure that this tent would blow away, and we'd be wrapped up in it too.

I twiddled my thumbs at one point, and I continued to ponder about the decision that I had made that night. Of course, you might say that I was rethinking this whole thing, but I thought no. I can't rethink this, I've got to get this bounty, and

I'm not going to let a couple of crazy stories stop me either.

Needless to say, there was a lot going through my mind that night. Sure, I was a man on logical stand points, but this was something beyond me. But what if this was indeed real? I'm not sure if I'm cut out for this here vampire hunt? I couldn't believe I was thinking these thoughts, but I was. To calm my mind, I began to zone out all of the troubles, and before I knew it, I began to drift off to sleep. The sound of the wind that had kept hitting our tent, began to zone out, and even that smell of Florence's right foot went as well. I didn't care anymore, I was tired, it had been a long hard day, and now I was on the verge of entering into a world of uncertainty. I had no idea what was out there, or even if those stories that Dietrich and Florence told were true? I had too much to think about at this point, so I just dozed off, and then eventually I had fallen onto the edges of a deep and dark sleep. Just as I had slipped into another world of slumber, I caught the last whiff of our dying fire, and in that dying flame I heard the slight bit of what sounded like a woman. I then went off to sleep from there, and I dreamt.

Chapter 4

The sleep that had found me, was much more blissful than I had ever thought it would be. Though it was cold outside, that didn't matter any more, because now I was dreaming about seeing my wife again. Her name is Anna Gerald Hill; she has skin like alabaster, dark black hair that shines like the most radiant jewel imaginable, and she has a smile that only God would give her. We are at this friend's homecoming event, a plantation home located just outside of Austin, and I knew exactly where this dream was heading. Everyone at this gathering seems so happy to be there, friends and neighbors are all gathered here. I eventually got a good look at this home, it was the home of my dear friend and Texas Ranger Jefferson Overfelt, and the look upon his face and everyone's is definitely welcoming. It wasn't clear as to who we were holding this gathering for, but one thing's for sure, we are all happy to be there. It's the Summer season outside, because the air feels moist and humid. There were no cold, violent winds outside, no, this was a pure blissful evening. There were fireflies outside, and Overfelt's children were catching all of the fireflies. I could hear the crickets chirping too, and the wind in this dream felt like a gentle Summer breeze for sure. My Lord, this was perfect.

To make my dream even better, my wife was in it, and I had missed her for so long. It was so nice to finally be back in her company, and again she looked perfect. I couldn't stop holding her hand, and I felt so happy around her. Honestly though, I couldn't blame myself for feeling this way, she was a true woman, and she was somebody that I had fought very hard for. At one point in this dream, we proposed a toast, and the drinks we were all drinking ranged from hard whiskey to very fine wine. Regardless, we were all in this moment, and everyone around me was happy. There were many games being played, there were many songs being sung, and there were many stories being told. It was certainly a wonderful moment that nobody on this Earth should miss.

Soon, I found myself in a study, my wife had taken me by the hand to announce some news to me. The look upon her face showed happiness, and she soon sat me down and discussed what had been making her so anxious all evening. "So, what's this thing you've been chomping at the bit to tell me?" I happily asked Anna.

"Well, I didn't want to tell you in there, because I still want to keep it a secret, but what is something you've always wanted?" Anna inquired.

At this point, there were many things that I had yearned for, but one thing that stayed in my mind was the idea of becoming a father, and without much hesitation I responded with this. "Well, to be honest with you pretty little lady, I think I've always wanted a little tiny, itty-bitty, version of me," I responded with.

"Well," Anna gleefully smiled. "What if I were carrying that little tiny, itty-bitty, version of you? Right now? What would you have to say to that?" She asked.

"I guess I'd say," I began calmly, but soon I became overjoyed. "I'd have to say that I'm tickled to death, my darling," I smiled.

At this point, we both hugged and kissed. This was the news that I had been longing for my whole entire life. The chance to be a father, and to raise a child of my own. Of course, I was beyond excited, but the news was certainly a surprise to say the least. This great night had just gotten greater, and for most of the night I couldn't stop smiling. Anna, I knew would make a perfect mother. Anna was hard working, determined, and she was also very loving and full of life. As the party began to wrap, and as Anna and I made our way back to our home in Austin, we couldn't stop talking about our future baby. We thought up every name in the book, and we even thought of ways that we would spoil it. It was truly a happy time, but all this I knew was a dream, and my dear Anna was still far away from me.

It saddened me that this event seemed so distant from me, but it was still wonderful for the few moments that it had lasted. Pretty soon though, I felt the chill morning air return, and from that I knew I was waking up from my dream. Quickly, I caught back the stench of Florence's feet. Shit, it smelt like pure shit! Though, I also could smell something cooking, it must've been Dietrich?

I rose from my slumber, then I slowly turned back the tent's entry, and from that I saw Dietrich cooking what appeared to be a quail. It smelt delicious, and the turning of it on the spit made me want it even more. The flames had charred it, and now I had gained an appetite in an instance. "Ah, good morning Mister Hill, care to have a bit of bird?" Dietrich inquired.

"Certainly," I responded, knowing that I had become famished. "You killed that this morning?" I asked.

"Yes, found it over there," Dietrich then pointed over into the direction of a group of trees on an adjacent hillside. I then stood up from my tent, and walked over into the space of Dietrich. Dietrich then added, "Killed it around seven this morning, you and Florence must've been deep in a sleep."

"Surprised the gun fire didn't wake us up," I stated, as Dietrich handed me a piece of the freshly cooked pheasant.

"Oh, yes," Dietrich responded, with a calm and collective attitude.

"Smells good though, that's all that matters to me, my dear friend...at this point, I could eat a cooked pile of shit on a plate and I'd still be happy," I cheerfully stated, as I sat down onto a rock around our fire.

"Well, I'm glad that you think so," Dietrich responded in happiness, he then continued. "I hope it tastes well done, my father had taught me years ago on how to cook a pheasant, and usually from what I remembered, it's a very particular way," Dietrich said.

Dietrich smiled at his comments, as he sat down on a rock as well, opposite of me. I then chimed in, "Yeah, you got to get them bastards cooked right, or else we'll be bending over on our hands and knees in the creek," I then snickered at my comment, Dietrich laughed lightly at my statements as he then took a bite into his part of the quail.

With a mouth full of quail, Dietrich asked, "So, Mister Hill...what are some areas we should look in?"

"Well," I hesitantly began, "I'm not a vampire myself or anything, but you may have a point... On the whole they'll be hiding out here like the rest of the crooks will gig," I then added, taking a huge bite out of my pheasant. With my mouth full, I continued, "One area we should seek out, is about five miles from here, over in that direction," I then pointed my finger towards the northeast.

"Well, all I know is vampires need a food supply, what is over in that direction?" Dietrich asked.

"Oh, there's a food supply, tons of desperados hide out over there, but the funny thing is...It's all about embracing this one thing that I hate to obtain," I responded.

"What's that?" Dietrich inquired.

"Patience, doc," I replied, "We need to be patient, and we need to be smart about where we're looking," I then added.

"More than likely they're hiding out in caves," Dietrich stated. "Vampires are creatures of the night, and they rely on sleeping in dark places during the day...However some of them do tend to get out in the day, mainly when it's an overcast, but most of the time I guarantee you...You will only find them hiding in the very depths of darkness itself," Dietrich chillingly added.

"That should complicate things," I replied with disgust. "You said that they suck the blood of the living?" I asked.

"Yes, but some vampires do need a food supply... This only occurs when they are running out of blood, and are starving for something...They basically drain out all life as we know it," Dietrich said with a tremble.

At this statement, I became quite nervous. Not only were these vampires seeking out the blood of the living, but it was now possible that they were indeed cannibals. My God, were these foul creatures really that desperate? Now, as I continued to indulge in my quail, I couldn't help but think about the worse. This journey to find Fredrick, though it seemed promising, seemed also quite uncertain. The more that the doctor would add into his stories, the more anxious I would get. I knew that I was a non-believer in this whole journey, but these stories for some reason, caused an uneasy feeling in the pit of my stomach. It wasn't the fact that this was a terrible mistake, but it was the fact that I had to come to terms and accept this here situation. Needless to say, it was tough for sure, but I sat there, on that rock, freezing my ass off, and I smiled at every story that Dietrich had to tell. I must've looked like the biggest jackass on this Earth.

Thankfully, there were the occasional good thoughts, like the fact that I get to be accompanied by different people. It has gotten very lonely out here in the wilderness, but now I get to tag along with an old friend and possibly a new friend. At the end of it all, I was going to receive that five hundred dollars that I had longed for. Honestly, the trip didn't seem too bad. I chewed on a couple more bites, but eventually my quail had become all bone, so I put it down on the cold, dirty ground. I then chewed the last remaining bite, and then I swallowed the delicious food with ease. I had become quite thirsty after this meal, so I asked, "You got something I can swallow this here quail down with? Something to make it a little easier?"

"Well," the doctor began, struggling as he did, he was chewing. "We have this," he then reached behind him, and I thought to myself it could be anything. Personally, I had become immensely thirsty, and a jar of piss would have probably satisfied me at this point. "We have a good old friend with us right here," Dietrich then showcased a bottle of whiskey.

I smiled at this, "Usually the morning ain't the best place to start your drinking at…But what the hell, I guess?" Dietrich and I both laughed at the inquiry I had made. Dietrich then readied himself and I two empty tin cups; both of them had handles on them. He poured me just a little bit, he did the same for himself, and then he handed me my cup. "So, you got a name for this here group of men y'all huntin'?" I asked.

"Name?" Dietrich wondered.

"Yeah, don't y'all know it's bad luck to not give your bounty, or group that y'all huntin' a nickname?" I asked, smiling as I did.

Dietrich paused for a moment, "Well, I guess we'll just call these here men, the Fang Gang...How's that ring?" Dietrich asked.

"The Fang Gang," I commented, then I thought the nickname was quite smart. "That's pretty clever, doc, and I like it."

"To the Fang Gang then," Dietrich then raised his cup for me to touch it, to which I did. "May we vanquish all evil from this Earth," Dietrich added.

"To Fredrick, may I kick his ass when I find 'em," I gleefully commented, then we both took a drink. Dietrich had a smile upon his face, and so did I. The whiskey had a slight burn, but it wasn't as hot as other whiskeys that I had drunk earlier in life. In fact, this whiskey was drier than most. I swallowed the shot down, as I then turned my direction towards the tent; Florence was just now waking up. "Well, bout' time you opened them eyes," I stated, laughing and grinning as I did.

To which Florence responded in a groggy voice, "Well, a good morning to you too."

Dietrich smiled at our exchange, "I'm hoping you'll grab you some breakfast sheriff?" Dietrich inquired.

"What the hell y'all eating?" Florence asked.

"Quail, my good man, killed it this morning around seven," Dietrich responded, as he began cutting off Florence's piece to eat.

"It actually ain't too bad," I commented.

"Well, it definitely wakes you up, that's for sure," Florence responded. Immediately, Florence then went for the whiskey bottle, to which he did not pour a cup. Instead he was drinking what was left in the bottle. "Y'all want more whiskey?" Florence asked, as he began moving the bottle towards his lips. The funny thing was, he actually let his lips touch the bottle, and he had asked this question far too late.

"Nah, I'm good," I replied.

"Already had my fix, thank you," Dietrich replied, with a smile.

Florence then took a bite into his quail, he then commented on it, "My God! That's pretty damn good there, doc," Florence said.

"Thank you, I told Mister Hill earlier, that quails are probably one of the most difficult meats to cook, so I'm glad that you like it," Dietrich replied.

"Yeah it's pretty good," Florence then swallowed a huge bite, he coughed as he did. He must've been starving like I was. He then took a few swigs of his whiskey, then he continued. "So, Terence?"

"Yes," I responded.

"Where the hell are we headed? I'm not the one who makes a ton of trips out here...So if you know where some of these here criminals hide, please let us know, because I'm sure just right around the bend are those spawns of satan too," Florence then took another bite out of his quail.

"For one thing, are y'all sure that these here vampires have fled? The ones you've counted?" I asked.

"Yes, all the ones that were remaining, you see Mister Hill," Dietrich calmly intervened. "We blessed that whole town...We placed mustard seeds all around, crucifixes, and so on...We narrowed it down to those six, they fled quickly, and all that remained were those who thankfully hadn't fallen prey to them," Dietrich said.

"Well, if there's a great place to start," I began, standing as I did, and again I pointed towards the northeast. "We need to make our way over Clay Mountain here, and head towards that direction," my finger pointing with authority as I instructed.

"Is that Indian Territory?" Florence asked with a full mouth of pheasant.

"Indeed, it is," I responded, then continued. "That mountain, then dips downward into a flat land, and in between the mountain and this flat plain, there is a large forest. That over there, might just be a great place to search," I stated sternly.

"Do you know if there are many caves?" Dietrich asked.

"Oh yes," I responded. "I've been out that way numerous times to hunt, and I used to hide myself in those caves," I said.

"Well, then that is where we will search immediately," Dietrich responded, hesitantly as he did.

Immediately after Dietrich responded, Florence had finished up his food, and then he finished off what was left in the whiskey bottle. For the most part we stayed to ourselves for most of the morning. It wasn't until nine before we even set off, the sun had already peaked long before, and it was now in the middle part of the sky above. We demolished our tents, we put out our fire, and then we packed up all of our supplies. The horses seemed healthy and well kept, the carriage seemed to be well kept as well, and for coming this far out into the wilderness I'd say that Dietrich and Florence had one great transport. While Dietrich fed the horses, I then told Florence, "Hey, once we make our way into the valley, pass the cedar forest, there's a little river that runs through there…I was thinking maybe we could stop there and let the horses get a drink," I said.

"That don't bother me a bit," Florence responded.

"Good," I replied. From that small exchange, we then set off on our journey, deep into the woods of Clay Mountain.

The morning was quite brisk; you could easily see my breath. However, once we made our way out of the ravine, and into the outermost part of the hills it began to warm up a bit. It was most certainly a surprise to see it so warm, considering that the last few days had been colder than any other days. Maybe now we were heading into a much nicer break in weather? That certainly didn't bother me at all, and I for one was getting too damn tired of all this bullshit cold weather.

I'd rather it be hotter than hell itself, because personally, the cold has never really been a friend of mine. By the time it had warmed up a bit, I began to notice my various surroundings. Dietrich was driving along the carriage into the woods of Clay; the forest was covered with many cedars and pines. The sun began to beat down on us, it must've been around spring temperatures now, because I began to sweat a bit, especially around my neck. Florence was in the back of the carriage, where he had his window opened, and Florence and I kept a conversation brewing every so often. We all had our guns by our sides, and we never put ourselves off guard at all. At this point in our journey, the best thing we could do was be humbly prepared, and more importantly we needed to be cunning and smart. Who knows what kind of cave or dwelling that these here creatures were hiding in? If these creatures even existed at all. That was another problem that continued to brew in my mind, and I mean it brewed to the point of where I had a massive headache.

By this point, it wasn't a good thing to have such an excruciating pain in my head, but I did. We had started making our way up Clay Mountain, and these trails were something straight out of a nightmare itself, I swear. Though the trail did start out promising, being that it was wide and all, it wasn't long until the trail began to get smaller and smaller in width.

Within about an hour, we had cleared one side of Clay Mountain, but the only way to get over the mountain was to take a very narrow and jagged trail. I had taken this damn thing before, and I remembered it was a pain in the ass the whole way. But I guess at this point, none of those complaints really mattered. The carriage struggled a bit, being that it had to push its way up the mountain, but to much of my surprise it actually did pretty well considering all things considered. Dietrich bounced about on the carriage, while I continued to clear the pathway. By now, we were on the edge of a cliff, but thankfully the road wasn't quite so narrow. We still stayed on guard, and we still carefully drove through those cliffs like we were carrying the president. At one point, Florence got out of the carriage, and retrieved a horse from the front as Dietrich halted. He hopped upon the stead, and then helped me lead ahead as we both kept ourselves on guard.

We passed a part of Clay Mountain, where we noticed a massive landslide, which had happened thankfully right below. The mud on this mountain was a clay-like color, hence this is why the name of the mountain is Clay. We observed our surroundings, in fact, I don't think I have ever seen such gorgeous views, such as this. We got many overlooks; where we saw plains, river valleys, and we could even see what appeared to be a distant lake. Soon, we moved along a flat part of the mountain ridge, and then eventually we began to descend on the other side of the mountain.

Now going up was certainly a chore, however, going down, that was a whole new story. Dietrich was driving the horses steadily, while Florence and I continued to keep the horses on track and safe. Florence was now walking on foot, and I remained on my horse. At one point, we hit many rocks, I mean there were rocks everywhere! I felt so bad for the horses at this point, the fact that they had to walk on such hellish terrain, that just made my heart sink a little if I'm honest. However, you've got to do what you've got to do. There was one problem though, and it wasn't with the horses or anything. No, there was now a problem at the top of my ass crack.

There was this burning sensation occurring right above my ass, and it was giving hell to me the whole way. I knew it was from where I had been riding my stead for so many days, but now it was at a whole new stage of pain. Every single bump or jiggle that the horse would make, this area around my tailbone would seem to flare up. My God, it was the absolute worst pain. It literally felt like somebody was stabbing me with my bowie knife, and that bowie was piercing right into the top of my ass with much tension too. I couldn't imagine what kind of a God-awful smell had accompanied it. Either way, I sat there and took it in the ass the whole trip. To make matters worse, it started to get hotter. Now the weather had gone from freezing my tits off, to now sweating them off, and at this point I don't think the sweat was helping my problem at all. I grimaced the whole trip, and I certainly had become madder than hell.

I may have been pissed off and everything, but for the most part, it was nice to be in the company of my former deputy. It was also nice to have met such a down to Earth fellow, like Dietrich himself. I thought very highly of Dietrich, he seemed to know a lot about these here vampires. I had heard about vampires through various ghost stories, many of which were told to me as a kid. Like most of us here in Texas though, we just brushed them off as pure myth. Now however, it was a different situation. I had trusted Florence, and I had taken the good word of the doctor. Right now though, it was hard to tell how I was feeling about this. A part of me believed in every word that was coming out of their mouths. While the other part, seemed to raise an eyebrow, and I for one knew that all stemmed from me being a pure asshole and skeptic.

Though I was trying to play nice and all, I couldn't help but feel urgent, and uneasy about the whole situation. I must say though, in this part of our journey, again, the views were only getting prettier. More and more overlooks accompanied our ride, and more trees entered our surroundings too. The forests of Texas were quite pristine, but the forests of Indian Territory were even more magnificent. Acres upon acres of wilderness, all of which one day may or may not belong to the United States. There were grasslands upon the bottom of the mountain, and at this point we found ourselves at the edge of an open forest. The trees became much more separated, and the grass became much greener.

There were no more signs of rocks, and now the ground had become much more stable. As we had reached the bottom, we got a clear view of our surroundings/ Blue sky and nothing but blue sky, consumed the air around us. There were no clouds, and I swear we had entered into a whole new season. By this point, I knew we had been traveling around three to four hours now. This meant it was now time for somebody to take a piss break, and at this point I had been holding my juices in far too long. We eventually found a good spot; below in a ravine, which had a magnificent view, of the other side of Clay Mountain. Wanting to give my whole problem a break, I quickly climbed off of my horse. I was utterly shocked though, that my makeshift sled, which was still carrying my two dead bounties, was still intact, and unharmed. I could smell shit though, both of their bodies must've voided their bowels or something? It was now a chore to keep these bodies preserved, and I was hoping that it wouldn't get too warm the rest of the way. Though I didn't mind the warmth or anything, the cold did preserve my dead bodies better. I was now thinking to myself, would I have made better time alone? I guess honestly it didn't matter, I wanted Fredrick, and I wanted his bounty bad. Five hundred dollars, ain't something you get every day, that's for sure. This was money within my reach, though maybe Fredrick may not be normal or anything. Though I guess if the doctor and Florence have agreed on me taking Fredrick then it can't be that bad.

I fixed my saddle a bit, then I walked up to my horse's head, and I began rubbing its face very gently. I talked very low to the horse, "There, there, that's a good girl," I whispered.

"How far away are we from this here river, Ter?" Florence inquired.

"Ah, it ain't but about a few ridges over maybe…We've got to make our way through these hills and this forest first, and then it'll be on the edge of these trees," I replied, breathing heavily as I did.

"Well good God!" Florence exclaimed, "Feels like we should be there by now, I'm starting to get the blackouts."

"Well here," I reached into my saddle bag, and then handed Florence the flask that I had taken from the campsite of my bounties last night. "Here, get you some water, you look as white as your hat, old boy."

Florence really did look like hell; he was pale and sweating vigorously. He then added as he took a swig, "Thank you, hopefully there's enough in here?" He inquired.

"Oh, yes," I replied, "The whole damn thing was full when I left them dipshits' camp last night."

As Florence enjoyed his sips of water, I then went back over to my compass; which was nicely snuggled in my saddle bag. I then took it out and leveled it. We were indeed going in the right direction, northeast, and we were well on our way into Indian Territory. I then shut the compass and drank a bit of my water from my flask. The water had this tin-like taste, which made sense. It had been sitting in this damn thing for days on end now. To be honest though, this water might as well be poisoned. I didn't give a horse's ass at this point, water was water, and I've been thirsty the whole morning. After I finished a few gulps; I then noticed that my flask had started to become low, and at this I was saddened. However, I knew we weren't far from that river. There I'd get some fresh water from the gentle flow, and just the thought of that made me anxious. From the right side of me, I then heard Dietrich ask, "So, bounty hunter, I hope you read northeast?"

To which I replied, "Hell yeah, heading northeast, my friend."

"Good, good," Dietrich replied.

I then inquired myself, curious questions that continued to plague my mind, "Doc, I've got this question here that's been bugging the piss out of me ever since you starting mentioning that you blessed Canden…But how do you know that these here foul beasts, won't find their ways into other towns and start the curse all over again? Be it, they haven't already?"

"Well, that my friend, was handled, thanks to your wonderful pony express," Dietrich giddily replied. "I sent out some telegrams, warning all surrounding towns about the matter, so we should not have nothing to worry about."

"Well, there's just one other scenario that I just don't quite understand?" I questioned.

"What's that?" Dietrich asked.

"I'm sure them town's people thought you were plum bat shit crazy, didn't they?" I inquired with a grin.

Dietrich smiled at my remark, "No, not exactly…In fact it took some persuasion, but in an instance, they got back to me…They blessed their towns from top to bottom, I can assure you that."

"What did you both use for persuasion?" I asked, I then whipped out a cigar, and placed it on my lips.

"Well, do you remember Deacon James?" Dietrich asked.

"Deacon? The photographer?" I inquired, lighting my match, and then lighting my cigar.

"Yes, well…We had him photograph the decapitated head of one of those beasts," Dietrich replied, lightly laughing as he did. "Needless to say, that persuasion…worked."

I then laughed at Dietrich's remark, "Yeah, I think that would do it there, no doubts."

We continued snickering at each other, then Dietrich added, "I'm sure those towns have more crosses in them than the whole city of the Vatican does."

"I'd say, you drove them out, and kept them out," I said, then I added, after taking a long puff of smoke, "That's smart thinking, doc."

"Yes, I'm sure by now they have nowhere to run…Maybe they have places to hide, here and there, But soon these vampires will run out of everything; food sources, blood, and soon they'll be reduced to the resort of killing and eating each

61

other…Savages I tell you…They don't call them the spawns of hell for nothing," Dietrich said.

"You sure they're around here, Ter?" Florence asked.

"Oh absolutely," I replied, "There ain't no other towns around here, and the closest people are thirty miles away at Hank's Lodge."

"Where are all of the Native Americans at?" Dietrich asked, "This is Indian Territory isn't it?"

"Well, there is the Comanche, but the nearest tribe resides about fifty miles northwest of here," I replied.

"Them tribes use this land for hunting," Florence chimed in.

"Yeah, but they don't come down here until the Summer months…The tribe usually stays up in the plains, and I can assure ain't none of them waddling their asses down here," I said.

"Still though, we should keep our eyes peeled," Florence added.

"That we should," I responded, "If we ever do come into contact with one of them Natives, you gentlemen have nothing to fear, I know a thing or two about negotiating."

"Let's pray we never have to face such a situation," Dietrich said.

I then walked back over towards Florence, all to retrieve my flask that he had been drinking out of. The air around me felt warm, and it was very comfortable up here on this hill. A light breeze blew through, and I thought for sure it was Spring time already. It made me think for a second, back to that wonderful dream that I had last night, where everything seemed blissful again, and I was back in the presence of my woman. It was most certainly a place I wouldn't mind being in right now. Florence was sitting on his stead; looking as prideful as a farmer after he had just plowed his field. "I'm sure your thirst is happy now?" I asked.

"Yes indeed, thanks for the swigs," Florence replied.

"Alright, I guess with that, we will set off again," I stated, turning around and heading back over to my horse.

Once I reached my horse; I felt that sharp pain again, around the top of my ass crack. It was on fire, like hell itself, and I was certainly dreading the ride from here on outward. However, I toughened up and pulled myself back up onto my horse As I sat down on my saddle, I grimaced a bit. When I made this face, it caught the attention of Florence, who then asked, "Everything alright?"

"Yeah," I replied, then I added, with much embarrassment, "It's just that, well...The top of my ass is sore as hell right now," I added.

Florence then of course laughed at my statements, "My Lord man, has that there horse given you the clap already?" Florence asked, he was now losing it.

I then rolled my eyes, "Nah, it's just sore from where I've been riding for the past few days."

"Yeah, sure it is," Florence responded, "Hey, no worries, maybe once we get up to this here river you speak of, maybe I can help you wash it up a bit," Florence jokingly commented, winking as he did.

"Oh yeah, very funny," I sarcastically responded. "But I've got one pain in the ass on this trip already, and I don't need another one, thank you."

Then jokingly, Florence wondered, "Hey, maybe Dietrich could clean you up? He's a doctor?"

Right as Florence made this comment, he then motioned for his horse to lead, and we then followed. To which Dietrich followed behind, pulling the horses along in his carriage, and at

Florence's comment Dietrich asked, "I thought you said you could sheriff?"

There was a million-dollar grin on Dietrich's face now, "No, I ain't touching Terence's ass," Florence stated, still laughing as he did.

"I don't know, hey Terence, how much are those two bounties worth?" Dietrich inquired.

"They're both worth two-hundred," I replied.

"Hey, there you go Florence, once he gets back to Austin, maybe he'll get two-hundred for you...I don't know, two-hundred dollars for cleaning an ass certainly sounds like a great bargain deal to me," Dietrich said with laughter.

"No, in all seriousness, I wouldn't clean Terence's ass for two thousand," Florence said.

"Oh, come on, my ass can't be that bad," I commented, snickering as I did.

"Well if you say so...But Ter, I think I'm gonna start calling you sore ass the rest of the trip, if that's fine with you?" Florence asked, laughing as he did.

To which I replied, with slight laughter, "Yeah sure, call me that...I don't think that's the worst you could come up with?" We continued laughing at one another, as our horses continued to push forward, further into Indian Territory. We were now edging closer, to the very edge of Clay Mountain. Pretty soon we'd hit that cedar forest, then we'd hit the plains, and then finally that river where we could let the horses get their water and where we could finally cool off in this unseasonably warm weather.

Chapter 5

Okay, maybe my ass was sore and all, and maybe this weather was hotter than Satan's loins. But one thing's for sure, our joking and picking back and forth never let up. The sun continued to beam down, as we rode along through beautiful forests and grasslands. The forest was quite calm, though it was the afternoon, I was surprised at just how empty it was. There was the occasional bird we'd hear, and sometimes we would spot a deer or two. However, for the most part, it seemed very dead in these woods. The smell of the forest, however, was quite fresh, and it made me feel good. There is nothing like the smell of cedars and pines. I continued to smoke on my cigar; it was from the pack of cigars that I had taken away back at my two bounties' camp site and it still was a mystery flavor to me. I swear, this was bugging the shit out of me, was this blueberry, or blackberry? It was weird, I couldn't tell really, a part of it had this blueberry initial taste, but then it had this after taste, which had a blackberry flavor to it. Regardless, it relaxed my mind, and the smell of it made Florence want one himself. I swear, that man kept eyeing my cigar, and I could tell he was picking up on the scent. "My Lord, that smells good," he commented. "What the hell kind of a flavor is that?" Florence asked.

"To be honest, I really can't decide…I think it's blueberry, but it does have this strange blackberry taste too," I replied.

"Blueberry or blackberry, it don't matter to me, I love me a good cigar every so often, where did you get them?" Florence inquired.

"Well, let's just say I borrowed them…From them two bounties," I said, grinning as I did.

At this I knew Florence had picked up on the fact that I had stolen them, "Oh I see," he stated.

"Hopefully you won't arrest me now sheriff, but all I wanted was a smoke break," I joyfully responded.

"Oh yeah, I hear you," Florence responded, grinning. "But I guess I could give you a pass there sheriff, or should I say bounty hunter?" Florence inquired.

"My appreciation, deputy," I nodded at Florence. "Here, and as my thank you, you get yourself a free cigar."

I then tossed over a cigar to Florence, he caught it instantly. Quickly, he whipped out a match and lit it. It took him a bit to inhale the smoke; but by the look on his face, he showed much happiness that's for sure. He exhaled the smoke slowly, and then he sighed in pure relief. I could tell that he was under a lot of tension, and I am sure all of this here vampire bullshit probably drove him to the point of insanity. I then turned my attention over towards the doctor; he was still driving the carriage, struggling to keep it on course, and now he was directly behind me. "Hey, doctor!" I shouted.

"Yes sir?" He inquired.

"How would you like a little free peace and relaxation? I'm telling you, these here cigars make you feel like you are on top of the world?" I asked.

"No, I don't think so," Dietrich replied. "The last time I had a cigar was way back, four years ago in New Orleans, when one of those crazed voodoo queens introduced me to this here peace and relaxation that you speak of…Let's just say there wasn't very much peace, nor was there any relaxation, because all evening, all I did, was cough my lungs up, and I really don't want a repeat of that again but thank you very much my good man," Dietrich smiled.

"Oh, I understand," I replied, "But if you ever feel like you need one, do let me know."

"I will, but personally I've got to be really stressed and panicked before I need one of them things," Dietrich replied, with a slight bit of laughter.

"I figured that this journey here would make you do such a thing?" Florence asked.

No, not really," Dietrich replied. "It takes a lot for me to get concerned, feared, or even frightened for that matter."

"You don't scare easily, do you doctor?" I asked.

"No not all, in fact, whenever I do find myself in situations such as that, I never really find myself in fear and agony...I'm not afraid of death either, I know where I am headed," Dietrich proudly said.

"I wish I had your strong will, doc," I said, with a smile.

"Nah, it's not really strong per say, it's just age teaches you many valid lessons...I'm sure that one day, when you get to be as old as I am, you'll see that," Dietrich responded, smirking.

"So, I guess you've gotten used to a lot of bullshit then?" I asked.

"When you word it that way, yes, I guess you could say that...Our lives are the greatest mystery of all...God is an even bigger mystery...I always wonder what my purpose is here…Who knows? Maybe there was a reason Vera left me? Something from above, had a plan for me to become a doctor, and to come here and slay these foul beasts? Maybe there is a purpose for us all?" Dietrich questioned.

"Yeah, I'm almost thirty-eight myself, and I'm still trying to figure that shit out," I sarcastically responded.

By now, we were getting closer and closer to the edge, where the mountain kissed the edge of the great plains of Indian Territory. There was a slight breeze that slithered its way up through the edge of the mountain, and the forest continued to go on and on. Once we had come to an opening, on the side of a hill, our horses then became startled. My horse reared back a little, snorting and hollering. Dietrich's horses, and Florence's horse did the same thing. It was like total chaos had entered the air around us, and I was confused by such a matter. I immediately jumped off my horse, trying to keep it calm, while both Dietrich and Florence began calming the carriage horses. Florence had thankfully calmed his horse down, but something didn't seem right with these animals. Perhaps something, or someone, was watching us in these trees. I became unsettled, that is for certain. However, Dietrich seemed as calm as the breeze that gently tapped against my face. Florence was frantic for a bit, but soon the horses quit carrying on, and we soon found this to be the perfect opportunity to stop and take a rest.

By now the temperature had risen slightly, and my jacket had no longer seemed to be a good idea anymore. I quickly took it off, and then I placed myself down onto a rock; which was perfectly stuck into the side of the grassy hill that we had stopped on. I took a puff of my cigar, Florence was finishing his off as well, and all three of us found ourselves in the midst of a much-needed break. We were getting so close to the river, and I could almost smell it. As we sat there; Dietrich fiddled with a few items in his carriage and Florence sat on a stump right next to me. We both remained to ourselves for a few moments. "So, is it blueberry or blackberry?' I asked Florence.

"Possibly a mixture? But whatever it is, it's a pretty damn good cigar," Florence said.

"Glad you like it, these two dips might be low lifes, but they sure as hell know how to pick out a mighty fine container of smokes," I stated.

"Oh yeah," Florence replied, "So, two-hundred dollars each, for them?" Florence then asked.

"Yep, plus the five-hundred I'll make on this expedition here...That'll put it right at nine-hundred dollars, and that my friend is a song I love to hear," I said with pride.

"Gosh, you must be drowning in it?' Dietrich inquired.

"Nah, I mean, I'm still a fresh bounty hunter and all…To be honest, them two men, are my very first kills," I replied, taking a puff as I did.

"Get the hell out of Dodge!" Florence exclaimed, "You've been doing this shit how long?" Florence then asked.

"Well, since September, but again, as I mentioned to the doctor earlier, it's all about enquiring about this one little thing that drives me crazy," I replied.

"Patience, isn't it?" Dietrich asked.

"Bingo! You've got that right, and a shit ton of it too!" I exclaimed.

"Well, you can keep that strength you got there Ter, I ain't one to be all that patient myself," Florence said.

"Nah, it ain't all that bad," I said.

"There was definitely a lot of patience tested back in Canden, that's for sure," Dietrich commented.

"Yeah, speaking of patience, my penis has been impatient for about forty-five minutes, about two groves back…My back teeth are floating, so if y'all will excuse me, I'm going to go take a piss now," Florence stated, standing up as he did.

"Alrighty then," I said, "Make sure you go far enough away, please."

"Yeah, I'm going about a hundred yards over that way, and oh by the way Terence?" Florence inquired.

"Yes sir?" I asked.

"This be a good time to check your little sore ass problem?" Florence asked, he then smiled.

I could hear Dietrich laughing under his breath, I smiled to myself. I then replied, "Nah, that whole situation, I hope, is improving."

All three of us laughed ever so slightly, but soon all went back to seriousness; the horses were startled again. Dietrich then remarked, "My God, what in the hell is wrong with those nags?"

Running quickly, I tended to my horse, grabbing both reins, and trying to keep my horse calm. The sled was moving back and forth as the horse went frantic, something was not right. Florence tended to his horse, however his horse started running frantically around in circles, and as for the carriage horses they too were frantic. All three of us struggled to calm the horses, for what seemed like an eternity, but soon all of them got calm again. After the chaos had ended, I then turned towards Florence, "Alright, go take your piss, we'll wait right here, and make sure you take your Winchester with you," I instructed.

"Alright, will do boss," Florence replied, and with that he turned and walked out of sight into the forest, with his gun fully loaded in hand.

"It can't be them; I know it can't?" Dietrich questioned himself.

"You said they're night dwellers, right?" I asked.

"Right, a vampire would not dare step foot out into this sunshine," Dietrich said.

"Well, there ain't a ton of dwellings around here," I stated, "A lot of the caves up on that ridge there, are too small to even fit a rabbit in."

"That's very informative to know," Dietrich commented, "But you see, I'm also keeping my nostrils on the prowl."

Curious by the doctor's statement, I then asked, "You mean, you're actually keeping your sense of smell in tune here?"

"Yes, I'm keeping my nose peeled, for anything that smells like rotting flesh," Dietrich replied.

"What kind of flesh?" I asked.

"That all depends, preferably animal, but I do expect to maybe pick up on the scent of humans too," Dietrich said trembly.

"Might be a food supply, ain't it?" I inquired.

"Well yes," Dietrich replied, "You see, a vampire is just like any other type of animal...When the food supply runs low, they become desperate, and they'll suck the blood from any deer, rabbit, bear, coyote, or even human...Of course, human blood is what they seek, but they'll do anything to survive."

"They'll eventually die, right?" I asked.

"Just like anything that loses the will to live, anything that runs out of its resources, and trust me they have their weaknesses...Like I mentioned last night; the cross, garlic, holy water, and even mirrors...Vampires fear much, time is their greatest enemy above all though," Dietrich replied, he then sat down on the same stump as Florence had sat on. "But I assure you, they will die...Eventually."

"Well, I surely hope to God, we ain't running out of time," I said.

"No worries," Dietrich happily commented, "I have much faith in our expedition."

"Even though you're having to tag along with a bunch of dipshits like us?" I jokingly asked.

Dietrich laughed under his breath, "Nah, it's quite alright...You two are doing great," Dietrich said with a grin.

"I take it you and old Flor seem to get along quite well?" I inquired.

"Yes, he's not too bad actually," Dietrich replied, smiling. "He's a very hard working and devoted man, I tell you."

"Yeah, he was that...Way back when I worked with him...But he sure as hell loves his bottle," I said.

"Oh God yes," Dietrich responded, "I think he drinks that saloon dry, back at home."

"My friend, if Florence could marry a bottle of whiskey, I guarantee you, for all of what my bounties are worth, he'd do it," I said.

Dietrich grinned at my comments. "I think he would, but make sure you've got a little money leftover yourself," Dietrich said, making quotation marks, with his hands. Dietrich and I then joined into a parade of laughter.

"God, I swear, he'll keep giving me hell for that, this whole trip," I stated, gently laughing as I did.

We laughed for a few more moments, then Dietrich inquired, "In all seriousness though, how long were you two acquainted back in Canden?"

"My friend, Florence and I were actually like brothers growing up...Though Flor definitely had the shittier end of the stick if I'm honest...He grew up without a father...A man shot his father down in a saloon when he was no more than ten...His mother was there for him, well as much as a prostitute could be, but for the most part I actually grew up with, and raised Florence myself...He soon found the bottle and everything, but I tried to keep him in line the best I could, and now ever since I left Canden to go off to Austin and start a new life...To find me an old gal and all...It seems looking back, he was again like the brother, that I never had...However doc, I believe he's fallen far from grace, because let me just say that Florence ain't what he used to be," I said.

"Well, he does love his bottle much, I can tell you that," Dietrich commented.

"You know, he's one hell of a guy, and he'd do anything between hell and damnation for you...But even before I left a few years back, I could tell it had started to get worse," I said.

"There is some humor in it though," Dietrich jokingly stated.

"What's that supposed to mean?" I asked.

"Well, let's just say the first time I met Florence, this was months back, I can remember his greeting quite well, and you see that all took place on a Friday evening," Dietrich replied.

"Oh, for the love of God, that's when Florence gets really shitfaced," I then rolled my eyes, and continued hearing Dietrich's story.

"Oh yes, shitfaced indeed, but anyways...I was at Manny's Boarding House, where I lived, and Florence lived there too...I can remember, I was walking down this hall towards my room, and I heard this hooping and yelling...Of course being curious as I was, I opened the door to his quarters...And what I saw there, would surely shock the hell out of even the most tolerable man," Dietrich said.

"What the hell was he doing?" I asked.

"Well, he was rolling back and forth on his stomach, complaining about his drunkenness...Then it got worse," Dietrich gently replied with a smirk. "He then got up, got out of bed, and said I gotta 'piss, bad!'...Then he pulled down his pants, whipped out his manhood, and urinated all over the room...I was frozen for sure," Dietrich said in shock. He and I then both laughed at this.

"He's one crazy son of bitch I tell you, he used to do that kind of shit when we both got wasted," I said.

"Yes…so yes, that was my wonderful introduction to your dear sheriff of Canden, and there were many more moments like that again…Like another moment in time, when he was drunk, and his arm had this great big cut, up it," Dietrich said, running his index finger along the skin up his arm.

"My Lord," I reacted.

"It was deep, but I had to help clean it and bandage it up…My Lord, that was like wrestling with a rhinoceros!" Dietrich said.

I grinned at his comment, "Yeah, I'm sure that dumbass was one."

"No doubts and my God it was a mess, and I'd like to leave it at that, but Terence, tell me about your life? How's Austin treating you? You got that wife and everything too?" Dietrich inquired.

Just before I could answer Dietrich's question; I heard a startling *roar*, it echoed up the hillside, and I could hear what sounded like Florence in distress. Immediately, I sprang into action, grabbing my shotgun, and I began looking down a hill. But I still only saw the gentle blowing breeze, brushing up against the cedars and pines. The *roar* sent chills down my back and I knew that something was in close range of Florence. I kept my eyes locked; I was now staring at a few trees which made their way down into an opening and I was just waiting. Any second now, I knew old Florence would pop out from behind the left side of these trees. Dietrich was now behind me, and I'm sure he was feeling just as uneasy as I was. I then cocked back my shotgun; I was ready for anything. "What in the hell?" I whispered. "Hey! Florence, you alright in there!" I shouted.

I got no response, then the horses became startled again, and this time we were too late to respond. They took off down the hill, and from that I knew. Whatever was making this hellish sound, this was more than likely what had startled them earlier, and I knew we were up shit creek now. "Ah, shit!" I exclaimed, "Just let them nags go, all of them!" I stepped forward, ever so lightly.

Then I heard Florence, "Run like hell! Run like hell!" He exclaimed, then he popped into view.

An uneasy feeling came over me, my heart pounded, and I asked myself, was this truly the end? Florence had terror written all over his face, and I knew this was not good at all. He darted right past my left shoulder, and Florence never stopped either. Then I got a good look at what was chasing him; my God it was a grizzly bear! This grizzly looked like it was beyond grown! It had gotten warm, and this bear was coming out of its sleep more drowsy and hungry than ever! I was shocked and frozen; for a moment all I could see was a massive ton bear coming at me and it had razor sharp teeth and razor-sharp claws beneath. I was petrified! I didn't hesitate at all, I took off, and I mean fast! Dietrich and Florence were well ahead of me, maybe no more than twenty feet, but I eventually caught up with them. We were now running in the direction of where the horses took off to.

I can take a lot of shit, but this is something entirely new for me. All of us just pressed ahead, breathing heavily as we did, and I must've said "shit" about eighty-two times. However, many of us were speaking up to the good Lord, some good, and some bad. We ran fast down the hill, and at this point we were edging closer and closer to the edge of the mountain. Maybe this bear was leading us out of here quicker? However, I had but one thing on my mind, and that was I didn't want to die over and over again. This bear would surely rip us to shreds though, I was frightened.

We pressed on for what seemed like a mile; cedars and pines became much sparser, and soon we all caught a glimpse of the river. I eventually found a great spot to maybe turn around and attempt to possibly bring down the massive grizzly. I fired off about two shots; I was no more than a hundred yards away, and while I did hit the bear around the top part of his torso it still wasn't enough. Eventually I stopped shooting, and because of this, Dietrich and Florence were now way far ahead of me. I would say no more than five hundred yards now. I ran like I had never ran before, and at this point nothing mattered. It was all about keeping my ass alive.

Up ahead though, there was a bit of hope; there appeared to be a hill of some sorts and it looked like it dipped its way down into the river and grasslands below. Regardless, I continued to run, and at this point I'm pretty sure I had swallowed the remainder of my cigar. Scared, wasn't enough to describe how I was feeling, and I was hoping that we'd soon find our horses. Looking up ahead; I had noticed the hill, it was now but fifty feet away, but there was no Dietrich or Florence in sight? Running quickly, and being stubborn that I was, I took one more shot at the big bear. I fired one; hitting the grizzly right in his chest, but I was running backwards, and I guess I had forgotten what was underneath my feet.

Eventually, I came into contact with a damn rock! Planted neatly in the ground! It met my spurs, and soon I was tumbling backwards down the long hill.

I tumbled for what seemed like forever; I then let go of my shotgun. I was hoping, too, that on the way down, I wouldn't hit my head on another rock. I could taste the grass on the way down, entering in and out of my mouth. It, of course, hurt like hell the whole way, and my head throbbed to the point of which I thought it might roll off. I cussed the whole way and much of the ramblings were quite a colorful vocabulary. Pretty soon, I was able to fix my fall slightly, from a tumble, to a light rolling.

However it still stung like hell. The bear now; sounded much further away. I don't think that damn thing was interested in chasing our asses down here. Maybe we were in luck? However, all that luck changed, when my back hit a rock in the hill! My Lord it smashed hard! But nothing compared to what I hit next. My head then made contact with another rock, "Ah, shit!" I exclaimed. Soon, I began to see darkness, I was blacking out, and just like that, all the chaos was no more. I could still feel myself rolling down the hill, but at this point I was starting to go numb, and my ears were starting to ring. The sounds of the big-ass bear; sounded so far away, and the warm grass that I had been feeling felt no more. I was still rolling down the hill, who knew if I would survive? I didn't quite know either, if I'd ever see Dietrich and Florence again? I also had no idea what would become of the horses, the carriage, the bounties, and if we would even make it to the river? I was drifting off again, but soon I found myself back into a great state of mind, I was soon back into the presence of my lovely wife.

Chapter 6

Nothing bothered me now, because I was now back in the Summer season in Austin. I was back at my home; a two story, white house, made out of nothing but some molding, plaster, stone, and wood. This day was humid, the sun beat down upon the adjacent field to us, and all of God's creatures were in full livelihood. I was walking here; the gentle Summer breeze whipped against my face and it didn't seem harsh at all. Up against an old hickory tree, at the end of our property, was my beautiful Anna once more, and she radiated like the sun itself. Her skin was tan, due to the fact of the season, and the smile upon her face showed great joy. I think I smiled for a moment, as I was walked towards her. Once I got close to her, I held her, and I held her like I'd never let go. She felt so warm close to me, the yearning had now become pure blissful satisfaction, and I hoped nothing on this Earth would ever ruin this moment. I didn't want to leave her, and I think I would give up anything to be with her here again.

This gave me hope again, as I had missed my dear Anna so much, and I knew it wouldn't be long till I was home again. The baby that we were about to receive in a short while; had now made its presence ever so known, as now my darling wife had a bump on the middle part of her torso. "It won't be long," Anna happily said.

"I know my darling, I can hardly wait," I said.

"I know you've always wanted a girl, but what if it's a boy?" Anna asked.

"Well, I guess I'd have to treat him like a boy then...No worries, I'll teach him how to shoot, skin, and hunt," I replied, excited to say the least.

"Sounds like to me you want a boy?" Anna wondered.

"Well...maybe," I responded, "But I guess in the long run, it really don't matter, because I'll be happy with whatever the child is."

I then kissed Anna's neck, and held her from the back. She then said, "You'll do great, this I know you will, and Terence?" Anna then inquired.

"Yes?" I asked.

"Please promise me that when this baby arrives, you won't spend too much time working...Please promise me that?" Anna asked.

"I promise my darling," I replied.

"I know you said you were interested in bounty hunting, but please, if you do that, please don't be gone for so long," Anna was now trembling.

"I won't my dear, I'll only do what I think is best, and I'll do what's best for you," I then caressed her face, and then I kissed her lips. It was a beautiful moment, no questions about it.

All that bliss changed though, again. This time, I wasn't waking up fully rested in a tent, and it wasn't morning either. Instead, I awoke to the smell of a fresh fire; I could hear it *crackle* and *pop*, and from that I figured my misery had returned. Suddenly; I felt a very sharp pain in the back of my head, it was sore, and it hurt like a son of a bitch! I grimaced a bit, I also felt light headed, and I had an aching pain in my head. I was also short of breath, but it didn't feel like I was dying. I had no idea where the hell I was? Slowly, I lifted my head, it instantly pounded, and in fact, it felt entirely sore. I wondered; did I break my neck?

Thankfully though, not to my surprise either, I was not alone. I could hear two men talking, and I knew it must be Dietrich and Florence. I laid there though for a few moments, and at this point I didn't feel like springing up like a sunflower. I stayed immobile, not moving a muscle. Soon as time ticked, I had that will to get up again, and trust me it was a good time to well up too. It was now twilight, the night was creeping in, and the temperature had dropped to where it was now freezing again. I could smell something cooking; it smelt like deer meat. Deer sounded heavenly, as it was one of my favorite meats to eat.

Slowly and in much pain, I stood to my feet. I got a good look at my surroundings; we were there at last. It was a beautiful looking river which flowed gracefully by, and it was in the middle of this grassland and valley. There were woodlands and a bunch of overgrown bushes up ahead, but for the most part we were in a clearing. I turned around; the horses, all of them, were standing and sitting. Thankfully, thanks to the grace of God, the carriage was still intact, and it looked like most of the supplies had made it down the mountain. I turned and looked over towards the fire; Dietrich and Florence were sitting around it. They were warming their hands, and eating a beautifully cooked deer. The deer hide was lying on the ground, and the guts were right next to it. I could see intestines, the liver, and even the stomach. This deer had been gutted well. I knew I had taught Florence good on something for a change, besides drinking that is. As I walked over, Florence asked, with a mouth full of food, "How's that noggin of yours, Ter?"

Slowly I replied, "Hopefully it's good?"

"Oh, no worries my dear man," Dietrich smiled, "You should be springing in no time, you just got a good hit on your head...I stitched a small part at the back of your cranium...And from what I examined you didn't break anything," Dietrich said.

"Talk about the grace of God," I said.

"For sure," Dietrich grinned, "Oh and by the way, I did finally treat myself to one of your sticks of peace and relaxation...That bear did it for sure," Dietrich then lightly laughed.

"No offense taken, remember it's free, anytime you feel like you need one," I responded. "When did you shoot this deer?" I asked.

"I shot him about two hours ago, of course you were out when I gutted it and everything," Florence replied.

"Yeah, about that...How long have I been out?" I asked, rubbing my head.

"Oh, you were out for about six hours...Around one I would say, and it took a lot of searching to find you too," Dietrich said.

"Yeah, we found you at the bottom, in some mud," Florence commented.

"That'd be why I feel so moist," I said. I then stretched for a bit, then I put my fingers to my face, and from that, my indexes collected a little bit of mud. I then added with disgust, "I guess I'll go rinse this shit off of my face."

"Alright," Florence replied, Dietrich tried to reply too, but at the moment, his mouth was filled to the brim with food.

Curious, I asked, walking away, "Did most of the supplies make it?"

"Yeah," Dietrich stated, swallowing the rest of his food. "Thank the heavens, we both recovered all of the defenses that we needed."

I then saw Florence lean forward, he muttered, with me clearly hearing, "Should we tell him?"

Dietrich shook his head; I was confused as all get out. "Tell me what?" I asked.

"Nothing," Dietrich smiled. Now I was more suspicious than ever at this. I turned around and started my way towards the river, and then I noticed the situation that caused my suspicions. I saw my horse, and my small makeshift sled. However, no Roger, it was only just Patrick. One of my bounties had gotten lost in the chaos. I turned towards Dietrich, who then remarked, "Well, I guess you'll find out on your own then."

"Son...of a filthy bitch!" I reacted; I then collected my breath. "No Roger I see."

"Now look Ter," Florence chimed in, "Please don't lose your marbles...We looked all over God's green creation, couldn't find him anywhere...I guess the damn bear got him."

I began to process this, I was angry, but not as much as I could be. "I'm starting to think that this here expedition may have been a dumb idea after all," I stated. "Ah shit! I guess I still got Boothe, but dang it! That there was two hundred, wasted down the shithole!"

"Alright look, Mister Hill," Dietrich chimed in. "How about I make you deal, are you listening?" He then asked.

"I'm listening, just hope I hear something good," I replied.

"Well, for your troubles, and for all that you have been through today...I will personally pay you back in full, how much was that bounty again?" Dietrich asked.

"Two hundred dollars," I responded.

"Two hundred," Dietrich repeated. "I will give you two hundred dollars then, plus an additional five hundred...And all of that will come from my very own life savings when we get back to Canden...I already make enough, and I feel like you deserve it."

Okay now I felt bad, but to be honest, it didn't sound like a bad deal at all, "I'll take you up on that offer...Hell, I guess at this point Boothe's all I need anyways," I remarked.

"You still look a little disgusted," Florence commented.

Though I may have seemed disgusted, I wasn't. "Nah, I'll be fine...Now I'm gonna head down to the river and wash my face," I said.

"Are you sure you're fine with my deal?" Dietrich asked.

"Yes doc, all of it sounds wonderful, and I really appreciate it...But to be honest with you I've got the shits building up, so I'll be back shortly," I stated, huffing impatiently under my breath.

"Didn't need to know that," Florence commented, taking a massive bite out of a piece of deer meat.

"Well, now you do," I sarcastically responded, "I'll be right back." I then turned and walked away from the camp. I could hear both men behind me talking again, but the further I walked towards the river in the tall grass, the more their voices got lower. Eventually I was far enough at the river's edge that I could not hear them at all. In fact, all I could hear was the gently flowing water that was gracefully moving downstream. I bent down on both of my knees, then I cupped both of my hands together, and splashed icy cold river water in my face. I grimaced at the cold water; it stung my face. However, I was able to rinse off most of the mud from my cheeks and forehead. I rubbed the back of my head a little; it still throbbed with much intensity. Now came the toughest decision I'd make on this entire expedition. I've done it multiple times, but it blows a big one every time. I don't know much about killing these here vampires, and how tough that'll be. But the hardest situation I think I'll ever have to face on this trip; is pulling down my drawers, squatting, and then sticking my bare ass out in front of God and the whole western world. I was about to do this, but then I felt a presence around me. I felt like I was being watched by someone.

I looked up towards the adjacent riverbank; there I heard the strangest and most ominous sounds I think I had ever heard. They sounded like a million voices; voices that would make any man's skin crawl. They certainly caught my attention, and I soon became drawn towards the adjacent wooded area across from me. All I saw on the other side of this river; was nothing but tall grass, and as I mentioned a wooded area. This area led into a small flat forest; most of which looked pitch black. However, out of the pitch black; came this figure. At first I wasn't too sure as to what it was, then it was clear. I was staring at what looked to be a woman.

She came to the edge of the river, but for some reason she was startled by the flowing water. I began to move along the riverbank; she followed me as I did. I locked eyes upon her, she was a beautiful woman/ She had dark hair, and her skin was so fine. Though she looked beautiful, she looked as if she was a whore. I mean this by the clothing that she was wearing. She had a little bit of cleavage showing, and she looked seductive to say it best. Her eyes were locked upon me, and then she did the unthinkable. She began to untie her top; she had a white corset with it, but that disappeared quickly. Soon, her torso was completely nude, and her breasts were exposed. I became aroused by this, no questions asked. I quickly forgot about my shit, as my eyes became so dead set on this woman. I couldn't control myself either. I was blank now; then the woman removed her bottom half. After that, I was then out of existence it seemed.

Her eyes now seemed to be the main focus point; I was drawn by those dark and stimulating eyes. The back part of mind was wondering, what in the hell is happening to me? I feel weak, but strong. Then in front of me and coming from behind was a crucifix. It waved in front of my face, pointed towards the strange incubus, and within a split second, my eyes began to burn. "Ah shit!" I screamed. I then heard the demonic-like woman scurry away, and she made a horrible sound too. It sounded like millions of demons; all chiming in at once. The sound sort of made me sick to my stomach, and I tried to endure the pain to my eyes. I then proclaimed, "Ah, dang it! What the hell is happening to my eyes?!" God the pain hurt, it felt like my eyes had hot rocks placed in them. They were hotter than a steaming pile of shit, on the hottest day in July. I continued screaming in agony, "Shit! Shit! Shit!"

I then heard Dietrich's voice from behind me, "You're going to be fine, Mister Hill!"

"It hurts dang, it!" I exclaimed.

I then heard Florence too, speak, I was blinded, "Was that Elizabeth?!" Florence asked.

"Doesn't matter, here grab that arm, we're going to help him back to the fire," Dietrich said.

"Shouldn't we put some cold water in his eyes?!" Florence asked, I could tell both men were in distress and worried for my sake.

"It won't help…we'll have to give it about five minutes to wear off," Dietrich replied.

Then I became disgusted, inquiring, "What the hell?! Five minutes?!" Both men then grabbed me by both arms and helped my blinded ass back towards camp. I could hear us scramble through some tall grass, I could feel cold air hit my cheeks, and I could hear both men breathing heavily. I could feel my heartbeat throbbing fast; I couldn't see a damn thing now. Everything was pitch black in my vision, and I didn't know why my heart was going a mile a second? My eyes still burned like the most dangerous inferno, and I didn't know if I'd ever see again or not? We continued to scramble though, and before it had started, we finally found our way back to our camp. I could tell we were back there; because I could smell the smoke coming from our fire. I was then placed down on some kind of hide; I think it was a bear hide that Florence had brought with him. I was placed down gently upon the hide; then I heard Dietrich and Florence walk away from where I was at. I continued to grimace in pain; my eyes were literally about to blow up in a blaze.

I put my hands over my eyes, and at this I heard Dietrich come in, "That won't help very much...You must be patient Mister Hill," Dietrich said.

"Oh, dear!" I proclaimed, "My eyes are on fucking fire right now!"

"Yes, I know Terence, but you need to give them a few more minutes, they'll be as good as new, I promise you this," Dietrich comfortably stated. I then heard Dietrich walk away from my position.

Then I smelt the deer; I felt a presence over me, it was Florence I knew it, "Hey, Ter…Everything's going to be fine old buddy."

At Florence's soothing voice, I replied, "God, I sure as hell hope so."

"Hey, if this makes you feel any happier, you did get to see a woman naked," Florence jokingly stated, in my right ear.

"Shut up," I replied, laughing as I did.

"I mean she wasn't bad looking at all…Minus her big old bush, I'd say she was as perfect as Bathsheba on the rooftop bathing," Florence remarked.

"Well, that doesn't sound too bad at all," I replied, then laughed.

"There you are," Florence remarked. "Did you ever do your business?" Florence asked.

Florence laughed, and I continued laughing too, "No…Was about to, until that whore showed up, and swooned me," I replied.

"Everything's going to be good, I promise Ter," Florence stated.

"I know," I replied. I then proceeded breathing ever so carefully; in and out slowly. I remained calm and to myself. I could still feel Florence's presence by my side; he was comforting me. Eventually, I began to see a light; slightly dim but it was a light. My vision had started to return, and I began to see a twilight sky from behind our camp. I saw Clay Mountain off in the distance behind us; Dietrich was in view and he was grabbing a few items from his bag. He pulled out a bag of mustard seeds, a necklace that had garlic cloves wreathed around it, and a small bottle of what appeared to be some kind of a liquid. "What's that bottle full of?" I asked.

"Holy Water, my good man," Dietrich replied. "Also, nice to see your vision has welcomed itself back," Dietrich commented.

"Yeah, but nevermind that it still burns like hell," I said.

"You will be fine, now...We'll proceed onward into that forest, adjacent to you, and we'd like you to come join us, Mister Hill," Dietrich said.

Petrified, I simply responded, "Hell no! My eyes were just set on fire, and you want me to follow you in there?"

"Well, I'd certainly hate to leave you here alone...What if she shows up again here? Then you would not have any means of defense necessary?" Dietrich wondered and concluded to himself.

"Listen, I ain't going through that there predicament again," I said.

"Ter, you're going to need to join us…The doc's right, we can't leave you here," Florence said, with much concern.

"I ain't going in there," I insisted, I then pulled out a cigar from my moist jacket pocket. However, I never got the cigar properly lit; it was too wet. At this, I muttered to myself, "Piece of shit."

"Mister Hill…we cannot, and I repeat we will not leave you here. You want to believe this here, right?" Dietrich then asked.

"I mean yeah," I stated, I then put my hand to my chest; right around my heart. My heart started beating ever so fast.

"Everything alright Ter?" Florence inquired.

"I think so," I replied. "My heart's losing its mind I think?" I wondered to myself.

Dietrich had a look of confusion upon his face, "Your heart faces the right side?" He inquired.

"I guess so…That's just usually where I feel it beating at," I stated, rubbing my right breast.

"You must have Dextrocardia...Usually the majority of your heart faces towards your left, very interesting," Dietrich replied.

"Dextro? What the hell did you just say?" I asked.

"Nothing, it's not important right now... Are you fine?" Dietrich asked.

"Yeah, I just witnessed a bunch of crazy shit...That's all," I sarcastically responded.

"Well, that's just a shock for your senses, now you need to join us on our hunt, Mister Hill," Dietrich urged.

I finally gave in to both men's wishes, "Alright, alright...alright...I'll join you both, but I better come out of this alive," I said.

"No worries Ter, I've gotten a lot of experience back in Canden," Florence stated. I then stood to my feet; however, my head began to spin ever so slightly. I caught my balance, and eventually I was back into myself. We collected a few supplies, and then eventually we walked out of our camp. We had two lanterns with us; one was red with an old rusted handle, that was Florence and I's lantern. Dietrich had a tall green lantern; and it looked to be brand new. As we left, going towards the river; Dietrich placed crosses all around the perimeter. This would ward off any of these so-called vampires away from our site.

I was still in a slight bit of shock it seemed though. My logic and reason was beginning to be thrown into the wind. I had no idea what kind of a shit show I had entered? A part of me was scared, though it seemed silly, I knew something was out of place here. As we entered the location, where my encounter with the whore from Canden went wrong; I began to feel sick to my stomach. My head got dizzy, and all surroundings seemed otherworldly to say it best. I felt as if I was in the presence of something far beyond human comprehension. I wasn't so sure as if I would ever come out of this, but I kept walking forward with Dietrich and Florence.

We crossed the river; it was very cold. Thankfully though, the deepest it ever got was two feet or so. As I pressed onward; I had a necklace filled with cloves of garlic on it. I smelt like shit, and I looked like a complete and total dumbass. But if this was all to protect me, and keep me from entering a certain fate, then I was all for it.

Eventually, we found ourselves at the end of the forest tree line; it was mainly a forest filled with many cedar and pines. The forest however looked pitch black; as now the sun had gone to sleep over the horizon. It felt eerie here; everything seemed so lifeless and without motion. It was pure silence. We entered into the forest and walked our way towards the western part of it.

Then I heard both Dietrich and Florence begin to mutter. It sounded like a little bit of prayer, and the voices seemed to be quite trembling upon release. Both men were muttering what sounded like scripture, "God is our refuge and strength, a very present help in trouble. Therefore will not we fear, though the earth be removed, and though the mountains be carried into the midst of the sea; Though the waters thereof roar and be troubled, though the mountains shake with swelling thereof. Selah," Dietrich spoke.

"Sounds like you're quoting the scripture," I stated. At this point it was starting to get much darker; Dietrich had his oil lantern, while Florence and I still had ours as well. Our lights illuminated the whole dark, and lifeless forest up.

"We're quoting the forty-sixth Psalm," Florence said, then he added, "Feel free to join us."

"Oh no, I'm afraid I'm not one to recite a scripture from the Bible, word by word," I replied.

"Well, I hope for your sake Mister Hill, you're at least praying?" Dietrich inquired.

"Oh don't you worry about that doc…I've been praying and cussing both at the same time," I replied.

Our conversations; echoed throughout the forest. It was an immense, dark, and lonely place.

No man would dare enter such an abyss of uncertainty. We continued forward but remained silent the whole way. We must've walked around a mile or so? Though we never saw anything whatsoever. The trees got closer and closer together, and the forest floor was a rough dirty terrain. Some trees poked up out of the ground; I even tripped over one. To which I replied, "What the hell?"

"What in the Sam hell is going on?" Florence asked me.

I looked down and saw a large root, strung all the way across the forest floor. "Hey, y'all watch out for these here tree roots," I said.

"We need to be looking down upon the ground anyways," Dietrich stated. Then he added, "Look for any signs of footprints."

Just as Dietrich had stated this; I heard the *snap* of a tree branch. Florence and Dietrich both heard it too. We all stopped dead in our tracks, and we remained silent again. Now, all we heard were the small echoes of silence and silence itself. Not one of us said a word; I could again feel my heartbeat fast. Panic had started to set in over my mind, however, I never lost my mind or anything. We stood there for only a few moments; until I then concluded, "Probably just a deer."

"Stay on your guard," Dietrich said, trembling as he did.

We then resumed our journey; none of us said a word. A few more minutes had passed; by now we had traveled about five hundred yards further into the woods from where we had heard the tree *snap*. Our breaths could be seen now; it must've dropped a few more in temperature. However, my blood was boiling at this point, and I really didn't give a rat's ass about temperature. I was too scared now. Yes, I'm a grown man and all, but I felt as if we were in grave danger. We then stopped; our breaths began to get thicker, and somehow it seemed to have gotten colder without any explanation. We were frozen, still as a blue sky on a clear day. We had walked into the middle part of this clearing, and we examined all of our surroundings. There was no signs of the whore anywhere, but I still felt as if somebody was right next to me. It also raised a huge eyebrow, as I quickly noticed the temperature in that vicinity began to drop further and further? Mysteriously, there were no signs of life in this forest; it felt like everything around us was pure dead. We proceed onward again; digging deeper into this eerie forest. We could hear the pines *creak* as a gentle cold, and brisk breeze ran by us. The *creaking* of these trees was unsettling to say it best, and my stomach sank to my toes.

None of us really knew what the hell was going on, but we continued to push regardless. We may meet a fate of death, but to be honest, all was unclear at this point? We walked another hundred feet or so; the cold air was getting too cold now. We had to stop in another clearing. This clearing in the forest; was much smaller than the last one, and it had four giant rocks in it. We all three took a seat on these rocks, and all of us blew warm air from our mouths into our hands. Our lanterns still lit up the whole forest, and our repellents still stayed by our side.

I was of course nervous as hell. But to calm this anxious feeling, I then quickly reached into my breast pocket, and pulled out another cigar. My hands were shaking; not because I was anxious, but because like I had mentioned a million times before, I was freezing my ass off out here. At this point in our journey; Florence had the lantern, and from the look in their lighting, I could tell they were just as miserable as I was. Florence had noticed me with my cigar, somehow. He then asked, "Do you ever not smoke, Ter?"

"Yeah," I replied. Then I added with a smile, "Once my cigar gets so small, and there ain't nothing left of it."

"I'd hate to see how your lungs are functioning now," Dietrich jokingly added.

"Well, I'm sure at this point in life…None of that really makes a damn bit of a difference," I said, laughing under my breath.

As soon as I stated this, Florence intervened, "Well enough of that…Shall we load our guns doc?" Florence asked.

"Yes that may be a great idea," Dietrich said.

"We gonna load them guns with them there sacred bullets that you mentioned about earlier?" I inquired, as I removed a match from my pocket, and then removed my Colt from my holster.

"Yes, what type of gun do you have?" Florence asked.

"I've got a Colt Forty-Five," I replied.

"Here," Dietrich stated, handing me a small glass, which had no top on it. "That's Holy Water…Just pour it upon your bullets that Florence gave you…Then softly dry it on your pants or something?"

It sounded like some crazy shit, but I did as Dietrich and Florence instructed. "Hope y'all ain't wrong here," I muttered to myself. I then poured the Holy Water on my bullets that Florence had handed me, and then quickly I rubbed the small form of liquid off on the outer edge of my fur coat. I then quickly loaded my chamber. I had a few regular bullets in the chamber too, but I too poured them with Holy Water.

As we sat there; it continued to get colder. The air got heavier, in fact, I could feel some sort of pressure upon my chest. We were all loading, sharpening, and cocking back our weapons. Florence had a large Bowie Knife, and he was sharpening it on the rock he was sitting at. There was one problem though, I had apparently left my bowie knife back at camp. I guess the gun was my main line of defense in this here situation? Just as we were sitting in a stillness, everything got eerily motionless. I lit my match, and then put it up to my cigar that was dangling from my mouth still as it was moments earlier. But just as I was lighting my cigar; a look of terror came upon both Dietrich and Florence's face. Apparently the light from my match; had shown the presence of some other entity from behind! Dietrich and Florence both sprang up; Dietrich whipped out his crucifix again, and Florence then threw a garlic clove right over my right shoulder. I then heard this horrid, demonic *shriek*. It made me jump too, and it freaked the fuck out of me. I quickly turned around to see what it was that both men caught a glimpse of. My light lost all visual of this apparent being! The dreaded undead vampire had apparently vanished out of our sight. "The hell was that?!" I asked.

"It was her…Oh my God it was her!" Florence exclaimed.

"Shine your lantern! Over in the tree line!" Dietrich shouted. His voice echoed throughout the forest.

We all shined our lanterns; all we could see though was darkness. Then we saw the whore again, suddenly too! She darted quickly from one tree to the other. She was still giving off this ungodly *shriek*, and the whore was completely nude. I was shaking in my boots, and I wasn't sure as to what move to make next? We all were breathing heavily; our breaths continued to show in the eerie lantern light. Dietrich then exclaimed, "We need to trap her! You men run to the right, and I'll run to the left! We'll throw mustard seeds on the ground, here!"

Dietrich then handed Florence and me a bag full of mustard seeds. "Alright," Florence stated, "Let's get the hell going!"

"Alrighty," I reacted with confusion.

With that, we all three took off in different directions. Florence and I both threw mustard seeds into a long line of trees in which the whore had descended into. My God my breath was like a ton, and each step I took, I wondered, would it be my last? We ran and ran. We must've ran about five hundred or so yards, and we also made our way down this hill. I could hear Dietrich on the other side, he was screaming gibberish, "What the hell is Dietrich saying?!" I asked.

"He's speaking in Hebrew tongue," Florence replied, he could barely breathe at this point. We could still hear something rustling in the dead leaves, but we weren't sure if it was Dietrich or the whore Elizabeth? By now we reached a point where we had repelled her enough, and we had now enclosed her area. We had her trapped within the seeds; she had no escape. We stopped throwing the seeds and found our way at a part where we might encounter the mysterious undead woman. However, we came full circle around and met Dietrich? We were hoping that it'd be Elizabeth, but it wasn't. Dietrich was breathing heavily, and he had a look of disorientation and confusion upon his face. "Doc, we were thinking that you were Elizabeth…The damn whore must still be in there?!" Florence angrily inquired.

"She's probably in the middle of the trees," Dietrich said, he then pointed to the middle of the trees.

"Did you see her?!" I asked Dietrich.

"I mean, I heard her moving, but—"

Just before Dietrich could finish, and as we were walking forward towards the middle, another Dietrich came right in front of us. There were two

Dietrichs, and apparently the one behind us wasn't who they appeared to be? The whore had tricked us. Dietrich's eyes, in front of us, got wide; he then whipped up his cross again. Now I knew, the second Dietrich, was the real Dietrich. We then turned and saw the most horrid looking nightmare I think I've ever seen. Elizabeth had now shapeshifted from Dietrich; to looking like this hellish, demonic beast looking creature. It was all black and had these ominous and dark red eyes!

"Holy shit!" I exclaimed. I quickly whipped out my Colt and fired a bullet right into the creature's torso. Once the bullet hit; it caused the area to burst into flames. Dietrich was speaking Hebrew; Florence was petrified. The demonic creature, despite being shot at numerous times, continued to come at us. Dietrich still held that cross high, and the creature continued to stay back. The creature I swear, was something that the devil himself would kick out of hell, I bet you he would. It was tall, I'd say a little taller than Florence and me; it had these long fingers and it had hair on its chest. Every inch of me was trembling with fear as we shot a few more shots at the vampire's torso. Blood was spurting from the point of impact, and everything all around was chaos. Even our lanterns' lights began to go dim, and the winds began to howl around us.

"Get out your knife!" Dietrich exclaimed to Florence.

"Hold your fire, Ter!" Florence shouted at me.

As soon as Florence had shouted, I let my gun down. He then approached the foul creature; throwing mustard seeds in its direction. Dietrich continued shouting in Hebrew. I was beyond the point of shock, my gun remained steady and loaded; I was ready for anything. As we began to weaken and corner the beast; Florence got no more than two feet from it. He had his Bowie Knife ready, and the creature continued to *shriek*. My God, the sound of this beast, would make any man's skin crawl, and make any man tremble with dread. Then, Florence was no more than a foot from the creature; the garlic also continued to repel and I was still beyond the point of disbelief. Then the creature got pissed; it struck back, and its sharp fingernails struck right at Florence's face. He reacted with much pain, "Ah, you bitch!"

The creature then came at us with such aggression, "Keep him back!" Dietrich exclaimed.

I grabbed Florence by his right shoulder and pulled him back from the creature. Then Florence shouted with disgust, "Where the hell is my knife?!"

Apparently, Florence had dropped his knife when the creature had struck him. "I don't know? Shine the light over there!" I exclaimed.

Under the creature; was Florence's knife, and now we had a serious problem. Florence was bleeding all across his face, and he had noticeable claws marks from the attack. I fired off some bullets, but all they did was slow the vampire down, "Will this damn thing ever die?!" I inquired.

"The bullets only weaken it, turn it to flames! We must at least pierce its heart!" Dietrich shouted.

Thinking quickly; I fired two more bullets right at its head. Blood was spraying everywhere, and flames were beginning to engulf the creature, but it wouldn't die. We then found a way to get Florence's knife into reach; to which we did thanks to Dietrich's wielding of the crucifix. "For God's sake, kill that whore!" Florence exclaimed.

I had plenty of cover at the moment; but my heart was still pounding like a drum. I quickly knelt down at the creature, and then I swiftly tumbled under the creature's legs. The creature was now in flames; I even felt those flames lick my body as I tumbled under it. I was moving so quickly, and my trembling was way beyond the point of normality. I grabbed Florence's knife in the tumble; then quickly I turned around at the back of the creature's body, and then swiftly stabbed the beast in the back. I lashed at its back multiple times; flames still licked me and I wasn't sure if I'd have any eyebrows after this or not? The creature then finally fell face first, but then it rolled over. Eventually, I was wrestling with the foul creature, but then it did the unthinkable. As I lashed at the vampire's chest; it quickly grabbed my neck and put me in this unbearable choke hold. I could still hear Dietrich shouting, and Florence was losing his shit too. At this point, I'm dead for sure. The knife was no more than two inches from its chest; I started to use all of my strength. I pushed with everything that I had in me, inching closer and closer towards the creature's chest. It was getting there, I knew it. Then I heard Florence load his gun; he then swiftly fired a few shouts at the vampire's head. Blood spurted from its wounds, but that did nothing but piss it off. The creature made the most horrid sounds; again, Satan would've probably kicked this thing's ass out of hell, no doubts.

I pushed and pushed. My arms started to shake; I was so terrified. But finally, the creature gave in, and I slowly then pushed inward into the creature's chest. For good measure; Florence shot another shot at its head, and I drove that knife in deep. I mean that son of a bitch was hitting the soil, I swear. It was dead, finally. I then backed up; the creature was now fully engulfed in flames. The wind had died down, and everything around us became silent again. I breathed in slowly, and then I got up onto my feet again. Dietrich then placed a garlic clove into the creature's mouth; it looked mangled now, and hopeless through the flames, but at least this shit, was over. As we stood there for a few moments, and examined the burning carcass,. Suddenly, I then felt a burning sensation around my arm. I looked down, "Shit fire!" I yelled. My arm was in flames from the scuffle!

Quickly Florence whipped out his cantine and calmed the flames all over my right arm. "Let me drench you there old boy!" Florence exclaimed.

"Ah shit!" I exclaimed. "Thankfully it ain't too bad I guess?! Do you see any more flames?!" I inquired.

"Nah, I think that's it?" Florence said. He was breathing heavily. The flames *sizzled* away quickly; we all three then stood there for what seemed like forever trying to collect our calm again.

Then after a few moments; Dietrich had this to say with a smirk, "Well, that worked out splendid gentlemen…Let's try that again, five more times."

Chapter 7

We eventually found ourselves walking back to our camp; not one of us spoke a word. I guess at this point, I had become a true believer of this here predicament, but a part of me had a hard time swallowing the circumstances. The night was still chilling my bones; the only noises I could hear were the rustling of our feet as we made our way back towards the edge of the forest. Our breaths were still thick and at the moment, Florence had the burnt carcass of the vampire over his shoulders. We had wrapped up the remains in a big gray clothed blanket, and then tied twine around both ends. It sort of looked like how my bounties would look, after I had shot them. As we were approaching the edge of the trees; I started hearing the faint noise of flowing water. My heart and head were still pounding at the moment, and I think my state of shock wasn't going anywhere at the moment. It was very hard to accept this fact, that is for sure. "Which one of the six was that again, Flor?" I asked Florence.

"This one here was Elizabeth, the whore," Florence replied.

"Y'all sure?" I asked. "You know, it was blacker than midnight there?"

"Nah, I know that was her...I never forget a pair of knockers like that," Florence jokingly replied.

"That...I did not need to know," I replied.

"Well what? I slept with her many times...Not as much as you did old buddy," Florence then turned, and winked at me in my lantern light.

"Oh my Lord, you and Elizabeth were involved?" Dietrich asked.

I laughed at Dietrich's remark, "We weren't much of anything," I then shook my head.

"Well, she was a very beautiful woman, swooning all those men as she did...It's just a shame she gave into a life of prostitution," Dietrich remarked.

"Doc, that was the main reason we never really worked out," I said.

"So, you two were serious?" Florence asked.

"Okay, sure we were, but I never really envisioned myself in a life with her like that, I guess I would consider myself a family man," I replied.

"So, is that why you moved to Austin?' Florence asked.

"You know damn good and well why I went down there...It was all for the Texas Ranger position, trust me, a woman was the least of my worries I can assure you that," I said.

"From what I overheard; you did settle down?" Florence asked.

"I did, with a woman named Anna," I said.

"Well, I would say, a family man now, would be the best way to describe you...But you had some rowdy times with old Liz here, let's not forget that," Florence said.

"We've all had our wild oats sown at some time, Flor," I said.

"I'd like to eventually find me a woman too, but I don't know...I like raising hell too much," Florence stated.

"Like I said before, some things never change," I said.

"I'll eventually come to my senses, but I'm enjoying the life of not having to care for anybody else but me, and me alone...You know honestly Ter, not sure why in the hell you gave up that life?" Florence inquired.

"Simply put, I needed a change of scenery I guess, and family was one of the biggest obstacles in my mind and heart," I stated.

"So, it sounds like to me, you've gone a bit soft there old buddy?" Florence asked.

"I'm not sure if soft's the word you're looking for…I've still got a spit of fire in my veins," I replied.

"Mister Hill, it sounds like to me a woman was one of your main concerns," Dietrich said.

"Okay, maybe it was, but I still put my ass to hard work for that ranger job," I stated.

"Still sounds like you've changed a bit though," Florence said.

"Maybe I have, it's a half and half deal I guess," I responded.

"Well, all I can say is, I can't wait to get back to camp, this dead body's starting to kill me…God almighty," Florence remarked.

"Well, the creature did have hair on it, then add that to the mix of burning flesh," Dietrich remarked; as we then began to cross the icy cold river.

"This ain't the same spot where we came in at," I said.

I had noticed in the light that the embankment looked a lot different, Florence noticed as well, he then commented, "Yeah doc, I think old sore ass is right, this ain't the spot where we came in at. There were also a lot fewer trees on the embankment where we entered too."

I rolled my eyes at Florence's remark, then I commented, "I think Florence is right…This don't look too familiar."

"Well gentlemen, we can't be that far off, I mean we stayed in a pretty straight line I thought?" Dietrich pondered.

"I think we went a little bit southwest if you ask me," I stated.

Just as I had stated my comment; we heard the faint sounds of our horses. It was coming in the direction of the northeast, which fit my claim correctly. We had exited the forest a little further towards the west. However, this wasn't a huge problem, we just simply shrugged it off, and continued in the direction of where we heard our horses. We walked about a hundred feet on the embankment; which had begun to flatten, when we then heard the horses again. This time, it sounded as if the horses were in distress. "We better go and see what those nags are crying about this time," Dietrich said.

"Indeed, we better hustle our asses...Here, Flor, let me carry Liz for a bit," I said, knowing that Florence had become exhausted.

"That ain't gonna bother me a bit," Florence commented.

Florence then handed the wrapped-up corpse to me; to which I flung it over my back just as Florence had done. Elizabeth was quite heavy; the stench was unbearable too. My feet are cold now, and I can barely feel them from where the water had soaked them. However, I continued forward, we were now worried for the sake of the horses. What were these animals crying out over? Yes, these were cries, something was startling them, I could tell. We had walked around a hundred feet or so, then the cries got closer; we were headed in the right direction. Though I carried the weighted foul creature upon my back with ease, it was still hard to breathe and the air still felt thick. However, again, something felt off, and then it felt like someone else was watching us. At this point, I wasn't feeling too good about all of this. This here predicament, is really starting to piss me off, and I don't feel like killing another vampire. I swear, all I want to do is get back to camp, and settle in. I'm wore the fuck out, and all of this chaos is not what I need right now. As we got closer; I began to smell the smell of that deer that Florence had prepared earlier. I even smelt the faint smell of our fire; which Dietrich had put out earlier before we had left.

We came back into the clearing where our camp was; there were the horses, and they were losing their shit. They were jumping up in the air, kicking as they did, and they were *shrieking* loudly as all get out. I put down Elizabeth's corpse; while Dietrich and Florence made their way over towards the horses. Just like earlier, we tried everything in our powers to get these mighty creatures calm and silent. I went over to my horse; which had started running back and forth throughout our camp. The horses at the carriage; weren't quite as rowdy as Florence and I's horses. It took a lot of patience, that is for sure, but eventually they got calm. I then saw Dietrich bent over; he was examining the ground in his lantern light. "Hey boys!" He shouted. "Come and take a look at this."

Florence and I walked over to Dietrich, "What in the hell are you looking at doc?" Florence asked.

"Do you see these," Dietrich was pointing; it appeared to be tracks in the ground, "Somebody's been here...Recently," Dietrich nervously stated.

"Looks like a pair of cavalry boots," I said.

"I know who wears those types," Florence commented.

"How do you know? Tons of people wear them types of boots," I said.

"Well, Marcy wears some like them, but I don't know if that's him or not?" Florence pondered.

"Look, there's another set of prints, them look like bare feet," I said.

On the ground, was indeed that; a set of bare footprints. "Looks like they belong to a woman, because them ones are small," Florence stated.

"I suggest we throw more seeds around our camp," Dietrich stated.

"Looks like them first set of seeds warded them off while we were gone, cause ain't none of them stepped in here," I said.

"You see Mister Hill; aren't you glad you came with us?" Dietrich inquired, with a smile.

"Sure am, but there's just one problem," I stated.

"What's that?" Dietrich asked.

"These footprints, they vanish," I said; my light was shining on the ground, as the prints of bare feet and boots seemed to have gone out of sight.

"Son of a bitch they do," Florence remarked.

"They shapeshifted...I would've swore that these would have been another couple, but now I know this must be them, we've certainly grabbed their attention," Dietrich said.

"Maybe the wind blew the rest of them tracks," Florence stated.

"Not likely, but I would stay on our guards tonight, we've got a long sleep ahead of us," Dietrich responded.

"What the hell," I said. "What are they? Ghost too?" I then asked.

"They took on the form of some kind of vapor or fog," Dietrich said. "However, that's not important, we need to start planning our next move here…Because they're somewhere nearby that is for sure."

"Well, there's a ridge up there about three or so miles, it's at the end of Wilmer's Peak," I said.

"Lots of caves up there?" Dietrich inquired; as he started to start another fire. Florence was putting away a few items.

I then joined Dietrich in starting another inferno. "Well, I know for a fact old Roger and Patrick hid up there for a few days, it's so secluded really," I replied.

"Interesting…We'll head that way first thing tomorrow," Dietrich said.

We then found ourselves in a state of absolute rest. As soon as we started our fire; all three of us then sat down on some rocks and began to lean back. We pissed around for a while. Eventually, Florence drifted off to sleep, and Dietrich and I sat in deep thought as we stared at the fire. "Terence?" Dietrich asked.

"What is it?" I inquired.

"I just wanted to thank you for coming along with us…I know it's all in an effort to get your bounty, but extra help is extra help," Dietrich said.

"Well, I'm much obliged to your statements, doc," I said; I then whipped out another cigar, and swiftly lit it. "It's certainly become an educational experience," I then added; as I then took a puff.

"You're certainly taking this situation here a lot better than I thought you would," Dietrich said.

"Well, I'm still racking a lot of clutter in my brain right now, shit, I didn't believe in these here vampires until no more than two hours ago," I stated.

"I know it is much to process, but I know you shall receive a large reward in the end…So, exactly how long has Fredrick been running?" Dietrich inquired.

"Well, I heard about his bounty back in late autumn, and that was just when I left Austin," I then took a large puff of my cigar. "Anyways, long story short, Roger and Patrick were top priority, then I heard of Fredrick's whereabouts…Heard he was around Canden, and then I heard he was in Indian Territory…Basically, I took a valuable detour," I said.

"I hope that the detour will be well worth it for you," Dietrich stated.

"Oh, I know it will," I confidently responded. "Honestly doc, if it hadn't been for you saving my ass back there at that river, I wouldn't be sitting here talking to you, ain't no doubt there," I then said with a grin.

"It's no problem my good man," Dietrich said.

"So, what's this here Julius like? How'd he get out?" I asked.

"Verna is intelligent…He knew of the plot against him long before we ridded the town of evil," Dietrich said.

"How did he get into the company of Thomas and Fredrick?" I asked.

"They had met in the Canden Saloon…They'd win just about every card game, and I believe they took much advantage of their newfound powers," Dietrich replied.

"Wait, they got inside people's heads?" I asked.

"Indeed, and not just that...Hypnotism is a vampire's strongest ally, and we must keep our heads strong and keep our defenses by us at all times," Dietrich responded.

"I'll tell you this though, ain't no blood sucking demon getting control over this body," I stated.

"Well, you were under Elizabeth's control temporarily," Dietrich said.

Acknowledging that situation with a grin, I then stated, "Well, maybe one can...But I'll tell you this, it ain't happening again, I can assure you that."

"I would hope not...But as for Julius, he was the main carrier of that dreaded curse when he came into our town, and it was only by the grace of God himself that we were able to drive a few of them out," Dietrich said.

"Thank the heavenly father," I said.

"Indeed...But in all seriousness Mister Hill, do not underestimate the powers of the vampire, especially Julius, that man is a true monster," Dietrich stated, trembling as he did.

"As for Thomas and Fredrick?" I inquired.

"I'd keep my head strong with them as well…Again, do not underestimate them, they may be Julius's side acts, but they're powerful and intelligent too," Dietrich replied.

"I'll keep that in the top part of my brain, doc," I responded.

"That would be very important," Dietrich said. "Well, Mister Hill, we have much ahead in our travels tomorrow, how long should it take to get up on that peak that you had spoken of?" Dietrich then asked.

"Should take no more than a morning's travel…Then I'll show you boys the way towards the caverns, those were the caves I referred to earlier this morning," I replied.

"That sounds splendid, my good man," Dietrich responded, giddily.

"Hell yeah," I said. "Let's have whiskey for good luck."

"Don't think I will, it doesn't settle the greatest with me…Being that it is so late you see," Dietrich said.

"I understand doc, but I'm craving a stiff one myself," I said. I then got up and went over to my saddle bag. I pulled out a bottle of Old Forester whiskey; it hadn't been opened the whole journey, and I think now was the perfect time. I quickly then grabbed my tin cup, and then slowly drowned it. "Well, this here drink, is dedicated to the killings of this here Fang Gang," I then raised my cup; I was laughing under my breath, and Dietrich was grinning too. "To the Fang Gang."

"To the Fang Gang," Dietrich muttered, tilting his head forward in my direction.

I swallowed the whiskey; God almighty, it was some strong stuff. But I had craved a good swig, and this felt like pure bliss indeed. Dietrich and I then pitched both tents. Dietrich then woke up Florence; who then groggily walked his way over towards his newly pitched tent, and I then joined him. Again, I slept with my head one way, and Florence had his head at my feet. We then both drifted off; all while terrible thoughts swarmed through my head. I was now feeling uneasy about this here predicament, and I didn't know if I should be afraid? Or if I should be shrugging this whole thing off? It was certainly peculiar; I felt comfortable being a hunter of the undead but I also felt beyond mortified. Maybe the shock had worn away a lot quicker than I thought it would? But shit, I didn't know how to feel? Would this work? I asked so many questions like that; I was now scared but secured in my own comfort. My mind had so many problems; but the brewing of these here thoughts, soon led to my mind growing weary. I soon then slipped away into an immense abyss of absolute slumber.

Chapter 8

This sleep was just like any other, but again I had another dream; it was my darling Anna once more. Oh my, my sweet Anna; she looked fresher than a summer's rain in July. I was walking with her, hand in hand, through one of our many pastures located on our land in Austin. We were happy there, but something felt off. Though the day was bright, and the sun beamed upon us like heaven's light itself, something felt wrong. It felt as if an omen was steadily approaching our lives and I could feel this feeling of uneasiness come over me. I can remember I was looking down at one point; my mind was going through all of the emotions of what it would be like to be a father and Anna I'm sure was thinking the same. Only her thoughts were of being a mother, of course. I then looked up towards Anna; she had this graceful smile upon her face. She looked very much at peace, and I could tell that she was feeling absolute ecstasy at this moment in time.

Then suddenly; that face of joy and grace was no more. She then turned white; whiter than the whitest blizzard. A feeling of panic came over me, what should I do? I seemed helpless to her in this dream. I caught her in my arms as she fell forward towards me, and now there was a chance to save her, I thought? Maybe she was hot from the weather? I didn't know what was going on for a second, but then my consciousness caught up with me, this was all in the past.

I then blanked out for a second; I think a part of my soul was trying to outrun the inevitable fate of Anna. I knew what had happened, and I began to squirm in my sleep. I could feel myself moving about in my hide; I then felt that same old blast of frosty air, that I had felt a million times before, and it hit my back with such force. I awoke; I jolted up. I was breathing heavily, and I was looking around frantically. I looked over at Florence; he was still fast asleep. He was snoring, and oh my, I think he was sucking all of the air out of our tent too. I then pulled myself up and exited our tent. The air this morning; was certainly brisk indeed, and the bite of it was tough.

I then gritted my teeth and crossed both of my arms. Though I was warm ever so slightly, it was still colder than Jack Frost's pecker. My breath was still quite thick, and at this point, the spring months could not have come faster. I'm seriously really sick of this bullshit. Either way, a part of me was freezing, but one thing that remained, was that bad vision of my dear Anna. I guess I could not accept that fate, much like I could not accept this here predicament, that I had gotten myself into. I was anxious to see where our journey might take us today now, because all that mattered still was getting Fredrick.

That old bastard is really giving me the throb in my head, and I'm so close to him and his other two cronies, that I can almost smell it. In fact, I think it could be possible that maybe these vampires might be all hiding up on Wilmer's Peak? It's certainly something to think on, but I know we're close to at least two more, because they were just here last night. I looked off into the distant morning sky, my God, it was like something that only Winslow Homer himself would illustrate. The sky was filled with many colors; orange along with a little purple here and there and what looked to be a green star of some sorts? The sun had not quite kissed the horizon, but I knew any minute now it would. Dietrich and Florence both would arise from their slumbers as well. By now I was starving, and I knew that one of the best foods to eat right now would be a nice and juicy wild boar. I knew that many of them shuffled around here, and it's now or never about hunting. However, first things first, a bath was one of the most important elements on my mind. I still thought about it; mainly because I still smelt like the inside of someone's asshole. Honestly though, a nice dip in a nearby hot spring would surely brighten my mood. I gazed around our campsite; all of the crosses that Dietrich had placed down the night before, were still accounted for.

I then walked over to my horse; who was now seated upon the cold and dirty ground. I could hear the rustling of the cold brisk wind hit the tall grass that surrounded us; oh boy, it was like music to my ears. I loved the sound of softly swaying tall grass in a field, it always took me back to my home in Austin, the home where my dear Anna was. However, those grasslands were miles away, but just the thought took me there, and I felt a sense of peace and comfort. Though this journey by now has had its troubles, it's the little things like this that really outweigh the bad, I think. My biggest concern though, was getting this ungodly smell off of my body. I swear, at this point, I'm getting so sick and tired of smelling like shit and cigars. My body is starting to become irritated; I've got rashes in places where rashes shouldn't be and my ass still feels like Satan lit a match at the top of it.

I grabbed a few items out of my saddle bag; the first was a small glass bottle of cologne as well as a small sponge in which I would bathe with/ I also grabbed another cigar for the hell of it. I then began my walk out of our camp; there is much grass that surrounds us still. I can also still see Clay Mountain off in the distance; as well as

Wilmer's Peak to the right of me and in the distance are a few forests and woodlands. It's mostly flat out here, with the exception of a few hills here and there. This land is meant for no man, and that's why it still belongs to the Comanche.

I had picked up one of the many crosses that Dietrich had staked into the ground and began carrying it with me in my right hand. I was well prepared for anything this time; however I still trembled at the thought of what had happened last night. Seeing that creature, whatever the hell Elizabeth had become, certainly made my mind run a million miles an hour. But all that seemed like a week ago, mysteriously. Though it was crazy last night, it seemed almost like a distant memory. I guess at this point, hunting vampires was like hunting bounties, and it was on to the next. I walked out about a hundred yards away; I then stopped for a second here. I whipped out a match, lit it, and then lit my cigar. The cigar as usual was warm, but the uneasiness of silence certainly ran my trembling fears high. Seriously, it was so quiet out here in the early morning, that I swear I could hear a hair drop. The silence was quite eerie too, but for some reason, I didn't feel the presence of anyone around me. I just felt cold, and lonely to say it best. I trucked onward; the terrain shifted from many hills to many flat straight walks. My breath could be seen, and the smoke from my cigar was making it thicker too. Each step I took, felt like a challenge of some sorts, and I could feel every joint in my bone structure tighten up. The cold was getting straight to my bones. I could feel it.

My hopes were high though, and maybe I've gone around a mile now, but at least this gives me a chance to be alone in my thoughts. Seriously, walking out here in this wilderness is much like a thirty-minute holiday. Not only did I get a chance to catch up with myself and dissect this here predicament, but I got a chance to see such a beautiful sunrise. I must've walked about a million steps it seemed, but up ahead, my hopes and prayers were finally being answered. I could see it; it appeared to be a slight vapor rising slowly out of the middle of this tall grassy area. Though I was tickled to piss, I began to have doubts in the back of my mind, but I was still hopeful to say it best. I picked up speed towards the rising steam; to which sure enough it was indeed mist rising out of a lone and small hot spring. Immediately I began to strip down naked; this was absolutely not the best idea right now especially with it being as cold as it was. But at this point, I needed a good bath, and I needed it in a good hot spring, this is for sure. Once I got naked, the cold snapped at my body, and instantly I began to go numb. Quickly though, I swiftly moved my way into the hot spring, and began rinsing myself with the warm and refreshing water.

I washed my privates, my arms, and my face really well. The sponge had a crusty feel to it, but I simply just kept washing anyway. This bath was pure bliss I tell you, nothing else on this Earth could feel as good as I do right now. The spring wasn't but only three or four feet deep, which made this bathing scenario much easier than it needed to be. Eventually, after I had rinsed all of the grime and more from my face, I began to slowly make my way over towards my clothes. Then suddenly, I heard what had sounded like a small *grunt* of something; I turned towards my left and emerging from the tall dead prairie was a wild boar. This was breakfast I thought, but there was but one problem. I was streak ass nude. I didn't want to get anywhere close to this creature; everybody knows you don't come anywhere near a wild and angry boar. He sniffed about the area; then the little shit decided to take a piss on my clothes. "You little bastard," I mumbled under my breath. Sure I was clean, but now I've got to walk back to camp, with clothes that smell like boar piss! My day wasn't starting out on the right foot. However, I began to slowly creep forward; the boar noticed me. He then started to stomp his right foot. At this I stopped creeping and remained in my place. Then, to add to the insult, the damn thing then proceeded to fiddle with my clothes. I had forgotten about a small piece of bread that I had left in my right coat pocket!

The stupid thing then proceeded into an all-out scuffle with my clothing, as it was trying to find the piece of bread in the process. Eventually, the hog did find the piece, but only after it had torn my long johns and shirt to shreds! Then the hog got its tusks caught into the belt loops of my pants. The creature went absolutely nuts after that. It was going into a state of panic. It then got its head tangled up well within my shirt. I initially reacted, "You little shit!" I shouted. The boar then stomped off into a set of bushes; he was carrying pretty much all of my clothing, because his right foot had taken my long johns and shirt with it. I quickly emerged from my warm spring and found myself naked and pissed. The boar had left my boots and coat, that was all I had to wear! I picked up the boots and gave them a good sniff. "Dear God," I stated. The smell of boar piss was absolutely unbearable, and my coat didn't suit any better either. I quickly threw the coat on; despite the fact that my good old boy, Mister Johnson, was still dangling out in the brisk cold morning air! By this of course, I'm referring to my stone cold penis! I threw on my boots as well, and in general, I guess you could say now, that I looked like a complete and total dumbass.

I had no idea how I was going to explain this here situation to Dietrich and Florence when I got back? Regardless, I still needed to salvage some of my clothes; I needed something to hide my junk. As I approached the shrubs; I heard a rustle, then I saw a few bushes bash about. It must be the boar charging? I thought, so calmly I backed away. However, that wasn't enough, this boar was pissed off, way more pissed than I was! Then suddenly, the damn thing emerged from the bushes; it was snorting and squealing. I quickly ran in the other direction; a look of terror upon my face said it all. Now here I was; bare ass nude, wearing nothing but a coat and boots and I'm running for my life. The boar that was chasing me, couldn't be no more than five hundred pounds, but I wasn't about to find that out. I wasn't one who wanted to know how it feels to be gauged and gored by a big boar. This boar was fast too, despite the fact that he was big, he wasn't no more than fifty to hundred yards behind me now. I then quickly shifted my running, towards the direction of our camp. I was breathing heavily of course, and every stride that I took, it became harder to breathe. My whole naked body was becoming numb instantly. Fortunately, there appeared to be a small group of bushes up ahead; I found this as a great opportunity to hide out from the creature. I proceeded towards the bushes; the boar had started to lose sight of me. I eventually found myself situated behind a few dead rose bushes; I carefully knelt down and waited to see if the boar would come any closer to my position.

My heart was pounding so hard, I thought it might actually explode. My blood was boiling like a pot of soup, but I stayed in my place, calm and reserved.

I knelt down for no more than a minute; eventually I concluded that my friend would not be making a surprise visit to me in these shrubs so I then stood. As I was walking away though; I felt the nastiest prick I think I've ever felt! A rose limb from the bush I was standing by had caught the top of my thighs, my pelvis, and worst of all, my pubic region and penis! It hurt like hell! I had about fifty or so thorns lodged into my skin now, and blood is starting to ooze from the puncture wounds. "Son...of a...bitch," I said. I stopped for a moment and collected my breath. I then inhaled and mustered up the strength. I carefully began to remove a set of thorns lodged in my thighs, which wasn't so bad. However, the removal of the thorns from my pelvic and pubic region were the absolute worst. One of the thorns had even become lodged in my urethra. I carefully pulled that out, "Fuck!" I yelled. I grimaced a majority of the time of course; it was at this point that I had thought I might actually bleed to death. My thighs and pubic hair were soaked with blood; dear God, no man should ever have to face this here predicament! Eventually, all the thorns that I saw were removed; then carefully I took a few steps forward. I minded my surroundings and watched for the wild hog too.

There was no hog in sight now; just me and the bushes. At the moment, my morning had obviously not started like it should have, but I still had a chance to seize this here day, despite the unfortunate circumstances! I carefully stepped out into the open of where these bushes were. Then out of the blue; I heard the sound of shuffling feet and rustling. Thinking it may be the hog, I began to then quickly shuffle my feet away from the direction to where the noises were coming from. I quickly walked away from the direction, over towards another adjacent shrubbery. Over by another set of bushes were a couple of small boulders sticking up out of the ground. I hid behind one of them and waited on the unknown assailant. The sounds were getting closer and closer; I crept over behind what looked to be a Barberry Bush. However, this sound didn't sound like an animal. I could hear the small faint sounds of spurs *clinging* as each step was taken, and at this thought, I knew, it must be Florence.

Of course now I'm in a state of panic and confusion. How in the name of all that's holy am I going to explain this? The spur *clings* got louder and louder, and my blood started cooking. Soon, Florence did reach the bushes to where I was at; he was now wearing what looked to be some kind of fur on his pants. Florence had a pipe in his mouth too and his eyes were traveling about the surrounding bushes. He had this dead look to his face; his eyes were kind of misty. "Ter, was that you? Where are you, old buddy?" Florence asked.

"Well, I'm over here behind this Barberry right now...Say, you wouldn't happen to have any bandages or wrappings on you?" I asked.

"No, why? What the hell did you get yourself into?" Florence inquired.

My face had started to turn as red as a beet. "Well, it's a long, sad, yet funny story," I said. "By the way, I need some clothes too, have you got any of those on you?" I clumsily asked.

"Don't tell me you're nude as a jaybird?" Florence asked.

"You see, this morning, I found me this here nice, warm, and comforting hot spring," I stated. I then slowly, but shamefully walked out into Florence's view; my head was hung low and my hands were covering my private areas. "Well, long story short, a damn boar came along and robbed me of my clothing...Left me with nothing but my jacket, which smells lovely now, by the way...Oh and the damn thing did happen to leave my boots, thankfully," I said, rolling my eyes as I did.

"What in God's name?" Florence asked himself. He paused for a moment or two; then he bursted into laughter. "Well my oh my, looks like that hog was trying to get himself a date I see!" Florence exclaimed; he was half dead from laughter.

"Should have stayed in the bushes," I said, rolling my eyes.

"No, no, this is too good!" Florence exclaimed.

"I tell you what Flor, I get myself into some of the shittiest predicaments...First thing this morning; damn boar pisses on my clothes! Then he chases my ass, while I'm running streak ass nude! Then to top it all off, my pecker's gotten a good prick from the thorn bush over there too! I swear to all that's holy!" I exclaimed.

Florence then interrupted my rant, "Alright, listen you crazy son of a gun; I'll take you back, and have the doc address your...Problem...Then we've got to get a move on, if we want to reach Hank's some time tonight or tomorrow," Florence said.

"I know we gotta get going, but dang it! Why me?!" I inquired angrily.

"So, you got your old John Thomas stuck in some thorns?" Florence asked, giggling as he did.

"Yeah, yeah, yeah...I know...Like I said, long, sad, but funny. Mostly though painful," I said with a grimace, as a sharp pain shot up my leg.

"My God Ter, you have the worst luck down there…First you ass was sore, and now this!" Florence laughed.

"Yeah I know, ha ha ha, very funny," I said.

"Screw the sore ass nickname, I'll just start calling you old prickly dick," Florence said; his laugh got more exaggerated.

We walked our way back over towards camp; the whole way over, Florence was of course giving me hell. It was all he'd ever do really; that bastard loved turning the most painful and out of line situations into his very own entertainment show. The whole time I kept myself tuned out; I looked down at my bare thighs the whole trip, hoping that they wouldn't turn purple. Frostbite was the last thing I needed right now, trust me. The blood from my puncture wounds around my pelvis; had started to freeze. It was certainly not a pretty sight, and this stroll back to camp couldn't go any faster it seemed. I actually hadn't stopped too far away; we merely walked a good one thousand feet, and then there it was. The camp; it was just as it was when I left it this morning. Florence or Dietrich, though, had started a fire. The hides were still strung out all over the place; there was a deer hide on the same rock that I had sat upon last night. I slowly sat upon the rock, and as soon as my nut sack had touched the top of that hair; a few spurts of sharp pain shot up through my testicles. Apparently there were still a few thorns still lodged there, "Mother of Joseph!" I exclaimed.

"What in the hell are you whining about now?" Florence sarcastically asked.

"There's still apparently some more thorns in my ball sack?!" I said.

"Well here," Florence said; he was reaching for another hide which appeared to be a bear. "Cover your legs and everything...I'm done staring at your ding dong for a little while."

"Son...Of a...Bastard!" I shouted.

"Ter!" Florence exclaimed, shocked it seemed from my swearing.

"Sorry, it just hurts, dang it!" I shouted.

"Well pull the little varmints out of there!" Florence shouted.

"Just give me a second here," I said, trying to collect my breath. It truly was painful; probably the worst pain I've ever felt.

"Well stay there...Pull the thorns out first off, and I'll see what the doc's got," Florence said.

"Alright," I responded. Florence then turned around; he descended into Dietrich's hide filled tent.

While Florence went in to talk with Dietrich; I began the long and painful process of plucking each thorn off of my scrotum. "Oh…Cow pie!" I said to myself, grimacing. I bit down on my lip too; one thorn at a time, I pulled one out after the other. Quickly, Florence then exited the tent; he had a look of confusion upon his face. "Where the hell's the doc?" I asked.

"I don't know?" Florence wondered; he looked bewildered. "Doc!" Florence shouted out. There was no reply.

I then joined in, "Doc! Where the hell are you?!" I shouted.

"Hey Dietrich, where are you man!" Florence yelled once more. We searched our whole surroundings, not a trace of Dietrich anywhere? "It's not like him to just take off," Florence said.

As soon as Florence made his statement; I then noticed Dietrich's cross that he had around his neck last night. It was laying on the same rock that he had sat on yesterday evening. "Hey Flor, look," I said.

Florence gazed at the crucifix, "It's the doc's cross," Florence said. He picked up the cross and examined it. "He usually wears this thing twenty-four hours a day," Florence commented.

"Well, he clearly ain't wearing it this hour," I said.

"You don't think he?" Florence asked.

"You don't think he, what?" I inquired.

"I know I've only known these here vampires for a mere short while, but they do know how to lure someone, just look at what happened to you last night," Florence said.

"I thought the doc said they usually don't come out in the daylight?" I asked.

"Well they may not, but that doesn't mean they can't lure somebody in from it…They ain't got to worry about nothing…No worries of the sun hitting their skins, just fresh blood at their disposal I guess?" Florence wondered.

"We need to go search upon Wilmer's Peak," I said.

"Why there?" Florence asked.

"Well, that's the only place that's got a million dark caves…Plus it's the closest…That might be where these here blood lusters hide, and besides, that was our destination for the day anyways," I replied.

"We'll head up there then…Did he walk on foot?" Florence asked, sounding baffled as he did.

I gazed over to my right to where the horses and carriage were resting; I noticed that one horse was missing, "Looks like he took one of them nags," I replied.

"We'll have to get a move on, but first things first old buddy," Florence said.

"What's that?" I asked.

"Go into my leather bag, it's in our tent, I brought along a spare set of clothes," Florence stated.

"I need to at least wrap up my…Problem first," I said with embarrassment.

"We got some bandages, in the doc's handbag…Hold on a moment," Florence said; he then walked into Dietrich's quarters. He pulled out what looked to be a black carrying bag; it must've housed a few medical supplies? "Here, this ought to fix you up really good," Florence stated, as he started to unwind a big strip of wrapping.

"Well thank you, old boy," I said.

"I ain't wrapping you by the way, you'll just have to do that whole endeavor yourself," Florence said.

"Oh come on Flor, you said you wouldn't mind cleaning the top of my ass crack, so this can't be any worse," I said, laughing under my breath.

"Never said such a thing there, old sore ass…Or I mean, old prickly dick," Florence responded; shining a big grin on his face.

Florence and I exchanged a few smiles back and forth for a moment. I then proceeded to tightly wrap up my puncture wounds. By this point; the pain was non-existent. Probably due to the fact that I had no feeling in my thighs at the moment. The cold I swear was getting to me; I was surprised I was even still standing. I wrapped my wounds well; Florence was loading up a few supplies as I did. I eventually had everything bandaged and ready. By the time Florence had gathered his garlic cloves, sacred bullets, and crucifixes I had already thrown on my new get up. I have to say, I really liked old Flor's style. He gave me a spare outfit; it was very similar to what he was wearing only it was much more of a darker brown. It had those tassels hanging down all along the sleeves, and the pants fit tighter than a corset on an overweight woman. I gathered up my shotgun, I also gathered up my rifle too. We then got our horses together and set off in the direction of Wilmer's Peak. Just beyond the peak, a mere ten miles away, was Hank's Lodge. It was a place that we had muttered about before, and our goal was to hopefully reach it by nightfall tonight or tomorrow. However, because of the strange disappearance now of our dear doctor, it doesn't look like we're going to make it up there tonight. Who knows how far Dietrich went? Who knows if the man even went up to Wilmer's? All I knew was, something, or someone, called him up there, and caused him to blank out of reality.

Chapter 9

Our journey into this uncharted wilderness was certainly mind boggling. This part of Indian Territory was nothing short of God's country. Florence and I were steadily making our way along this valley. Surrounding us on both ends were a set of ridges and peaks. The sun had risen upon this land like a man rising from his early morning slumber, and the sky had consumed the air around us with the most absolute bluest blue I've ever seen. It was starting to warm up by this point in our journey; we had traveled for a little over two hours, and we were hot on the trail of Wilmer's Peak. Florence and I kept our horses on this trail; from the looks of the dead soil, we could see what appeared to be hoof prints, and the prints seemed to have stayed perfectly in line with our journey too. The prints appeared to be much farther apart than normal; this indicated that Dietrich's horse had been running, not casually strolling. We didn't want to give ourselves a way by trotting fast up through the valley, simply because both of us had not one clue of Dietrich's whereabouts? We were just casually strolling. However, we weren't exactly going slow by any means. Our horses kept a good fast pace the whole way. We didn't know what we might encounter in our trek, so we stayed on our guards as much as we could. "We might need to pick up the pace here," Florence suggested.

"No, we'll go at the pace we've been going...There's no need for panic in a situation like this," I said.

"Hell Ter, I bet you the son of bitch went sleepwalking," Florence said.

"On a horse?" I inquired.

"Well maybe, I don't know?" Florence asked himself.

"Sleepwalkers walk on foot, they're also not very well coordinated either," I said.

"It was just a suggestion," Florence hastily responded, almost as if he was annoyed with my smartass response.

"Listen, I'm sorry, I wasn't trying to be a smartass, but this whole situation is quite odd, and honestly I don't know where he is?" I wondered.

"Thought you said he was at Wilmer's?" Florence inquired.

"I said it might be a good spot for these here vampires to hide out, but I never said it was absolutely certain though," I replied.

"Well, that's just great, now we have no idea if what the hell we're doing is right or not!" Florence exclaimed.

"That ain't going to be the case old boy, we will find Dietrich, that is a promise that I swear on my father's grave," I said.

"We better find him, we still have to find five others after this," Florence said.

"I know what we have to do, and as Dietrich said, we will do what we have to do…Regardless if we find the doc or not," I said.

"We are not losing him, old buddy," Florence commented.

"Never said we were," I said.

"I know you didn't…It's just that, I'm scared as hell right now," Florence stated.

"Why should you be? We've got all of the supplies, ain't that protection enough?" I asked.

"Well, I ain't going out without living life first," Florence replied.

"What do you mean by that? You've had a wonderful life," I asked and commented.

"Yeah, but I never got to experience certain things yet," Florence said.

"What the hell does that mean?" I asked.

"Well, I've never been as far as the northeastern and northwestern parts of the state…I've always wanted to travel the country, you know," Florence stated.

"Well, you're traveling through some country right now, and we're in the central northern part too," I remarked, grinning as I did.

"Yeah sure, but I've always wanted to see California," Florence said.

"Oh Flor, would you stop it, we're going to get out of this here predicament, I can promise you this," I said.

"You know, you're taking this here vampire problem with the utmost confidence," Florence remarked; he then whipped out a cigar from his breast pocket and lit it.

"I don't know if it's confidence that I have…It's been a long haul for me, and this here face I put on might just be a little bit of shock, I don't know?" I wondered. "I tend to show my emotions more differently than you think," I then added.

"Well you've been taking it a lot better than I have," Florence remarked. By now, we were edging nearer to the edge of Wilmer's Peak. The sun was crawling to the top of the sky like a spider. This part of the wilderness showed much life; within the regards of more pines and cedars that is. It was beautiful, but everything around us was dead still due to the fact that winter still had much more thriving to do. We eventually found ourselves along this river; it looked to be the same one that flowed into Texas, the same river that I was at earlier the day before yesterday. Honestly, I didn't quite know where we were at? But Wilmer's Peak was a mountain that I had seen a hundred times before out here, only I had never made the journey up here to it. It was, though, an absolute sight to behold. We had stopped our horses in the river so they could get something to drink; both of our horses seemed to have stumbled along the latter part of our trek.

The river that we were in was below this small drop off, adjacent to our vantage point. There were plenty of pine trees around our surroundings, and the river that was slowly flowing by us was nothing short of cold. Despite the cold river; it was pleasantly warm outside for this time of the year. I had started to feel small drops of sweat trickle down my forehead. I slowly pulled my hat off and began to wave it in my face to cool myself down. The horses drank with such aggression, as Florence and I both pulled ourselves down off of them. "Be careful where your spurs hit when you get down, old boy!" I shouted out to Florence.

"Why's this?" Florence asked.

"Well, I've got a shitload of gunpowder in these bags, both of them! Don't want all of that everywhere! Very explosive stuff you know!" I exclaimed.

"Says the man that smokes often!" Florence sniped back.

"Yeah, yeah, yeah," I muttered to myself.

As we pulled ourselves down, we gazed around at our settings; upon the ground I noticed more of the hoofprints. Though they soon began to weave their way off into the cold icy river. This disappointed me, as now I had no clue as to how far the horse had moved upstream through the waters? "Shit! The damn prints exit right into the stream! Who knows how far it went through the water?" I wondered.

"Let's take a load off for a while Ter, I'm deader than my eyes after I've had about five shots of Overholt," Florence stated.

"That don't sound too bad, partner," I commented.

Florence and I sat down on two small rocks; however they were very firm and well stabled. The dirt along the river was dry, and it had very little life within it. There were mostly other rocks and twigs throughout the ground. Florence smoked his cigar; the aroma of it smelt like strawberry. "Terence, there's something that I've been meaning to talk with you about," Florence said.

"Well, I ain't never heard you say my name like that before," I remarked. "Only time you call me Terence is when it's something serious," I then added; I then pulled out my knife to sharpen it.

"Maybe it is, but I've been meaning to ask you something, mainly about your choice to become a bounty hunter," Florence said.

"What did you want to ask me?" I inquired.

"Well, it's just that...I never would've thought in the years that I've known you, that you'd even consider doing something like this," Florence remarked.

"Well, it was a choice...I guess I made it because of the state of my life at the time," I said.

"What does that mean?" Florence asked.

"Shit, I honestly don't know old boy? I guess...For one thing Flor, I made a decision that

I thought felt necessary, not because I thought of the reward, but because I had thought of my inner turmoil," I replied.

"I knew it," Florence remarked. He then took a puff of his cigar, then asked, "I knew you were upset, was it your woman?"

"I'd rather not touch on that subject, I've been through a lot of shit throughout the last half of last year…So…I'll just forget it," I said.

"Okay, I'll say no more, but I did want to ask you for advice on something," Florence said.

"What is that?" I asked.

"Well, women?" Florence asked.

"Oh Lord have mercy, I'm not even going to begin on that," I replied.

"Nah, it's just that Ter, I feel like I need to settle down myself too," Florence said. "You've been there for me since we were small boys, and I couldn't have asked for a better sheriff than you," Florence then complimented.

"Well, thank you," I responded.

"But I um…Really want to know what your secret was, and how you were able to find your one and only? Are you both still together?" Florence inquired.

"Well, again I ain't touching on that, but in order to truly find that woman, the one...You've got to show that one thing that we talked about earlier, and that's patience," I said. "She's out there old boy, you've just got to start looking in the right batch," I then added with a grin.

"So, you're telling me I should calm my old self down huh?" Florence asked, laughing as he did.

"Hell yeah brother, take it easy man, and just find the means of good change," I said. "This life's so precious my friend...We all have to make choices...It's just that...We sometimes have to make the wrong choices, before we get to the right ones," I then added; smiling as I did.

"I guess that ain't bad advice at all, it's just that, this life I've been living lately, has been so good, yet so empty...I need something more...Hopefully a woman will come my way, I don't know," Florence said.

"Oh she will, and she'll change everything for you," I said. My mind started to go blank for a moment; that was when I thought of Anna once more.

"Hope I'm not making you feel uncomfortable with me telling you these here desires of mine?" Florence inquired.

"No, not at all, old boy, you always were like a brother to me," I replied.

"I know, and you were as well like one to me," Florence responded; he took a long puff of his cigar as he spoke.

"Yes, and don't you worry yourself to death about women and all you have to live for…I assure you, as the sun sets in the west, you'll find you a gal one day," I said.

"I guess I've got to start learning that one action you just told?" Florence inquired.

"What? Patience?" I asked.

"Hell yes, that may not be my strongest point, but I'll certainly give it a try," Florence said.

"Yeah, like I said old boy, take it easy…The past is, well, the past, and you can't change that," I stated. "The real important thing to remember is, whenever you do find that gal you've been searching for, she better not only accept you for what you are now, but for what you were then," I then concluded; grinning as I did.

"Damn, life can surely take you on a shitty ride sometimes, can it?" Florence inquired.

"Oh absolutely, and you're going to make mistakes…That's all a part of being human…God knows we're going to screw up once in a while," I said.

"Yeah, I've certainly done my share of that," Florence said.

"Hey, remember what the doc said…He buried his past of loss in the deepest ocean…Don't you remember that old boy?" I inquired.

"Oh yeah, when he talked about his beloved," Florence responded.

"That's some advice I could use myself, if I'm being honest," I said.

"Terence?" Florence asked.

"Yes Flor?" I asked.

"What's really pestering you? You got that look in your eyes yourself that reads loss, are you going through something similar?" Florence asked.

"Again, if it involves anything to do with my beloved…Well, I'll just let you know later, cause it's a real long, long story," I replied.

"I understand old buddy," Florence said.

"Yes indeed," I said; I was still sharpening my knife on the edge of the rock that I was sitting at. "Well, speaking of the doc, we'd better get a move on up to that peak…God only knows where that crazy son of a bitch wandered off to?" I then added.

"I sure hope he's alright, I mean he left that cross back there...You think maybe them bloodsuckers got to him?" Florence asked.

"God I hope not, I'd certainly feel bad about that for probably the rest of my entire existence," I replied.

As soon as I spoke; Florence and I both stood. As soon as we did, we both felt an uneasiness come over us. Florence began to rub his head; I then began to rub mine too. I could feel this throbbing on the edges of my cranium, and I could feel every heartbeat pulse with absolute fury. I became lightheaded for a moment; it almost felt as if time itself had stopped. Something, perhaps another force of evil, was close by. Florence and I both looked at each other; we both knew something strange was happening, but we weren't sure as to what exactly? Then I looked down upon the water; instead of flowing towards the west it began to flow to the east within an instance. Every sparrow and every dove that had been singing had sung no more. Eventually all around us was dead; I felt coherent to my surroundings, and I was nothing like I was last night. However, both of us were completely in shock at what was happening. "What the hell is going on?" Florence asked.

I began to hear a ring in my ear. "Old boy, your question is about as good as mine," I replied.

Florence grimaced, I grimaced. Then suddenly without any explanation, the pandemonium and chaos stopped. Everything went back to normal. The waters flowed in the correct direction, and all of the birds had gone back to singing their beautiful songs. I had no idea what the hell just happened? I'm pretty sure whatever the hell it was, it certainly wasn't good. I felt a sense of fear come over me; I was shaking from my head to my feet. I gazed upon an adjacent ridge; I noticed what appeared to be buzzards up on the side of Wilmer's Peak. It seemed that they were no more than a mile away. "You notice them damn buzzards too, don't you?" Florence inquired.

"Yeah, let's walk up there and see what in God's name they're circling," I replied.

"Don't forget all of the supplies," Florence reminded me.

"Oh trust me, I ain't forgetting that shit," I responded.

"Here, put this around your neck," Florence said; handing me a crucifix necklace.

"Thanks old boy, but I think I have enough with this wooden one I picked up back at camp," I said.

"Trust me on this one Ter," Florence began; we started walking towards the buzzards up on the ridge. "Them vampires can easily just knock down your little wimpey ass cross…I'm telling you, they can old buddy," Florence grinned.

"That may be but watch it!" I exclaimed.

"What's that?" Florence inquired.

"I'm not sure whether using wimpey ass and cross in the same sentence is necessary…Plus this little old cross did its job well last night, I'd say," I replied.

"That's true it did and sorry, my mouth's been looser than a goose," Florence replied.

"Yeah, uh-huh, you jumped all over my ass back at camp, so I'll just return the favor back," I responded; smiling as I did.

"Sorry, again," Florence said.

"Don't apologize to me, talk to Him," I said, pointing my finger up towards the sky.

With my remark, from that point on, it was nothing but silence between Florence and I. We walked up this hill; it was shrouded in trees and most of them were obviously dead. The soil was nothing but hard and dusty too. We began to notice more and more pines though, as we then began to climb higher and higher. There were also many roots from various shrubs and trees, protruding out of the side of the peak. There were a few large boulders in our view; some probably weighed a ton and some probably weighed no more than Florence and I put together. One thing was for certain though; we both were starting to pick up on the stench of rotting flesh. My mind began to go into panic; I was worried that quite possibly this rotting could be Dietrich. We could hear the buzzards cry out as we got closer and closer; Florence and I both continued to keep quiet as we were trying not to attract attention. My head still rumbled from our ordeal only moments earlier; an ordeal that almost felt as if the walls of Jericho had fallen. "I'm curious about that whole predicament back there, Flor? What the hell was that all about?" I asked with a loud whisper.

"Could be this?...The doc once told me back in Canden, that when you're in the presence of the undead, the Earth, the sky, the rocks, the trees, well, everything...It don't seem to flow with all of creation, everything comes out of order for some reason, the world don't exactly rotate right?" Florence replied; inquiring upon every statement made.

"Interesting, but I sure hope to God that the stench our nostrils caught wasn't the doc," I remarked.

"I'm hoping it ain't too…But old buddy, please keep it down, and proceed with caution," Florence stated.

"That's what I'm doing old boy," I said.

"I know, I just don't want our whole journey to blow up into smoke," Florence remarked.

We remained quiet and to ourselves the rest of the way up. By the time we had reached the side of the ridge where the buzzards were flying, we finally got a glimpse at what was stinking so bad. It wasn't the doc at all. Upon the ground lay dozens of coyotes, rabbits, bears, birds, and pretty much anything that walked on four legs. These animals weren't just drained of blood; the innards had been practically mutilated and every animal had looked to be eaten with savagery. The sight of this was truly grim and I didn't know if I should run or if I should stay still and look in horror? My thoughts ran like how I ran earlier from that grizzly. Whatever had done this, was not human at all. "What the hell?" I asked myself.

"This would be what was stinking up all creation," Florence muttered.

I then saw a man in the distance, he was standing motionless by the entrance into this cavern, "Look Flor," I pointed towards the man.

"The doc, I hope?" Florence inquired.

"Heaven I hope so, let's get closer and see," I said.

"Sure, but be on your guard old buddy," Florence stated.

"Come on old boy, do you really think I'm just gonna sprint up there and yell like a bunch of jail mates in Dodge?!" I hastily inquired, however, calmly speaking as I did.

"I'm just making sure you ain't gonna do something stupid," Florence angrily responded.

"Well I ain't, especially after what happened last night," I said.

We swiftly then moved ourselves up towards what we hopefully knew was Dietrich. As we approached the male; it became clear by the style of hair and the clothes that it was the doc. Though we needed to get a better look closer. We got into a clear range, we then saw our person, it was Dietrich, but he wasn't himself it seemed? The look upon Dietrich's face said terror and uncertainty, I began to talk to Dietrich, "Hey doc, everything alright old boy?" I asked.

I got no response from Dietrich, instead, I instantly got a response from some other force? "Piss off! You pieces of foul Earth!"

The voice was extremely demonic, and it instantly made me still in my place. My heart began to beat like a drum, and I could hear Florence's breath behind me breathe faster and faster. Then suddenly, I heard the sound of Florence running from his place, "Forget that!" Florence calmly muttered to himself.

I then instantly stopped Florence dead in his tracks, "Just hold your ass, we ain't going nowhere, till we kill whatever possessed the doc," I whispered to Florence.

"Be my guess, but I ain't never dealt with a vampire's ability like this before," Florence said.

"Well, I guess we'll have to just take a chance on this," I responded.

I then calmly collected my breath; I don't think I've ever been this nervous before. My heartbeat got faster, I gulped loudly, and I knew whatever had possessed Dietrich was probably feeding off of my fears right now. "Put that cross upon his head old buddy," Florence annoyingly commented.

"It seemed to have worked last night with me," I said.

Before I could even get the cross to Dietrich's forehead; Dietrich then lashed out, instantly coming at me with sheer strength. "Get that filthy object away from me!" The demonic voice exclaimed.

"Alright old boy, you might want to stay back, you already got a few marks on your face from last night," I commented to Florence.

"I can hold him from behind!" Florence exclaimed.

"Nah, I'll just use the cross," I said, pulling my crucifix into view.

"Get that away from me!" The demonic voice exclaimed; it then swatted at my hand.

I pulled back quickly, "The hell!" I shouted.

"You fool! I sense a great amount of fear in you! I dare you to try it with me!" The voice chillingly exclaimed.

"Alright, you've got it coming!" I yelled.

"Wait, Ter, don't!" Florence shouted.

I sprang forward upon Dietrich's forehead, but the cross did not do its job correctly. The cross was ineffective, and now Dietrich was pissed! Dietrich then grabbed my throat, "That should've worked!" I said, choking on my words.

"You have such little faith, misty eyes!" The demonic voice exclaimed.

Then from behind; Florence quickly dumped a small bag of mustard seeds upon Dietrich's back. Dietrich let go immediately; I coughed vigorously. "Here, give me that cross!" Florence exclaimed.

"Get that demon out of him!" I shouted; coughing vigorously once more.

"You shall be no more," Florence muttered to himself.

Florence then pressed the cross furiously to Dietrich's forehead; he immediately reacted with much pain and anguish. The front of his skull burned instantly; now there was a red imprint of a cross upon his forehead. Dietrich then reached for his eyes, "Ah! Dear God!" Dietrich shouted.

"Well, it's good to hear that voice again," Florence remarked.

"You've got that problem too huh?" I inquired.

"My eyes feel like an inferno on the sun!" Dietrich exclaimed.

"Well, I guess just give it five minutes," I responded; smiling brightly as I did.

Then out of nowhere, while Florence and I began calming Dietrich down and propping him up, something large had hit the ground behind us. It made a loud *thud*! It scared the living shit out of all of us! "What in the name of mercy was that?" Dietrich asked.

Florence and I turned, "Oh my God, they did it," Florence remarked.

In front of us was a grizzly sight; it was Dietrich's horse that he had rode up on. It was torn to shreds though. Nothing of it was left really; something had eaten through it?! Some bare bones were visible, and some inner organs too. The smell was God awful; I instantly covered my nose in disgust. "Dear God!" I exclaimed.

"Looks like they got hungry," Florence commented.

"Alright, while the doc's recovering, you and I are both heading in there…We're going to give that sucker hell!" I exclaimed.

I then heard Dietrich behind me, "Mister Hill, please stay where you're at, just give me a few more moments to recover," Dietrich stated.

"We ain't got no few moments doc! Flor grab everything we need! We're gonna get this shit done!" I shouted. I ignored the doc's warnings.

"Ter, maybe we better wait on the doc, or better yet plan this out more," Florence said.

Annoyed, I replied, "You must be the world's number one dumbass! Who knows where they're at? We need to get going! If there's one thing I've learnt from bounty hunting, it's never, never, ever slow down and plan!" I exclaimed; Florence then handed me a lantern and bag of mustard seeds.

"Bounty hunter, I think this is stupid," Dietrich commented; he was still holding his forehead and he was still in anguish.

I began to walk forward; approaching the cave with absolute determination, "Old boy you better be following my strides," I said to Florence.

Florence was far behind, hesitant to say it best. "Old buddy, if anyone's the world's number one dumbass, it's you!" Florence shouted.

"Stay close to me old boy, we'll get it done just like we got the other killing done last night," I said; we were now crossing over into the threshold of the cave.

"Bounty hunter, just give me a few minutes…You're a fool!" Dietrich exclaimed.

Pretty soon, Dietrich's presence was far behind, but Florence was oh so near. He seemed on edge, but who am I kidding, I was too. I was trying to be as brave and sure footed as I could be. This cavern was pretty wide and open. However, it was more black than the blackest black. I lit a lantern slowly; I began to turn myself around in the cave. I was looking for any possible signs of anything out of the ordinary. There were many burrows throughout the cave; some probably spread out for miles. It was brisk in this cave; our breaths had gotten thick again. I started to get a sharp pain in my head, my sides also ached, and my feet began to tremble. I could feel a possible presence nearby.

We then walked a little further into the cave; we had both noticed another exit up ahead. It seemed to be an outlet that was right next to the entrance where we had come in. I do remember a large pile of boulders and rocks separating our entrance. Then suddenly, as I shined my light towards the direction of a small hole; I noticed a foot that quickly descended into the hole! Florence and I both jumped at the sight, it must be Marcy or somebody? I quickly sprang into action; I handed Florence the mustard seeds. I had other remedies at the ready too. I shined the light into the small hole, however, all I saw was darkness? The strangest thing was, there was nothing in this hole? Just a dead end and a large number of rocks at the end.

I was certainly in bewilderment; did Marcy, or someone, just walk through a compounded wall? I continued to carefully shine my light into the hole. Florence was breathing heavily down my back. "What in the hell?" Florence whispered in my ear.

"That's what I was about to ask," I replied.

Then I noticed a bit of movement in the rocks, however, there was another presence that made itself known. Out of nowhere came this hand on top of Florence and I's head! We immediately jolted back with fright! "Sweet mother of mercy!" Florence exclaimed.

We got a good look at our culprit that had startled us; it was a large black arm and hand! Then another large arm and hand sprang out; it made the most devilish noises imaginable. It made my stomach turn. Creeping out of the walls of the cave was a being, but it was far beyond anything I could comprehend. It was tall and completely black looking. It almost looked like a rotted corpse, but it had not just two arms, but freaking six limbs! At this point I was beyond dazed; I fired at the creature. It crawled out of the wall like a spider. Florence threw mustard seeds at it and began waving the crucifix at it.

Looking at this foul creature, I think the worst element of all, was its cold and demonic-looking face. It had blue piercing eyes; its hair was very thin on top too and if anything it was nothing more than a skull! It had razor sharp teeth and it continued to *shriek* at us! My Lord, it was an unbearable sight!

The creature we were fighting almost looked pathetic and half decayed. I sort of felt sorry for the poor bastard. It was certainly Marcy though; I could tell by what was left of his clothing. Marcy always wore a puffy looking white shirt. I fired constantly though at the creature; flames shot up in the air and frantically Florence and I were scrambling about the cavern. We were backing away of course, and each moment, I could feel the vampire get weaker and weaker. It was insanely large; I'd say ten feet tall and again it ain't like nothing I had ever seen before! It stretched out its long spindly hands; they were disgusting and filled with hair. The creature lashed at Florence and I, but it was a failed attempt every time. It seemed that Marcy had run out of his time, his vampirism had started to wear away and there was no more fresh blood for him. "Shit!" I exclaimed.

"You got your knife on you this time? I hope?!" Florence loudly inquired over the noises.

"Hell yeah! I'm gonna send that sucker to hell!" I shouted.

Marcy by this point looked absolutely disgusting and pitiful. There was absolutely no bit of humanity left in him and honestly I think it was of best interest to take him out of his misery. To which I swiftly did. I quickly stepped forward and rammed my bowie knife deep within his half

175

mangled remains. He *shrieked* loudly; my heart skipped a beat! The killing though, had gone smoother than I thought it would. Again, like with Elizabeth, the flames from where our blessed bullets had hit, had graced fiercely on various parts of my body. I backed quickly away; as Marcy had inhaled his last bits of air. He fell flat on his back; flames were still dancing all over his body too. I then felt something hot on my right arm, I quickly raised it, and discovered a shocking sight again! "Shit on a grave!" I exclaimed; my right arm was in flames.

"Holy cow!" Florence exclaimed. "Let's get your flaming ass outside!"

We began to move; I took one last look at Marcy's half mangled and disgusting body. Then from out of nowhere another pale arm reached from in the darkness. Florence and I quickly jumped back. "Lord have mercy!" I shouted.

The arm grabbed my arm instantly. Then slowly, creeping into our viewpoint was this woman. I did not recognize her at all. She then violently raised my arm; she projectile vomited blood all over my fucking right sleeve! Good gosh it was absolutely insane. The blood did put the fire out, but right now, I could care less about the fire! Freaking death itself was staring at me in the eyes. She had sharp fangs, and she was wearing a gypsy-like wardrobe. She let out the most Godawful screams and instantly I fought. She still had a tight hold on my arm. At this point, Florence was just as shocked as I was. Now we were near the exit out of the cave, and from there within a few seconds, we heard this chatter. It was Dietrich, who had found his way around, and was now in our vicinity! He was speaking in tongues, and again he was waving the cross. The light from outside casted a shadow upon the woman's horrid face. The vampire instantly reacted with agony; she quickly let go of my arm. "This is why we work together, boys!" Dietrich shouted.

"Hey, this was, old ding-a-ling's idea!" Florence shouted, nodding my way.

"Hey, I'm just trying to get this here shit done!" I exclaimed angrily; we were shouting over the chaos.

"Gentlemen! Gentlemen! This is no time for pointless bickering! Florence throw what seeds you have left on you! Terence, have your knife at the ready!" Dietrich commanded.

"We gonna back that bitch up into the sunlight?!" Florence inquired loudly.

"Just do what I just told you!" Dietrich yelled.

We took cautious, but important steps towards the outside of the cave. The woman was backing up into the sunlight outside. The tensions were building now; they were boiling over the pot at this point. Florence threw his mustard seeds; I then drew my gun at the vampire. However, Dietrich stopped me. Dietrich waved his makeshift cross in front of the vampire; the woman was screaming for mercy! I swear the heavens could hear her by this point. We got closer, and soon the sunlight was only a few short steps away. Intensely, Dietrich spoke Hebrew like no other, shouting everything he had in him. Florence and I both just watched in shock. I could feel every bit of this moment well up like the deepest spring, and then suddenly, Dietrich had reached the sunlight. As soon as the horrid vampire had hit the sun; it instantly began to smoke. The woman screamed in terror; then she let out a demonic statement, "I hope you three go to hell! Cocksuckers!"

Then the woman instantly began melting; at this point it was beyond a gag. I put my hand to my mouth, shocked at just what the power of the sun can truly do to the powers of the evil and sickening undead. First her skin began to melt. Then I saw some veins, tissue, and eventually all of her was carnage! She eventually melted down to the bone, and she was still begging on her knees when she vanished, begging for mercy again. Then in a passing moment of time; all was quiet and still. "Again, this is why we work together," Dietrich firmly stated.

"Hey, I'm a stubborn jackass, and I'll do what I think is right," I said.

"Well, unstubborn yourself, this is something far greater, and something very evil Mister Hill...That being said, do what's right, but don't get yourself killed over it," Dietrich responded.

With our small exchange over; we gathered up what supplies we had up on Wilmer's. Then we went into the cave and grabbed Marcy's charred remains, followed shortly after, we picked up the bones of the unknown woman. "Shouldn't we entomb the bodies?...Then put crosses over them?" Florence inquired later, all while we were gathering up our essentials and leaving the cavern area.

"I was just about to suggest that, we did it in Canden," Dietrich said.

Going along with Dietrich and Florence's word; we hiked our way down the mountain a little ways. We stopped for a moment and took a good view as to where we would be heading next. We also searched high and low for valuable and rich soil. It took us a few hours to find a good spot for the burial, but eventually we found it at the edge of the peak. We were still up in elevation, but we were definitely much lower than before. There was a beautiful sunset; we dug our way into the soil using only one shovel that was housed in some supplies on the back of Florence's horse. We dug a hole about four feet deep, but at this point, anything was good enough. We threw both bodies down into the hole; Dietrich then spoke in tongues again, and Florence and I sprinkled mustard seeds all over the remains. Then we threw the makeshift cross down into the hole; Dietrich then kissed his crucifix. "May the powers of the Holy Spirit be with us," Dietrich stated. "And with these two," He then added.

We then covered up the hole and gazed one last look upon the setting sun. It was the kind of sunset that made you notice how precious and important life is. Thinking about the sunset, I also thought of Anna, God how I missed her. We smoked a few cigars and tickered around for a bit. Then quickly we hopped upon our horses, and rode off down the mountain. Dietrich rode on the back of Florence's saddle, and I had my horse to myself. There was so much work to be done and having these plaguing thoughts of my dear beloved Anna, weren't helping a bit. But it wasn't bad, it was good thoughts of Anna. However, it made it harder to focus on the journey at hand. Who knew what this night could hold? One thing's for certain though, this has been an expedition filled with crazier than shit moments.

Chapter 10

We were now taking this trail; it's a shortcut behind Wilmer's and it's substantially winding its way towards the outer edges of the mountain. This trail would eventually find its way to a small creek; I used to hunt down on this basin a few years ago. Then a mile ahead there's this flatland. Then from there; our camp should be no more than a couple of miles away. I had forgotten how unstable this terrain was, but if this was the quickest way, I really didn't see any problem with that at all. The sun had finally slipped into its slumber no more than an hour ago. The moon in the sky was no more than a crescent, and I could hear a hoot owl crying up in a far away tree. By the time we had reached the basin entrance; we were coming into a thick and dark forest. The forest floor was shrouded with dead leaves, and our lantern lights were the only element that kept our journey well lit and clear. Our minds, however, weren't quite as clear.

Many thoughts bumped about in my brain; from my dear Anna to the strange hellish creatures we witnessed in the cavern. This here predicament was starting to become personal.

Death was something I was used to in regards to my bounty hunting, but this shit was far beyond my own comprehension. My only dread was that this journey here may only get worse as we continued. Our breaths were thick; my head and chest were pounding. Our horses were doing substantially well considering how cold it was. They made their way, step after step, tumbling over any rock or obstacle that rested before these nags.

We were coming closer and closer to the creek that I had remembered, and with one signal from my hand we stopped dead in the forest. The stream was in view; no more than a couple of yards ahead. It was uncomfortably quiet, but I could feel something uneasy, and I knew it wasn't what we had just witnessed either. "Well doc, Flor," I began. "This right here should be a great place for us to catch the old wind," I said.

"Alright with me, the horses could also get something to drink too," Florence replied.

"My feet could use a little wake up too," Dietrich said.

Then all three of us climbed down off of our horses; we then cautiously led both of our horses towards the stream. We had our lanterns in hand and we were slowly looking at the cold dark forest. There wasn't a huge variety of trees here.

There were mainly just oaks, cedars, and a few maples here and there. As the horses began to drink; Dietrich and I made our way over towards an old fallen down tree trunk. Florence was reaching for something in his saddle bag. The tree was rotten; but it certainly made a great place for myself to stretch out my legs. Dietrich stayed upright; he then stretched out his lower back and moved his neck from one side to the other. Florence walked over to my position; he had cigars in his hand. "Care for a smoke there old prickly?" Florence inquired; grinning as he did.

"Why certainly, don't mind if I do," I replied.

"Prickly?" Dietrich wondered.

"Doc, it's a long, sad, painful, yet funny story," I responded; lighting my cigar as I did.

"You see doc, old Ter here got his man meat caught in a thorn bush this morning," Florence started to laugh.

"You're kidding?" Dietrich inquired; he was smiling and laughing under his breath.

I was smiling to myself, "I wish he would...Shit, he'll never let that story go," I said; I then took a long puff of my cigar.

"But get this Dietrich, the worst part was, a damn wild hog took his clothes off with him, and then he tried to chase down old Ter here, for a date!" Florence exclaimed, busting his gut.

"Oh my," Dietrich said.

"Yeah, oh my," I responded with annoyance.

"Well anyways, laughs are over, I've got to go drain my juices," Florence said.

Florence then wandered off into the woods behind me, to which I then shouted, "Hey old boy!"

"Yes sir?!" Florence replied.

"Just make sure you don't get into a prickly incident yourself in the dark...Watch out for them thorn bushes, you know!" I exclaimed.

"Keeping it locked in, old buddy!" Florence shouted; his voice echoed throughout the forest.

Florence's footsteps then got further and further away as he drifted off into the forest abyss. "Hey doc, you know you can sit down right," I said.

"Oh yes, I was getting a good stretch in my good man...My legs feel as if thousands of needles are penetrating them, my they're burning the dickens outta me," Dietrich said.

"Lord have mercy," I said; puffing in the middle of my speech. "That ain't the best feeling in the world," I then added.

"Indeed not," Dietrich stated.

"So, do you have any clue as to who that girl was back in the cavern?" I asked.

"To be honest, I'm not sure?" Dietrich replied; he then came over and sat by my side still pondering in thought.

"Four more of them damn things, is that right?" I inquired.

"Lord willing I hope so…Who knows, there may be unwary travelers involved in this dreaded curse?" Dietrich said; he then stroked his chin.

"Well, let's just pray to the good Lord that there ain't no more other ones than the ones were hunting down," I said.

"Believe me, I'm praying, my good man, just trying to keep that fearless spirit alive too you know," Dietrich said.

"Dear God, you certainly got it too, I mean you really know how to keep your shit together…I mean it's like back at the cave when you cut in and saved our asses, you battled that there ugly ass bitch like a boss," I stated.

"Well, I don't like to boast a lot, but I am much obliged to your compliments bounty hunter," Dietrich responded; he smiled like he had struck gold too.

"Hey brother, you complimented me, I'll return the favor," I said.

"Much appreciated my good man," Dietrich responded.

"God willing we make it through this here predicament," I said.

"Oh, I believe we will...Do not let your thoughts wander in the realm of the negative, my good man...We will make it, and even if, God forbidding we don't, we will lose this fight together," Dietrich stated; he then grinned and patted me on my shoulder.

"My mind just keeps on rattling on the idea of what this here Julius might be like, that's all that concerns me," I said.

"Oh yes, Julius is no normal man, for that matter, he is like no other vampire...I sense a great deal of hatred of course, but also I feel a great sense of deception within him too," Dietrich said.

"We'll get that son of a bitch though, I know we will doc," I said; I then took a puff of my cigar.

"We will, but we shall carry onward with our strides, how far do you think we are from camp?" Dietrich asked.

"I'd say maybe about five miles, it's in that direction," I replied, pointing my finger towards the east.

"Five's not too bad, I don't know about how you and Florence are feeling, but I'm starting to starve," Dietrich stated.

"You ain't the only one doc, my stomach's starting to make a fuss too," I said.

"Damn I tell you, vampire hunting certainly makes me famished, you know that," Dietrich stated; he then laughed.

"Hell yeah brother," I responded; taking a big puff as I did.

Suddenly from behind Dietrich and me; we heard the faint rustling of leaves. Dietrich and I both jolted to our feet; I ran over to my saddle bag and grabbed my gun while Dietrich went and grabbed his crucifix. Though it probably was an animal of some sorts, we were both not taking any chances. I pointed the lantern light in the direction of the sounds. It sounded as if something was stopping, and then walking again. It almost sounded like something was in distress. "Flor! Are you in there?!" I yelled out.

I got no reply, "Be ready for anything Mister Hill," Dietrich stated.

Our breaths fogged up the whole forest; we stood there waiting and anticipating for something. My heart began to take off again and I gulped really loud. Then from out of the darkness; we began to see a figure. At first we couldn't make the person out, but Dietrich and I still stood at the ready. The person was coming closer towards us, and then eventually we saw the unknown wanderer. It was Florence; however, he looked as if he was confused as hell. "Flor, dear God old boy, you had us in a frenzy," I said.

"Ah!" Florence shouted in pain.

"Florence, everything okay?' Dietrich inquired.

"Nah, I can't hear anything, and everything's all…Everything's all a twirl," Florence frantically commented. Then suddenly Florence collapsed to his knees. Dietrich and I sprang forward to help him up. We then led him to rest on a fallen tree.

"What the hell has gotten into you, old boy?" I asked; I was talking right in Florence's ear by this point.

"Hell if I know? I was just down yonder taking my leak, when everything around me started spinning…Good Lord I feel sick," Florence said.

"You probably need some water," Dietrich suggested.

I then walked over and collected a bit of water from the stream. I gathered the cold water into my tin cup that I had used earlier. Then without any warning; I heard Florence gag behind me. He started to violently cough, then suddenly, he threw up everywhere. "Ah shit!" He exclaimed.

"Well, the water may have to wait a bit," Dietrich said.

I then knelt down at Florence; his head was slumped down. "Hey old boy, chin up…That's not how a sheriff handles these predicaments…Now, is your hearing getting better?" I asked.

"Oh it's better, but everything's still spinning around in my head," Florence replied.

"Could be the sudden change in elevation," Dietrich commented.

"I don't know doc, he would've felt like this way back further," I said.

Then, coming from the distance of a cold night holler; we all heard what sounded to be an oncoming carriage. We could hear the sound of a lantern *squeak* as it swayed from side to side. We turned our visions downward to look. Sure enough, climbing up this small incline was what looked to be a gypsy carriage. It crept closer and closer; I could feel my blood start to boil. I was ready for anything. We all stood there silent; the carriage was now only but a hundred feet away. The *squeak* of the lantern naturally got louder, and it crept under my skin. Eventually we were able to make out a driver; he also had a passenger sitting right next to him. It looked to be a woman; the woman was covered in gypsy style tapestries. She had a white veil covering her face, and she looked to be wearing a wedding gown of some sorts? The driver then instantly acknowledged our presence. "Good evening, fine gentlemen!" The driver exclaimed. "Whoa now!" The driver halted his horses.

"A good evening to you too sir," Dietrich responded.

"This certainly is a lovely evening for sure, without a doubt...Forgive me, my name's Luke Grooms, and this right here is my new wife, Bertha May Grooms," Luke said.

"A pleasure to meet you both," Florence said, tilting his hat at the young couple.

"You'll have to forgive old Bertha though, she's a mute and can't talk unfortunately," Luke said.

"Oh I understand," Dietrich said.

"Yes siree, but she certainly is the greatest thing that's ever happened to me!...We're actually on our way to this little old lodge, it's owned by this little old plump feller, oh shit, what's his name?" Luke puzzled himself for a second or two, until I chimed in.

"Hank?" I asked.

"Yep, that's the guy, Hank! Interesting son of a gun from what I've heard," Luke commented.

"That he is," I replied.

"So, what in the name of Geronimo is y'all's story?" Luke asked.

I immediately wove a lie; I was not intending on giving away the true intentions of our expedition. "Well, I'm a Texas Ranger, Jeb Hanson, and these two here are my cronies," I then pointed towards Dietrich. "This here is a German, his name is Dietrich…We can't for the hell of us pronounce his last name, so we just call him Dietrich the German feller…We even gave him a nickname, old Sauerkraut…And this feller here," I then introduced Florence, "This is Sheriff Bill Layman."

"Bill?" Florence inquired in my ear softly.

Then under my breath I mumbled, "Just go with it old boy," I then smiled really big. "Well anyways!" I shouted. "We're currently seeking out a thief," I stated.

"Well my oh my, we got ourselves the law out here! I assure you gentlemen, I ain't done nothing wrong!" Luke exclaimed.

"Never said you did, but we three are searching for an unidentified male, about six feet tall...He was fairly decent looking from eyewitnesses, much like yourself," I said.

"Well, maybe it was my twin!" Luke laughed.

I smiled and grinned, "Maybe, maybe...But again, we ain't pressing anything against you, it's just that, this here criminal we seek stole a shit load of art paintings, jewelry, and valuables on a train inbound for Jackson, Mississippi...He had a wagon too...He was on his way to Glenn Hall, that's where this sheriff's from by the way...Anyways, the son of a bitch shot two men as well...You see where I'm going with this?" I asked.

"Well, Lord have mercy on his soul," Luke commented.

"Indeed sir," Dietrich spoke up. "As a detective, however, Mister Grooms, would you be free to let us search your carriage?" Dietrich asked, playing along with me.

Without any surprise, Luke looked quite nervous upon Dietrich's question. Something was wrong here, I knew it. "Sure, sure," Luke nervously replied. "I can't argue with an investigation, I guess," Luke laughed awkwardly under his breath.

"Well as a general rule, we shall have the right to search every inch if necessary, just to see if we find something that matches as to what we are looking for," Dietrich stated.

"Where's your papers though?" Luke hastily inquired.

"Well, you see, as a ranger, I don't need any type of search warrant, and since I'm the one leading this here search for a wanted man, I'd say you'll just have to keep your ass right where you are, and let us do our job," I sternly replied.

"Sure ranger, my apologies," Luke then tipped his hat.

"Apologies accepted," I responded; tipping my hat back at Luke. "Now, Flor, I mean...Bill," I then laughed as I caught my mistake. "Why don't you keep a watch on old Leroy here, while me and old Sauerkraut here search over his belongings," I instructed Florence.

"Sure ranger," Florence smiled. "Anything for you," he then smarted off in his added comment.

Florence then went over and grabbed his gun from behind his saddle bag. Dietrich and I then began our search through the carriage. We both had small lanterns in our hands. The carriage was made from wood of course, and it had a large white sheet draped over the top of it. It was truly the gypsy look. Either way, we were nervous, terrified, but also curious. Was this mysterious traveler, exactly what he appeared to be? We didn't know, so we took no hesitation here. Looking at the back portion of it; we saw nothing but wedding gifts. We found nothing of interest, just gypsy style tapestries, and loads of clothing. There was curiously no food of any kind here though? We then noticed this box, "We'll have a look in there," Dietrich whispered.

"What if they're actually…You know?" I asked.

"We need to make sure there's none that have hitched a ride, that's why we're doing this search," Dietrich then responded.

"Sure, whatever, I was just weaving along a little lie out there, just to see if they'd break character, I didn't know we were doing all this," I said; still keeping my speech down to a whisper.

"Hey, it's an investigation, so let's, well, investigate," Dietrich replied.

Without any more discussion, we continued our search in the back. We then finally opened the large wooden box that we had noticed; however it was nothing but more clothes. There wasn't anything out of the ordinary here, and I was baffled. I thought my little old tale of bullshit would make them break, but no, I was wrong.

We exited the back and returned towards the front. Florence was still keeping a close eye on the two travelers. "Well ranger, did you find anything bizarre?" Luke asked.

"Nothing, but there is this one problem though," I stated.

Nervously, Luke inquired, "Oh Lord, what is it?"

"Nothing really, just saw you both had a whole bunch of wedding gifts in there," I said.

"Oh yes, I tell you this, women and their clothes, am I right?" Luke asked.

"Yes, well, I saw a bunch of clothes in there though, and I had seen a few other valuables like a mirror, a few tapestries, and a table...But nothing that was in the missing cargo report," I said.

"Well, see you gentlemen, I told you, I'm as harmless as an oriole in a tree!" Luke exclaimed.

"My apologies for scaring you sir," Dietrich said.

"It's alright, you men are just doing y'all's job...Y'all have every right to do what you do," Luke said, laughing as he did.

I then saw Florence move towards the back of the carriage. "So, you two are going to Hank's lodge?" I asked.

"Yes siree, hoping to get a little romance in up there...If you know what I mean?" Luke inquired; again laughing hysterically as he did.

"Well, that's certainly a wonderful place to go, how many nights are both of y'all staying up there?" I asked.

"Just two," Luke replied.

"Well hey listen, Hank's crazy just to keep up with for one day," I said; we all three then laughed.

"This Hank feller certainly sounds like my type of man, he must be a tasteful feller," Luke replied.

"Tasteful?" Dietrich asked; his voice trembled.

"You know, he's a man with good taste, a great sense of humanity, and he has a great sense of humor," Luke replied.

"Oh I see, it sounded like you were going to eat him or something," I jokingly replied.

"Maybe I will," Luke replied; his face then got serious.

My heart skipped a beat, I then inquired seriously myself, "Excuse me?"

"I'm just messing with you ranger!" Luke then exclaimed, he continued laughing.

We all then tuned in to a great laugh too; though Dietrich's and my laughter both had turned awkward. Then from the left side of the carriage; out popped Florence, he was carrying a large mirror! "Sheriff?" I inquired.

Then everything got still; it was so quiet that I could hear the leaves talking at one point. I heard Florence whisper; he was aggressively in front of Luke at this point, "I know what you are," Florence said.

"What in the name of Sam are you talking about boy?" Luke inquired.

Then Florence put the large mirror directly into Luke's face, Bertha was also within its range. However there was no initial instant reaction, "What the hell sheriff, get that out of their faces!" I shouted.

"Sorry ranger, just wanted to—"

Then suddenly; popping out from the other side were these large hairy arms. They grabbed Florence in a choke hold; they shattered the mirror into a million pieces! Florence was then tossed aside like fodder scraps. Frightened, Dietrich and I then retreated towards our horses. We grabbed our guns and then opened fire on Bertha, who had also reacted. She turned into some kind of hellish looking, pale-skinned demon. Dietrich hit her directly in the chest; she burst into flames there and fell off the side. She let out a Godawful *roar*. Florence was still at mercy on the ground, so I then charged the carriage and whipped out my bowie knife. I thrusted the knife repeatedly into the stomach and chest of this large beast. Luke had shapeshifted into what looked like a wolf man. Luke *howled* like a wolf, and it gave me the shock that's for sure. Mortally wounded, Luke then fell to the ground, and rolled under the carriage, "Mister Hill, for God's sake help!" Dietrich shouted.

"Shit!" I exclaimed.

Bertha had Dietrich in a choke hold; Florence came to assist him. In the scramble Florence opened fire; all while I was now crouched down looking under the carriage for Luke. Every ounce of sweat was pouring from my body, and I could feel nothing, but fear come over me. I could hear the horrid scramble of Dietrich and Florence in my ear, but I had no time. "Flor! Help him! I gotta get this little bastard!" I shouted in wrath. I pointed my light under the carriage; instantly I saw the horrific sight of Luke. "Son of a bitch!" I slashed my knife at the creature, but it was a failed attempt. It lashed at me and scrambled quickly. It pushed me backwards into a small boulder on the ground behind me. "Shit!" I shouted. The wolf-like creature was making some horrifying sounds, *yelping* and *snarling*. I then tried to lash with my boot spur, but the creature just grabbed my right leg and held it. Luke then forced it backward, he then twisted my leg. "Ah! You piece of shit! Ah!" I exclaimed; the pain was beyond me at this point. It felt like my bone had even popped out through my skin. Though it didn't of course, so I kept fighting regardless.

Then coming to assist me, was again more gunfire. It was Florence; he had blood all over his torso. He was shaking in his very boots, I could tell. He had weakened the wolf, and at this point, it gave me a good opportunity to grab a broken tree limb from behind me. The creature continued to *snarl* and *yelp*. Flames were forming around his shoulders where Florence had hit his gunshots. I broke the tree a little more and made sure it had a sharp and pointy end. Then with all my force, I took Luke out of his misery. I rammed the tree limb hard into Luke's chest. He fell backwards; he then laid upon his back helpless. He was crying out in agonizing pain, and the sounds were making my stomach turn. He helplessly started waving his arms; he almost reminded me of how some insects look after you've flipped them over on their backs. He was kicking, he was screaming.

God it was awful, but not as bad as it was going to get.

Chapter 11

Obviously by this point, we had entered into the worst shit show imaginable. But unlike some acts, who knew how this would end? The wolf creature that Florence and I had vanquished was starting to shapeshift back into Luke again. Luke was now butt-ass naked, and he still had the tree limb lodged into his chest. He got extremely quiet, and the last of his yelps and screams had echoed out through the forest. There was blood all over us; all over the white sheet on the carriage and all over the forest floor. Then without warning; Luke regurgitated blood. It shot up through the air like a geyser. Florence and I were startled by this of course, we backed away instantly. We were as you'd expect, mortified and speechless.

Within the blink of the quickest winking eye; we all dashed quickly into action. I now hobbled along with a broken leg, or so it felt. I was yes, limping the whole way through the mysterious and unforgiving forest now. "She's gone! She's gone! I had her! She fled into the trees!" Dietrich screamed.

"Flor! Go! Move there!" I shouted, pointing my index finger into the darkness of a shadowy treeline.

Our lanterns were swinging constantly; our light created a strange mirage of twinkling flicker like none other. We looked like a million different stars; dancing within the vastness of that cold forest. Our breaths were getting thicker within the cold; it strangely felt colder within those few minutes. We frantically followed each other; quite drunkenly though I might add. We staggered carefully; though I did stumble a few times over a few protruded roots in the ground I quickly thought fast. Within the deadness however; I began to hear this constant ringing bell in my ear.

Though we yelled like a bunch of screaming drunk men; I still felt distant from the others for some strange reason. It almost felt as if I wasn't even a part of this world any longer. The spinning of it seemed out of line; the atmosphere not only felt cold but it felt very dense and heavy. The weight upon my lungs was like none other I had ever experienced before. The whole entire forest and its surroundings began to tilt ever so slightly. I soon found myself blacking out a bit. Then suddenly, within a quick instance; I stumbled quickly towards the ground. I caught myself in confusion, but continued pressing forward all the same. "Hurry! COME ON TER! I see her!" Florence yelled.

"Just give me…a bit…Old buddy!" I shouted back; struggling to speak as I picked myself up off of the ground a second time. My eyes were darting in over a million directions; I could feel cold, cold sweat start to pour. My heart was *thumping* fast and my hands were numb of course. Though I continued to stumble, Lord have mercy I fought, and I did fight hard. With every single ounce of whatever was left, I fought hard. Eventually, I felt this quick jolt on the upper right side of my arm, "Shit!" I reacted in surprise.

"It's me, bounty hunter!" Dietrich exclaimed. "You alright?!" He then inquired; running frantically along with me in the ever growing confusion of our lanterns flickering.

"Doing swell old doc! Hell no! I can't keep my staggering ass up I'm…Afraid!" I then shouted; again struggling to finish my sentences.

"We're in her presence now gentlemen! Keep all of your eyes peeled!" Dietrich exclaimed.

Just as I had blacked out for a second or two; I then quickly found myself staring at what appeared to be a large tall willow tree. I thought I was clear of obstruction, but I was dead wrong. It was more like a quick glance. Suddenly within the blink of an eye, I had made contact with one of its dangling tree limbs. Instantly I reacted in pain of course, "Shit! Hellfire! And damnation!" I quickly put my right hand to my mouth. Right in the vicinity of where the limb had hit me.

"Watch yourself!" Dietrich shouted.

"Not too easy right now for that, doc!" I comically exclaimed back.

Despite our mishap, we proceeded, never missing a step in that cold and uneven forest. My toes were numb, but somehow, by the Grace of God, we were continuing. I was honestly amazed by this point. Somehow, I had stayed intact on this journey; despite all of my crazy scenarios somehow. I was shocked, and by now, I was nothing more than a battle worn soldier, no doubt. With every breath though; I could tell I was only growing weaker, and it was by this point I began to think about my dear Anna. It was merely just small glimpses in all honesty, but I began to see her before me. I believed, for a second, that I was dying. It was a hallucination, but it seemed very real.

She was following me to the left; Dietrich still remained to the right of me. I looked forward, upwards toward her smiling face within the lantern light. I could tell in some way, she was helping, and leading me onward. It was the darndest thing, but it certainly felt comforting by this point in our chaotic run. I smiled ever so slightly at her; then suddenly Florence came right into her place. I quickly snapped back into reality. I jumped of course on the appearance of Florence, but I was also relieved all the same. "Dear God Ter! Your lip's cut real good!" He commented.

"Well, it could be a hell of a lot worse," I replied. In the flickering of our lanterns I then motioned for Dietrich to release me. "Thanks doc, everything seems normal now," I said.

Then there was this dead look within Dietrich. I could tell his confusion was beyond any notion of comprehension. I felt this violent tremble beneath his lip; his cheekbone sank in. He was nervous, in a state of utter silence. Then out of an unbelievable second; soon came another unbelievable sight. Through the dim flickering light; I noticed a figure coming right up from behind Dietrich and myself. I could tell Dietrich was listening to who was approaching from behind him, but all we did was remain frozen and still. We were much like that dense cold night air; very still and dead. Then within an instance; Dietrich reached up from behind him. He then violently pulled down a tree limb and broke it quickly into what appeared to be a sharp, natural weapon.

Then I saw the figure from behind; it was to my utter surprise Florence! Dear God! There were two of him! However, Dietrich knew of the identity of the right one. He quickly motioned towards me, "Get down!" Dietrich yelled.

He shouted so loud, my body had no choice but to cooperate. I quickly knelt down as Dietrich sprung forward toward the first Florence that had arrived on the scene. He rammed his sharp limb deep within the heart of Bertha; who had shapeshifted into Florence. She instantly reacted in pain; *shrieking* loudly as she was stabbed. I watched in shock; Florence's jaw hit the bottom of the forest floor. Dietrich might have barely missed me, but by grace he vanquished Bertha. Then nervously he yelled, "Garlic!"

Florence reached into his pocket, and rolled a clove over towards Dietrich. Dietrich then quickly placed the garlic clove down Bertha's throat.

"Dear God!" I yelled.

"Give me a moment, bounty hunter!" Dietrich sniped. I could see sweat starting to run down the back of his neck. I was sweating too and my heart was stunned. I wasn't sure if it had stopped or not? "Your knife!" Dietrich reached out for my bowie knife. I quickly handed it to him.

With no ounce of hesitation; Dietrich then forcibly thrust my knife into Bertha's stomach. He stabbed away; blood was flinging everywhere. In much honesty, it seemed like Dietrich may have gone a little too far by this point. I could tell he was in distress; repeatedly he was killing the creature and making sure she was dead beyond measure. Dietrich then fastly whipped out a crucifix and placed it upon her forehead. I was stunned, shocked, and somewhat baffled. "I think she's dead now doc! That's enough!" Florence shouted.

Quickly as he had begun his tirade; quickly so began his ease. Dietrich backed away slowly from the corpse. He dropped the knife; he was breathing heavily and trying to catch whatever breath he had in him now. He then rested himself on a small boulder from behind. Suddenly then, it was again, dead silent. Both Florence and I stared at Dietrich in worry. Dietrich then bent forward; he began rubbing his eyes. I sighed heavily. Then suddenly we heard Bertha again! She gagged a bit; it was loud and all of us jolted a bit. Then out of nowhere, she regurgitated up more blood. The blood shot up; it looked like a fountain of some sorts. All three of us backed away; closely watching and very intently waiting for more bad reactions. "Damn," Florence mumbled to himself.

"You've got that right, sheriff," Dietrich commented.

"How'd you figure it wasn't me?" Florence nervously asked.

"She didn't have a lantern, I put two and two together," Dietrich replied. He then leaned forward and breathed heavier. "Thank you for the assistance gentlemen…Your knife, bounty hunter," Dietrich, now half dead, added. He reached forward and handed me my knife, now drenched in blood. "On second thought no," He quickly pulled back; throwing the knife to the ground so I wouldn't retrieve it.

"Why not?" I asked.

"It's covered in cursed blood… We'll have to clean it and myself later," Dietrich responded.

I grinned ever so slightly; though quickly my mouth then positioned itself back into shock quickly. I was beyond petrified, but in a way, I was numb to all of my surroundings and life itself. Not just within regards to the cold weather, which certainly added to the atmosphere, but I was numb to my heart in much horror. That was when my eyes caught something that I quite honestly never wanted to witness. You may think it was just another undead being; pulsating itself towards us in a very horrific manner but no it wasn't even that. No. I noticed a slight bit of movement below the abdomen region of Bertha? In the lowly dimmed lantern light; all three of us approached the corpse, wanting a final glimpse and assertion that Bertha was indeed dead. "She's still moving…Or something is?…What the hell is that?" Florence chillingly asked.

"Not sure old buddy," I whispered anxiously in the dark.

"Careful gentlemen," Dietrich said.

With nothing more than silence accompanying us; the three of us couldn't believe our sights as we didn't know what to expect as we approached the corpse. There was this eerie look over her. The cold night air had begun consuming her skin; it had already appeared this way in our light. I began to feel every ounce of breath exit and I could feel my upper lip tremble. The corpse was also starting to slowly melt away and vanish before our very eyes. My hands sweat beneath my gloves; my feet and legs shook violently. That was when creepily; all three of our lamps caught sight of the unknown object. In the light, to my utter disbelief, there appeared to be a fetus. My eyes widened and my throat gulped in a sickening manner. "My Lord, it's a…It's a?" Florence couldn't even finish his question; I could tell he knew what it was too.

Then within a dead silence; Dietrich sprung forward and quickly grabbed his broken tree limb from earlier. As fast as he reached; I found myself in quick response too. I turned away quickly, not wanting to see what the doctor was about to commit. My stomach churned and rolled over a million times. My mind and heart did the same thing as well. I quickly then found myself transported back in time. To a moment that had a similar, yet unfortunate sight as well. It was supposed to be a happy day for my Anna and I, but no, it wasn't I'm afraid. It was months ago; right before I had myself in this here predicament. Right before I had pursued bounty hunting; my dear Anna was now in the final moments of childbirth. Little did I know that it would be the final moments for her own life, as well as for the infant that was crowning.

It was supposed to be filled in joy; though all I felt was this emptiness that day. Of course, dear Lord, I was torn apart. If you would, I was sucked dry; like as if one of these hell rounded vampires had gotten their hands on me. I was dead inside, cold and alone. Much like how I feel now. In much honesty, it was what led me out here. In many ways being a bounty hunter was my strange coping mechanism, but Lord have mercy, did this encounter only make matters worse. All of this killing was inhumane; I could feel every ounce of emotion take this notion up as I quickly walked away into the night back towards our horses and supplies.

I quickly saw within the memory; that horrid image of me holding my dead child, a girl within my hands as I helplessly wept. It was a warm day that day, but dear Lord, it certainly didn't feel that way.

It felt as dead and stone cold as this night that had accompanied my senses. I was of course numb in this memory; caught dead and confused within the confines of denial too. Though of course trauma was a part of it; a lot of it was for some reason my own guilt and doubt. Why in God's name did I lose my sweet Anna that day? Why did I lose my newborn? Dear Almighty I cried out in my mind; still locked within the carnage and disbelief of that childbirth death. As I shuffled away cold; I could hear Florence in my ear ask, "You alright Ter?!" He was concerned, of course.

However I never answered the question; I was too upset and traumatized by the event at hand. I mentally and spiritually was not prepared for the killing at hand. Nor was I in all honesty; prepared for the remainder of our expedition either.

Chapter 12

All I could hear now was my dear Anna cry. Her screams of pain echoed within my head over and over again. As for the infant; I heard not one cry. My newborn had died. In doing so, my newborn baby girl had complicated the childbirth for my dear Anna. Yes, in all honesty, though I may seem a bit rough around my outer shell, I am no more human than other person that walks these grounds. I think in many ways, this moment of unfortunate outcome has led to my life of bounty hunting. A life though too; littered completely in nothing but bitterness and regret.

I still beat the piss out of myself for what happened to my sweet Anna and my baby girl. However, I know there is nothing that nobody can do at this point. I'm still paralyzed and traumatized by the event. You see, I ain't always built out of steel. No, sometimes, underneath that grizzly man that I am, is still a husband and devoted provider for the good nature of a town and its law. I was once a sheriff upholding the law in Canden, also an up and coming Texas Ranger. However, now I was no more than this half-emptied man. I believed this duty would get me away from all of my past troubles, however this whole situation in the forest certainly proved otherwise. You could say, I was certainly thinking things over by this point.

I still remained smothered within the confines of my own regret and sorrow that cold, cold night. It certainly started to feel a bit colder as we soon approached the midnight hour. We sat around the fire; all of us were as still and silent as the dense cold that blanketed us. It certainly felt heavier in the air now; I could feel my breathing was starting to get much more taxing. Though in an anxious move, I found myself puffing on a cigar about three different times that evening. Our horses had become calm, our voices had become quieter, and our hearts had all returned to normal pulses. We were all nervous wrecks in much honesty; that was why we were all quiet to ourselves that night. It wasn't until twelve; that was when Florence and I had a final exchange. "The doc's knocked out cold," Florence subtly commented; tilting his head toward Dietrich who had slumped himself back and was now fast asleep.

"I don't blame him, old buddy," I responded; my teeth were chattering and I still had Anna on my mind.

"You seemed in a bit of a daze back there earlier? Was everything alright?" Florence asked.

"Yeah…Yeah old buddy, everything was fine," I nervously responded. I then took a quick puff of my cigar; all while Florence stood and walked over towards his horse and saddle bag.

"Lord knows this silence in the cold certainly feels welcoming…All that damn comotion earlier certainly had my head throbbing," Florence commented.

However, within the speech that Florence had been giving, so began my small blip away from reality. It was just merely a few seconds that I was zoned out, but it certainly felt longer. I could care less at this point; for that matter I didn't give two damns as to what Florence was telling me either. That was again when I thought of Anna; now I was at her burial ground in front of our once prosper land and house. She was buried there, and still is buried there along with the infant little girl that we never got to have together. It was torn and tattered, with nothing but sorrow, yet drenched in every ounce of sadness. I would do anything between Heaven and Earth to take the place of my wife, and my infant child that never was. I should be buried there, but I'm not. Instead I'm out here with this German doctor, I half-ass know from an Artesian well, and I'm having to fake my emotions with my once good friend Florence.

It certainly is not the expedition that I want to be a part of anymore. In some ways, I could give two shits if I ever finished my bounty hunt. Maybe I wasn't so hardened on the edges after all? Maybe I still have a lot more emotions at play than I ever believed? "Hey, Ter old boy," Florence then caught my attention as I then snapped back into the cold night air.

"Yeah, old buddy," I jumped a bit; clearing my throat as I did. "Sorry, just a little half-passed a doze," I jokingly commented.

"Well, I'm with you there too old pal, gonna probably hit the comforts here shortly," Florence said.

"Old doc's dead to the world, probably ought to check his pulse? Don't you think so?" I comically asked.

"Yeah buddy," Florence smiled; he reached over and nudged on Dietrich's shoulder. "Hey, doc?" He asked.

Dietrich awoke; he stretched out his arms and shivered within the protection of his, what looked to be, buffalo skin. "Yes sir, I'm awake," He said.

"Well doc, you might be drifting back off, but Florence and I, were checking on you…That's all," I said; grinning admirably at the doctor.

"Very thoughtful of you both," Dietrich said with a smile; he then slowly again closed his eyes.

"We'll all be up early again as usual, so get you some good shuteye, old pal," Florence told me.

"Oh trust me old buddy, after this one hell of a day, I do not doubt I will one bit," I responded.

"Night old pal," Florence said, as he began entering our tent. He began tucking himself comfortably into his animal skinned covers too.

"Night, old buddy," I then concluded.

Our voices from then on were all but quiet. However, within the bustling bells of my head and what was left of it, was nothing but a raging storm of anxiety and hopeless recollects. I laid down and drifted slowly off to sleep in the cold brisk night air. I could feel every ounce of breath enter and exit my mouth. I even at one point; could feel every single beat of my ever trembling heart. I counted all of the beats and all of the breaths. I felt distant from the others all night, but also too, distant within my very own self worth. I was taken back in my sleep, to this time, to a moment I long dreaded. Again like before, it was the day in which I buried my beloved Anna and our newborn baby girl.

I had named the girl Isabella, but none of it in the grand portrait of things really mattered. I believed on that day, my life was indeed over, and that there was no destination of prosperity moving forward. I could move on from this tragedy in my life; the tragedy of when I of course lost the only love of my life. Not just that love, but a newborn I never got to raise. I never got to be a father like I had planned on being. In many ways, fate had played its hand too much now, and now the time had come for me to stop facing that fate. That was when I devised a plan in the middle of my half drowned sleep. A plan to leave both Dietrich and my old pal Florence behind. I didn't care about the expedition or crusade at hand. No. I ain't giving this small blip of horror a try, I am tired of facing this death. This ever growing amount of chaos and agony. My leg is sprained good, my feet are as sore as hell, and my emotions all remain the same as they. Battered, beaten, and nearly, quite literally broken. I am leaving this mess; tomorrow morning no matter how much the other two want me to stay. I have some demons I need to sort out, and this certainly as hell isn't the scenario to do it in.

Chapter 13

I got not one lick of sleep that night. The ground in which I awoke upon was as stone cold as the deep chasms of my heart. My heart raced on and on all night. Though I almost froze to death; there were a few occasions in which I felt a slight bit of sweat pour down my neck and back. I felt dizzy throughout much of my sleep; though I knew eventually that sun would start to peak. With that, I knew the time would come at last. I'd haul my ass out of here and return back into a life of somewhat sanity. With all of this in mind; I found myself pondering on much of the conditioning of my now one dead bounty.

The cold we had experienced I'm sure had kept my bounty Patrick pleasantly preserved, but I was careful not to underestimate nature at this time. Trust me, whatever could go wrong, probably could go that way? By now though, I had no time to lose. Finally, the black dark, star-filled sky; finally transformed into a beautiful dark indigo. Then around thirty or so minutes past seven, I found myself staring at a lighter blue colored sky. With that change I quietly picked myself up and stretched. Standing on my feet; I instantly felt every nerve in my leg twitch. Then suddenly, there was a sharp, and I mean sharper than a jagged ravine rock pain! It was coming from right around my right shin. I instantly winced in pain and muttered in a whisper, "Son…of a…"

Not finishing my obscenity; I then reached down towards the area and slowly rubbed it. Though of course none of it helped; I found the small massage to be somewhat of a relief though. I knew I'd be hobbling along on the rest of my journey, but in all reality, I knew it wouldn't be so bad. Boy, Luke certainly took a hard gander at my leg last night! However, I won't let the pain phase me, because broken leg or not, I'm hauling my tattered ass out of here no matter what. I don't care if I've got one eyeball dangling out, I'm getting myself out of this whole mess entirely!

Yes, much of this I know is nothing but emotion and demons of the past. However, I'm facing a far greater problem than anything else I have ever faced. With much of my head bustling and my face wincing; I soon gathered up whatever supplies I thought would be essential. I then began my long and drawn out hobble back to my horse. That was when I heard footsteps behind me. "Where in God's name are you headed?" Florence's half-asleep voice asked.

I refused to answer; I kept walking forward ignoring much of Florence's presence. I reached my horse and supplies; all while from behind I then heard to my shock the *click* of a rifle. I could hear Florence breathe heavier now; I knew he was pointing the gun at me. I could feel his emotions of betrayal because of my acts and I understood his claim to some extent. However, I knew in my mind and heart that Florence wouldn't have the guts or willingness to shoot me in anger. He was quite honestly playing along in some act, I could tell easily. I slowly then turned with a smile; now facing him with a rifle pointed at me and trembling. "You won't shoot me, old buddy," I grinned.

"Don't test me!" Florence exclaimed in a whisper. "Why the hell are you leaving us? Huh!?" Florence inquired hastily; he was turning red hot in the face. His rifle was pointed at me; though it seemed a bit off putting in its aim.

"I have a pretty damn good reason old pal, but it's just that," I paused for a moment in thought; I then began walking forward towards Florence. "Well, I just ain't cut out for work like this," I said. "I've got a cursed spring welling up inside of me, and quite honestly I have so many different things that I have to sort out... I ain't got time for this here predicament anymore I'm afraid," I explained my position with much ease; though I could tell by the look upon Florence's face that he wasn't buying any of it.

"That's a half-assed excuse, and you're really going to expect me to leave you on that?" Florence angrily asked.

"No, because there ain't no excuse, old buddy," I responded; I was then right up on Florence's rifle barrel and it was pointed no more than a few inches from my face. "I've lost too much and if you'd put down your response of aggression and let me explain this, you might understand?" I wondered.

"You got ten seconds to explain your excuse," Florence then nervously stated.

"I lost her! I lost her," I subtly exclaimed; I then ended my statement with much ease. "I lost Anna, my wife, dear old friend…And the baby," I sulked a little upon my statements. "If you need anymore, then so be it, but in that case old buddy, just blow my face right off," I sarcastically concluded.

"What?" Florence asked, confused.

"Blow it right off, old buddy… I ain't got nothing left to live for now anyways," I hopelessly stated.

"Ter, old buddy, I understand that pain hurts, but right now this is way more crucial," Florence then slowly pointed downward his gun; nervously sighing and rubbing his forehead he then continued. "Listen, you ain't leaving us, because you're coming back with me…You're coming back with me and the doc to Canden…Where you belong…You get your shit right there, you understand?" Florence inquired.

"It's easier to speak those words old buddy, but you don't get it…The both of y'all never will," I then stated with an affirmative tone. "I can't do this, and I ain't gonna continue, because underneath this grizzled skin is still a heart and… Well in all honesty a man who's bent and broken…I guess last night old buddy, with that… Fetus…" I nodded up in my throat a bit; I then quickly turned away not finishing my sentence and not wanting to entangle with Florence at all face to face. I was upset, but also torn between continuing and or returning back to life of hunting and reward. I was at a loss at that moment, but I knew what I had to do, right then and there. I killed, but this to me, was starting to brew into a different kind of killing spree; one that quite frankly was above anything else that I had ever dealt with. "Listen old buddy, come and visit in the summer at the state capital…I wish you luck on the rest of your vampire hunt, but I'm afraid I must depart and return to a life I have found much comfort in," I said, I was now well content within my reasonings; though I was still caught in a crossfire between desertion of my friends and doing good for myself.

"Well, old Ter, if you must, but we'll miss you old pal," Florence with much sadness then stated.

"That I will to old buddy," I responded; I then pulled myself upon my horse and correctly positioned myself. "Keep the old doc straight," I then said with a grin; tipping my hat downward in a pleasant goodbye gesture.

With not very many words in our final exchange; I then motioned my horse with my spurs and trotted confidently away. I was gazing with determination; still pulling along that dinky old sled with Patrick still tied between the twine. I didn't turn back either, as I rode steadfast into that unforgiving; yet pristine and beauty drenched wilderness. I was leaving the expedition; not wanting any part in the sacrilegious killings and horrid discoveries of the great beyond. I had faced a force I wasn't prepared for; in many regards there were already many other forces of evil at play within my very own heart. I had to sort out the demons within me immediately, this I understood. I was leaving Florence and Dietrich to continue on their expedition; they were edging closer and closer towards Hank's lodge. From what I had gathered of Florence's word; a plan was in play to possibly intersect Julius and his gang there. Though my bounty Fredrick was more than likely along with him, I could care less by this point. I was broken now; back into the entanglements of my past and a truth of death that I was still having trouble coming to terms with. Yes, I hate death. In many ways, I hate its sudden act of taking away those whom you love, like for instance my dear Anna and my infant baby Isabella. I was still facing the fate that had met them, and that was again death. I wasn't sure if I was truly cut for this life at all? In all honesty. What would happen from my departure? Hell if I knew? Only time now, was telling my story. Trust me matters I felt were already becoming much more complicated, this I knew.

Chapter 14

I'd like to believe my departure from the group felt necessary. Though I wasn't certain? I still felt at ease with my decision in a small blip of thought. For once I felt nothing but peace; I felt it wholly as I trotted violently alone through that cold and untamable wilderness of Northeastern Texas. The winds had picked up as I rode about five miles along the side of Wilmer's Ridge; it was adjacent to Wilmer's Peak. I wore a pair of red spectacles; these helped protect my eyes in the case of flying debris and or in the case of cold snow flakes. Despite the whipping and violently brutal cold winds, I didn't feel any discomfort to my surprise.

I guess in many ways I had way too much on my mind. Anna and the baby crossed it over and over again. Much of the coldness that surrounded me certainly fit the mood and state of emotion that I was in right now. I was yes cold, but yet I didn't feel as if I was alone? Strangely, as the whole trek went through; I felt this uneasy feeling as if someone or something was following me. At one point, I even heard what I believed to be another rider? I glanced multiple times to both sides of my ever changing vantage points. I was riding fast; though my horse did keep a pretty good and steady pace. I was truthfully in no hurry to get back. At this point, my one lost bounty Roger was more than likely gone. By this I mean, wild animals or anything else that found the sight of his corpse, made it worth the scavenging. But just for shits and belly laughs; I was still trekking along in the same direction that all three of us had come in before; still pulling along Patrick's corpse.

I found myself back at the river, not at the same spot, but nearly identical to where I first encountered that whore Elizabeth and where I first encountered the sinister nature of the undead. My stomach felt a bit queasy, though this mainly could have been due to the nature of pain within my leg? I wasn't sure to be honest? I again, though, felt I wasn't alone here. I felt as if I was being watched as I trotted along carefully; gracefully making my way over the steady flowing stream and jagged cold rocks. The sounds of the river certainly felt soothing; for once I felt as if the pain in my leg had started to cease. Eventually, as the sun started to set over the mountains, further downstream; I came to a good stopping point where I could pause and refill my water. My horse had made a pretty good trip through the long and unforgiving ridges that day, and now came a perfect opportunity for my ride to finally receive a good bit of hydration and rest.

We were now tucked deep within this gently winding river bend. The cedar trees and cold hardened dirt carelessly sank into the river bed. It was a very beautiful sight and the perfect embodiment of peace. Yes, the scenery would certainly make any hardened man like myself cry. Now for a moment, just once, I had felt this sense of Heaven, despite all of the hell I had experienced earlier in my expedition. Though I felt peace, for just one blip of time; soon came back that uneasy feeling that I had felt earlier as I descended down into this holler. I felt all over; my body was being closely examined and every move made was being carefully watched. Much like I did with my bounties; only in this scenario I believed I most certainly was being hunted this time. I rubbed my horse's mane as its head bent forward and grabbed a quick gulp of icy cold water.

I was surprisingly not very thirsty; I was mainly distracted still by the sharp pain in my leg from earlier last night. I hobbled on it well though, which led me to believe that Luke didn't do as much damage as I thought he did. Still in many ways though; the pain was slightly agonizing. At one point in my stance, I felt this sharp pinch at the back of my calf muscle. Immediately I winced, sitting myself down slowly, yet promptly on a rock behind me. The waters were cold; colder than stone graves in the middle of a January night. However, I ignored the water for the most part; tenderly rubbing the sore and unquestionably fractured part of my leg. I was pretty sure something was broken, though I didn't know what the hell was? Regardless, I sat there on that rock, yes freezing my giblets off, but I found it to be soothing and relaxing despite all of my shortcomings. Dear Lord, for once I was able to kick my feet up, and never did the journey ahead ever cross my mind.

The loss of my one bounty Roger never once crossed my thought plain either. Sure I was anxious to get back to Austin and collect my money for Patrick but it was no hurry. I was cautious in my steps, believe me, I didn't want another grizzly bear with me, that's for sure! In much reality, I was anxious to get away from all of this terror and mayhem when it was all said and done. The living fire had been scared out of me; though facing death on this magnitude wasn't really the reason for my departure. In truth, it was the inhumane and sacreligious ways in which we killed those folks, if I'm frank! Just as a million different thoughts soon crossed my brain to ponder that thought; I heard a far off and ominous voice creepily rise through my eardrum.

Quickly I jolted myself up and turned in the direction of the strange voice. I even drew my gun quickly and pointed it towards the treeline in which I heard the voice eerily rise and fall in volume. Then strangely the voice darted fastly; it shot across to the right of my vision and then quickly towards the left. I cautiously stayed affixed to my position; still pointing my gun and eagerly ready for anything. Within a few moments, I soon found myself surrounded by silence again. However, that silence only lasted again a few moments. Suddenly I heard a *splash* from behind me in the body of rushing water; to which I quickly turned and looked. I found myself facing a figure covered in a bear skin; it looked exactly like the one Dietrich had worn when I had first met him on the night I was carrying back Roger and Patrick? Instinctively, I called out and asked, "Doc? Is that you?" I was surprised to say the least.

However, the man in the bearskin did not respond. All was still and silent; by now the sun had already sunk over the trees. I could barely tell by the height, if it was Dietrich or not? So as any normal person would do, I walked forward toward the unknown stranger. I was for sure it was Dietrich, but I found it odd he wasn't responding? As I walked carefully, hobbling along still, I also found it odd that Florence wasn't accompanying him? Regardless, I continued carefully forward; taking each stride through the ever moving waters with much anxiety. As I got closer and closer towards the stranger; I soon felt these uneasy knots within my stomach. Something felt out of place here; I felt as if I wasn't even a part of reality any more. The stranger remained there; he seemed to be hunched over and it almost appeared as if he or she were in some kind of pain? "Doc? You got old Florence with you?" I asked.

There was still no response from my question; so cautiously then I continued steadily forward. I then felt my heart start to race; suddenly I felt my hands start to sweat instantly too. My head started to throb; now I was no more than four feet away from the figure. .I then carefully reached forward with my hand, "Doc? Is that you?" I asked; this time impatience was embedded in my voice.

As soon as I asked; I small blip of silence overcame my eardrums. Then quickly the figure showcased his appearance. It was Dietrich! He *shrieked* God Awful at me, and he wasn't the Dietrich I had remembered either. Of course, the living shit was scared right out of me! I jolted back quickly as he came forward towards me. He had sharp fangs! Oh my God! He had become one of them! With no time to act; with much action behind my jumpy self I quickly pulled my trigger. Only nothing came out; my gun wouldn't fire. I panicked, quickly backing away and struggling over the rushing water. I fell backwards into the icy cold waters eventually, dropping my gun in the process. "Shit!" I exclaimed.

Springing to one side with no time to act, I quickly retrieved my gun. I *clicked* it back once more and aimed right at Dietrich. Though within my intensity I did not have the heart to kill him. I couldn't do it. Then suddenly from above; I saw Florence and dear God he was just like Dietrich! My mind was numb; my heart was off beat by over one hundred beats by now. I trembled so much; I believed for an instance that this might be my fateful end. I stumbled backwards toward my horse; who at this moment began going off in a frenzy! I was terrified, but not as terrified as I soon would be within the next moments. Out of nowhere I then heard another *shriek,* this time from behind me. I turned, and to my horror I then found myself staring upon the reflection of me? I was one of them too; yes I was hallucinating and I think I knew the reasons as to why!

Clearly I had deserted my friends, and now a heavy price was to be paid. Now humanity itself would become the undead; the world would be ruled by the vampires of hell and I was responsible!

Though it seemed crazy to think; it was most certainly true. I believe much of this was tainted with guilt, no questions asked. Realizing the downfall; I quickly closed my eyes not wanting to see the truth any longer. I whimpered a bit; though as a man I remained tough and to my own ground. I then opened my eyes once more; this time I was looking at myself dead on. Shockingly, I was having a staredown with myself. Suddenly my face quickly morphed; the nose fastly grew out and my teeth sharpened into what looked to be a thousand razor sharp fangs! Quite honestly, I looked to be what looked like a rabid and deranged dog. My God I looked horrifying! I closed my eyes again, it was horror, and I didn't want to see it anymore. Bravely I lay there; dreading on opening them back up and staring back once more. Foolishly I did once more, and within the horrible *shrieks* I soon found myself staring upon another person? This time it wasn't Dietrich, nor was it me or Florence. No.

It appeared to be a man for whom I had never seen before. He was well dressed for the cold; wearing a long trench coat and fur around his neck. He looked upon me with a glare that Satan himself would've worn. He creepily grinned at me; tipping his head forward he nodded in a very unsettling manner. "You can try to outrun your fears, bounty hunter, but you can't hide from them!" The man spoke. His voice sounded extremely faded though and very disorganized.

His spoken tongue of evil sent many chills up my spine. For one moment, I believed upon sight of this man, that it was indeed Julius! The man in which Dietrich and Florence were seeking out after. Though I knew he wasn't in the flesh and present; I found myself numb to the shock wave of power that the undead had brought on. This was a power in which I had no explanation for. I was petrified, so quickly, I found myself closing my eyes once more. I shut them tightly this time; though I kept hearing a million different demons screaming at once I did not find the urge to open them again. I lay there, shaking constantly as I awaited the departure of the horrid sounds within my ear. Hoping that all of this madness would cease, and praying that all reality would return to normal.

To much of my prayers being prayed and my hopes being hoped, I soon heard the sounds drown out slowly, and then eventually all was silent again. Quickly I heard nothing but the river, and the sounds of hooves on my frantically scared horse. To which I opened my eyes again; this time I saw not one soul. I sprang forward to assist my terrified stead; who at this point probably had no idea as to what in God's Name I was fighting?

"Woah! Easy! Easy!" I exclaimed; gently and cautiously grabbing a_hold of my horse's reins.

As quick as the chaotic behavior of my horse had started; much of it could be said for how it had ended. She calmed down within no time, and soon I found myself alone and in the company of silence once again. A sense of peace returned, though of course much of my emotions were affixed back towards the hallucinations I had just experienced. One question plagued me though as I drug my cold and damp self up the river bank. It was a question as to who that man was in my vision? I figured it must've been Juilius? However I was dumbfounded and somewhat confused as to the ordealings of this encounter. I was at the mercy, I knew it too. I was being observed from somewhere, but to be honest I had no clue? I couldn't understand this power, and nor could I understand the significance of this incident? I was blindly walking toward an undead grave, this I knew. A part of me was still terrified to return back to the expedition. I wanted to help, but to me at that moment, none of it was worth the loss of my very own sanity.

Chapter 15

I was sitting upon a stone cold, rock slab, and my dinner was nothing more than a small trout I had retrieved from the river after I had left the sight of my encounter. I had retrieved another three trout, but I was going to preserve them for later on, whenever I got hungry again. No more than an hour had passed. The sun had now fallen asleep in the west; though beautifully painted along the horizon was this beautiful array of deep orange, violet, and indigo colors. It was the true face of dusk light; a beautifully painted winter's twilight in the mountains of North Texas. I was numb to the cold; though also numb to every single thought that rattled within my brain. I believed that quite possibly, this hallucination may have been warranted by the lack of water I had been taking in. Though I tried to stay as well hydrated as possible; I still found myself feeling distraught with the vision I had seen. It was in much truth, way too consequential to be anything other than just dehydration.

In many good words, I believe it was a conflict within my soul, and much in which had manifested before me plain and simple. I was scared for my life; however on the outside again I tried to stay as tough and as fortified as I could. As the night grew darker; I started to notice the faint dim of winter stars start to grow in vast numbers. For being so cold; it was certainly a beautiful night no doubt. I laid back for about a half an hour or so; my brain of course running like a thousand different stampeding bison. I thought about my past and all of the hell that I had gone through. Of course I thought mostly about the actual hell I had just recently faced too. The undead, vampires. It was something that no mere mortal like myself was ready to face. I ain't no man that looks beyond the face of reality, but this expedition certainly made me see into the terrors of the other side and it's a sight I wish I never have to stare upon again. Though yes, I did worry for Florence and Dietrich's sake; I was however confident in the remaining part of their travels.

I had a feeling that a good night's stop at Hank's Lodge would suit them well. It'd be a perfect opportunity to quite possibly intersect this here Julius and his other two men. One of which being my bounty Fredrick; who by all means I had not one lick of interest in, anymore. Honest to the Lord, I could care less at this point. There was something deeper within my soul going on and I had to sort things through. Much of my sorting I was lacking, would have to be evaluated when I arrived back in Austin. I needed to get my life straightened, no doubts. As I pondered and pondered, thought after thought; I soon found myself in a slight moment of light dozing. I closed my eyes for a moment; listening to nothing but the fire *crack* and *snap*. I even heard the faint and off putting sounds of a group of coyotes. However this pack sounded so far away, that it quite honestly had become nothing to worry for.

'   As I rested my head back; I began to slowly drift away with the smells of soot and ash engulfing my senses. It had been no more than maybe a minute into my doze, when I all of a sudden heard the sounds of a tree limb *crack*. I then heard the sounds of shuffling feet; I quickly opened my eyes and jolted upward quickly. Standing quickly I looked around frantically; my horse was startled of course. I turned around quickly and calmed my horse. I then subtly whispered, "It's alright old girl." I then rubbed my horse's face. My breath had seemed thicker in its mist now; it felt as if the temperature had dropped within no time at all. I was sure footed though, absolutely prepared for the fateful inevitable. I reached into the back of my saddle bag and quickly grabbed a crucifix that Dietrich had given me earlier. I then reached forth and grabbed my colt revolver; I cocked it back and aimed it toward the treeline in which I had heard the movement. I stood there anxiously awaiting, I could see in the dim light of the flickering flames, of what looked to be a swaying of the pines. Somebody or something was moving about frantically. It appeared that whatever it was, it had struggled quite obviously, and it was drenched in its own stagger.

My heart began beating faster and faster; my hands began shaking like a tree being violently whipped in a severe storm of summer. Then for a moment all of the movement stopped; as did the subtle swaying of the trees and violently made sounds. I was scared that it might be a cougar or some other kind of furious animal. I figured it wouldn't be a grizzly since most were back to sleep now due to the weather getting colder. Regardless of whatever it may have been;

I wasn't truly prepared in much honesty. Then like a violent rolling thunder came crashing down into a view a nude man? I was of course startled, but I was also stunned by the appearance. He wasn't completely naked for truth's sake. He actually had wrapped around him what appeared to be a deerskin, but that honestly, was all that he had on him. He looked to be stumbling, but mostly he looked tired and obviously bitter cold. He was skinny, which honestly may have been due to the fact that he hadn't eaten in a long while. He knelt forward; breathing heavily and praying to his knees it appeared. He looked up quickly, gasping loudly. I jumped in fright, "AHHH!" He screamed aloud.

"You are a human!? Please tell me you are mortal?!" I inquired in a shout of desperation. I had my crucifix drawn and I was standing at the ready.

"Yes! For God/s…saa…akkk…ee!" The man shouted. He was struggling to speak; he was shivering violently and looked almost traumatized. He looked to be out of the most disastrous nightmare, this was for certain.

"Who are you?!" I asked; I was still trembling and I could feel my blood start to boil over.

"I'm…I'm," The man was too cold to talk; I could tell his face had become frostbit. I carefully walked forward; prepared for any sudden movement he might make on me. I believed him to be human; though a part of my mind was cautious otherwise. "Plee…asseee!" He exclaimed. "Help!" He then finished in a struggle.

"Certainly pal," I nervously replied. "Just let me get you some better clothes and get you some more suitable attire," I then shockingly delivered. I stuttered a bit over my words, but I was all willing at this point. He seemed legitimate; to which I reached forward; taking off a layer of my skin hide jacket, I quickly wrapped it around him.

Desperately he sprang forward; my heart skipped about forty beats and the wind was pushed from me it seemed. I was shaken upon his embrace and somewhat caught off guard. All I gathered from this was a man desperate for some warmth. It was a man drenched in sorrow and uncertainty as to what he had just witnessed. He was petrified and paralyzed by fear. In many ways, this man was almost suffering through the same trials as me. In some way, he was a frightening reflection of myself; a glimpse of somebody with nothing more than a hide on his back and the breath from his lungs.

Chapter 16

Within a single spark of time it appeared, before I knew it, all was calm again. I had sat back down and had let my confused and cold stranger have a break by the fire. He was frantic obviously; I had given him a pair of trousers and a spare shirt I hadn't worn yet. I let him keep my coat of course, and I let him have a bit of what was left of my trout. The stranger of course ate all three without any questions being asked. I then reached over and handed him a cup of hot water to sip on. He jolted at my presence as I touched him; he leaned forward still cold and shivering. "Here, warm up your insides," I said.

"Thanks," He said; he lifted the cup to his face, violently shaking. He struggled a bit on taking his first sip, but he eventually consumed the liquid.

Nervously I sat down; I then whipped out a cigar and lit it. "Well, who the hell are you? Furthermore," I then exhaled a long train of smoke, pausing. Catching myself in my sentence, I then continued inquiring, "Why in God's Name were you naked and bare assed? Just a little curious?" I then asked with a subtle grin.

"I thought you might be curious by this," The stranger replied, smiling slightly; though he then went right back to shivering and holding himself with much comfort. "I'm Nathanial... Na...Nathanial Austin," He then introduced himself; trembling and chattering his teeth as he did.

"Well what happened?" I asked.

"I'd rather not talk about the matter!" He quickly cut in; raising his voice in much aggression. "I ain't talking about what I saw! Or who I saw for that matter!" He exclaimed.

"Was it him? It was, wasn't it?" I chillingly asked.

"If you'd like to talk to me about something other than that, then please by all means do so," Nathaniel begged.

"I know it's hard to talk about, I saw the bastard too...In a vision really," I commented; I then deeply pondered for a moment.

"Yeah, well I saw that son of a bitch! Face to face!" Nathaniel barked back. "I saw him a couple of nights ago… I was traveling back with my dear brother Luke, and my wife Bertha," Nathaniel stated. At recognition of the names my eyes widened. He began to then subtly weep, "You know hunter, I ain't one to be fearful really, but I believe for once, just once…I believe I was just that! God I couldn't stop him!" Nathaniel exclaimed; by now tears were streaming, but he was still trying to hold everything together.

"Where did you see them?" I asked; having a bit of a nervous tone in my voice.

"Saw them over on the upper north side, right above Wilmer's!" Nathaniel frantically replied.

"Well, I'm hunting them, though I was hunting them," I then responded; correcting myself in the middle of my sentence. I then leaned forward; by now I was strangely starting to rethink my departure from Dietrich and Florence. "Please Nathaniel, where were they headed?" I asked.

"I for the life of me, couldn't say?" Nathaniel replied; he then caught himself from his continuously growing crying spree. "All I can remember vividly, were those eyes on that man… Dark, lifeless eyes…For God's sake the look in their eyes was true hell," Nathaniel described in horror. "These three came in the night and drank them dry! Dear Lord, I awoke the next morning and found my dear sweet Bertha, and my dear brother Luke that way! Dead! But they weren't!" A look of shock drenched Nathaniel's face. "I'll never know for the life of me why they didn't turn me undead? But I should have... I should have," Nathaniel couldn't finish; his delivery had grown very unorganized.

Looking towards Nathaniel's neck; I noticed a crucifix dangling. "You were probably wearing that? Weren't you?" I asked; nodding my head towards the crucifix.

"Yes, the Lord Jesus was with me! But!" Nathaniel began choking up in tears; though he remained calm in his cries all the same. "But! He took my brother! He took my dear Bertha and our unborn child! Lord they both came and tried to attack me the next night too! It wasn't truly them either! I couldn't do anything bounty hunter! So I just ran away from Bertha and Luke! I ran far away! That's how I got myself here, I'm afraid!" Nathaniel finally concluded; his tears ceased a bit, but I could still read loneliness within his completion.

"Pardon me for asking though, but how did you end up naked?" I asked in embarrassment.

"I slipped and fell this afternoon alongside the river...I got myself swept away in the waters...So I had no choice later when I pulled out, but to strip...Didn't want to catch pneumonia... Long story short though on the skin...I found the carcass of a doe when I had made my way up the side about a couple of minutes after I had stripped... Right place and the right time, you know," Nathaniel stated; he subtly smirked in my direction.

"I understand, pal," I said.

"However, please, do not think that I am telling these disorganized encounters for the sake of whistling out of my eyeballs! I swear to God above! I saw them come back! They returned from the dead! They weren't the same though! I had to run! I had to flee! I was scared! My God! They changed my dear Bertha! Dear Lord... I lost her and my brother!" Nathaniel then cried out; he then buried his head into his hands and began sobbing.

Of course I felt guilt return to my mind; I thought back to our group encounter with Bertha and Luke last night. Conclusively putting it together from the moment I heard Nathaniel speak of those names; I casually lowered my head in shame. I looked down in sorrow, I understood the pain that Nathaniel was facing, because much like him I had lost my dear wife too. It was ironic in a way; his pain was in much reflection to my hardships. "Do you know where they were headed?" I inquired.

Instantly, Nathaniel raised his head slowly; tears streamed and covered his face like a leaking spring from the inside of a boulder. "Bertha? Luke!?" Nathaniel wondered.

"No, the three you saw come to you? In the night?" I nervously asked.

"Again, Dear God! How am I supposed to know? All I know is, they were not of this world...I swear they must've come from the very ends and corners of hell itself...Dear Lord, I do not believe for once that the devil himself would want them! Do not underestimate what they will do! Dear God! I beg of you! If you are to hunt them out, please, please, do not underestimate their power!" Nathaniel eagerly warned; he had tears again welling mostly from fear this time.

"I have seen this power, I'm afraid, my dear friend... My mind is numb, and my soul remains the same," I said.

"From what I could tell, within their completions as I saw them, was they looked drained, this here strange foreigner and his men," Nathaniel then began with subtle hesitation. "They're probably headed towards Hank's Lodge where we had come from? I don't know? But I won't go with you my friend... I can't!" Nathaniel then cried out once more; he had petrification drenched all over his face.

"I won't let you go like this, pal," I said. I leaned forward; flicking my cigar as I did. "But if this here Julius is headed to Hank's, I'm not too sure if I'd be on the same ground as you?" I questioned myself. Now I wasn't sure if I should return back to Austin or not? Now I began to rethink my position on leaving; especially due to the circumstances of Nathaniel's experience.

"Whatever you do... Please... Please! He must be destroyed! All of them!" Nathaniel begged. I had never seen a man in more fear, than I had seen Nathaniel right then and there.

There was no doubt in my mind; Nathaniel's story, though seemingly disorganized, seemed quite legitimate. I believed every word he had spoken, and I saw the truth and fear once more within those pupils. I could read his intentions and they seemed authentic and beyond the point of honesty. For the rest of the night; I sat there in the cold with Nathaniel until he drifted off slowly to sleep. I watched him closely; making sure that his chest was well covered from the cold. The most important situation was making sure my new friend didn't die of a bad case hyportherma. Once all his vitals seemed normal and his breathing returned normally; I then leaned back and covered myself up for another long and cold night's sleep. I of course thought about everything, but in some ways I still remained numb. I was numb to this power of the undead. Numb to the decision of deserting my friends, and though numb to what power might be unleashed if this dreaded disease isn't contained. I wanted to help again on the expedition, but not as much as I didn't want to help. I was caught in a crossfire.

Chapter 17

My quality of sleep that night was of course unacceptable. I can not be more honest than that. I must've awakened about three or four times. I shivered in the cold; though I was buried deep within a bearskin I was still freezing my ass off. I was mainly nervous; anxiously I dug into the ends of my nubs on my fingernails and peeled them back. I peeled them so much; that eventually I started to feel blood pour out from the skin being pulled. It felt painful, yes, but in all honesty it was too cold to even feel that pain. At this point, I could care less, because trust me it wasn't the biggest plague upon my life.

Just as the dawn sky had painted its way across the clouds; I got up quickly and looked around. The fire had long been dead and my horse was now perched awaiting for me to assist her. I rubbed my eyes and stretched out. I yawned and pulled myself up slowly. My leg was now stiff in its nature; I was pretty sure it was all a simple bruise or quite possibly a fracture? To be honest, it didn't really worry me, because now I had the stories of Nathaniel and his encounters on my mind. I also regret now my departure from Dietrich and my old buddy Florence. I ain't one to own up to my mistakes if I'm truthful, but this time I was for sure feeling every ounce of guilt plague me. I knew this power of vampirism was far beyond anything I could comprehend, but then again so were the fabrications of my life in lighter words. I didn't want to go back, but now I was for certain; Dietrich and Florence may possibly be roaming into a trap.

Though I didn't think of it immediately when Nathaniel had spoken of Hank's and his lodge, now came this realization I'm afraid. The trap was maybe Hank's Lodge? Hank's was a good two day's trip, but if I went in a certain direction along Wilhemina's Ridge; I could possibly cut out about an entire day's travel? However, much of Wilhemina's Ridge and surrounding woodlands lay within Indian Territory, and this travel could possibly mean life or death? Despite this, I guess, I was willing to take a chance. I had traveled along Indian Territory before, but not for no more than a few miles. I'd more than likely stay as close to the river as possible; due to the fact that it acted as the border between Texas and Indian Territory. Though to be honest, I'd probably end up inside further without even trying. No matter the circumstances, the time was now to put my ass in motion. I had to return and I had to finish what I had started. I guess in many ways, I facing these Vampires, could've possibly reflected my life in turmoil right now? I've been facing my own personal demons lately, and now I am actually facing real life ones. I wasn't going to let their powers wreck havoc no longer. The place to be was Hank's, and the time I was aiming for was this evening.

Quickly I gathered my supplies together; checking over to be sure I had plenty of amenities for my long day's travel. I wouldn't have a lot of stops to make for the horse to drink, so whatever fluids had to be consumed it might as well be right now. I motioned for the horse; shaking the reins and nodding my head towards the river in which I had caught my dinner earlier the day before. As I walked towards the basin in which I was to take my stead, I walked carefully over, towards Nathaniel's deerskin. I noticed, as I approached to wake him, something odd? His skin looked quite barren and his belongings seemed quite fumbled about? I reached out slowly; my heart was actually beating frantically because I guess I didn't know as to what I'd find? To my surprise, I found no Nathaniel? "What the hell?" I asked myself in a mutter.

I shivered a bit; rising up back slowly I then heard the sounds of *splashing* water down below in the basin in which I was heading. Moving with no time to spare, I cut the rope to my sled that held Patrick's body from the horse. I was not caring at this point about collecting his bounty. I was to leave his corpse here to decay. At this point, Patrick was becoming a weight and drag. Regardless, I fastly walked down the hill into the rocky river shore. Within the rocks was of course again that infamously cold water. Though to my horror I saw Nathaniel walking slowly across the river; he was dragging himself like he had a piece of steel iron protruding out of his ass. He walked heavily; his head was down and he looked almost drunk. He was walking towards the other side; I dropped the reins to my horse and whistled loudly through my fingers towards him. Though the whistle was loud, he did not acknowledge my presence. "Hey Nate? The hell are you doing?" I asked; I noticed my voice had started to tremble.

Nervously I watched him; he did not acknowledge my voice either. I was bewildered of course so I began throwing small rocks in his general direction. Desperately I was trying to get his attention; however he remained all the same with his head hung low and feet shuffling heavily. He eventually reached the side of an embankment and pulled his sorry looking self up towards what appeared to a pile of small boulders. He then carefully stepped up onto the boulders and looked towards me with a very unsettling look. I then turned back toward my stead; I noticed that a small bit of my horse's rein had been cut off? Immediately my eyes widened; I now began to understand what Nathaniel was planning on. I quickly turned and now found the sight I had most dreaded. He had the piece of sliced off rein in his hand; to which he carefully tied over the limb of the tree branch right above him. He then tied it quickly around his neck. "Nate! No!" I screamed.

However, my cry and approach was too little, too late. He then jumped forward off the rocks; instantly his neck caught that jolt and before me now hung a man who had committed suicide. The tree limb made a *crack* sound, however it didn't break. It was sturdy enough to now hold up his now dangling, helplessly looking body in the air. It was the most grim looking sight I had ever seen up until that point in my travels. Quickly my once fast beating heart, now sank fast and my hands began to quiver. My mouth dropped; I then instantly put my right hand up to it in regards to the shocking events that had just transpired.

Now I had no idea what the hell to do? Of course the answer was clear, but my mind became fogged again. I understood why Nathaniel did what he did. He had probably felt there was no use to him continuing onward. Plain and simple as that. Within a few moments; I then sat myself down onto a rock and pondered for a few minutes. As I sat there, I stared hopelessly upon the cold hardened ground. Within that silence, nothing could be heard but the tree *creak* now in which Nathaniel was now hanging from. My horse then walked forward and put her head down into my arms. She was trying to get my attention from what I had assumed. I could tell that even she was upset and somewhat distraught with my emotions too. It's funny how animals can tell as to when you're down or saddened.

I rubbed her nose; calming her she instantly rustled her nose within my gloved hands. I blanked out for a second, not finding any ounce of motivation. Clearly I had seen a sight, I didn't wish for my own worst enemy to see. I had seen an innocent man, who had basically lost everything. His pride, his love, and his understanding of self worth within himself do the unspeakable. Again, this Nathaniel, I believed, reflected me in some ways. Though unlike him, I wasn't about to let these traumatic events plague my decision. With an angered look in my face I stood slowly to attention. I brushed off the dirt and readied my horse quickly. This tragedy that had manifested before me, was now merely a bleak and unimportant instance. I would not let this event stop me; come hell or high water above my head I'd push my ass forward. I needed to press on and put all of the demons of my yesterday behind me. As soon as my horse had drunk the last of her licks; I quickly sprang up on top and motioned quickly.

Like a fast zipping shooting star in the night, my stead and I were off. We moved carefully along the river shore; my horse's hooves lifted carefully over each and every single rock. The weather was actually quite pleasant as our journey continued throughout the daylight hours. Though once we began our climb up in slight elevation; I noticed a slight shift downward in the temperature. Around the afternoon we had made our way behind Wilhemina's Ridge; now we were in a small stretch of Indian Territory. Of course my nerves began to shock like a million lightning bolts and my heart rate began ramping up faster. I had no clue if I'd even make it out alive or not? I was an evil "white man" as the Comanche would refer to me as. I was number one on their hit list, this I was for sure. In pondering this, I perked up a bit; keeping close watch on all of my surroundings.

However, my horse and I still moved like a tempest, crazed wind. Though I wasn't trotting; I could feel my horse's exhaustion by this point. Despite this I still motioned for the horse to continue. She slowed up a bit as we made our way passed a small hollar; it was a set of trees that was connected to a small strip of Wilmer's Peak. The area looked familiar, though of course it was an area that no one ever dared to enter. My mouth was dry, my leg began hurting again, and my ass got sore too. In regards to these unfortunate endeavors; I could give two pisses at this point. I was a determined man that afternoon, and my horse was too, surprisingly. My mind was a muddled mess; all I could think about was the worst of the worst. I was waiting for one of the Comanche warriors to hunt me out of the bushes. They'd quickly shoot me down with an arrow and drag my fool hearted ass away, and not a one word would be spoken. As the day grew tired, so did I. My mouth got dry from dehydration and my stomach began to rumble from hunger. Again, I didn't care, I was a determined man.

I was hell bent; sending up every prayer under my breath as I edged closer and closer towards the lodge. Eventually, I found myself at an elevation at around fourteen hundred feet; this was one of the highest points in the state of Texas. I was eventually crossing over the Red River; though mainly I zigzagged along from one side of the shore to the other. I had to be careful due to the unknown nature of the terrain I was trotting upon. I'd be in Indian Territory for a few trots; then I'd be back in Texas, in no time at all. It was a never ending back and forth, confusing cycle. I found myself alone on multiple occasions, which certainly kept my eyes peeled, not only for the Natives, but for wild animals too like Cougars, Coyotes, and Bobcats. The water *splashed* about as I came in and out of the waters on my horse. I could feel the small brushes of icy cold water softly caress the edges of my spurs. I motioned the horse; constantly beating it over and over again. I could tell she was tired, but so was I. I felt all of my nerves shock at once; I felt my leg go numb on multiple occasions.

Before I could even blink; it was now around four in the evening. The sun was starting to settle slightly over the mountainside. Yet despite the positioning of the sun; much of the scenery still looked quite lively and bright. I could still see in front of me a good one thousand feet no trouble. Again I was on my toes and constantly on high alert for any Natives that might ambush me. I was relieved though as I now edged closer towards where the border of Texas met back with Indian Territory. I still had a good two miles to ride to the border. Despite much of that light, at the end of my tunnel, feeling so close; I found myself in the unsettling presence of somebody else. At first, I thought it was just simply the rustling of me upon my stead; the constant sounds of my horse's feet hitting the river and cold hard ground. No, it wasn't that at all. I could feel this predator watching me; though I knew it wasn't a cougar or coyote. I began to hear another shuffle to the right of my ear. It clearly sounded like another rider. As I got to around one mile from the border; I then heard clearly the sounds of another horse *snarling*. To my utter dread, I turned quickly towards my right; to which I saw a Commache warrior. He had his face fully painted and he sat upon his stead like a statue. His posture was perfect and he seemed ready.

In his right hand I noticed a bow and arrow. He remained silent though; never did he make a battle cry sound. He was stoic in his look; wearing a cougar skin for warmth, and buffalo skin pants. I winced of course; though my body was slightly numb from shock I had no time to react. I remained calm, cursing though under my breath and praying too all the same. Then suddenly, the warrior loaded his bow quiver and quickly, he shot fast! As I had my attention on the Comanche toward my right, I quickly knelt downward. I then heard an arrow *wizz* right past my left ear. I quickly jumped of course; though still keeping my stead in full maneuver forward. "Son of a!" I exclaimed; quickly lowering my head in a moment of quick half-assed reaction, I trembled once more.

I beat my horse further and further. My horse was trotting like fire upon the most violent winds now. My heart rate increased again; though it was cool outside I started to feel sweat pour down the upper part of my neck. Now I had another Comanche warrior coming along. This time riding from behind me to my left. I was being chased out of Indian Territory. Either ran off, or it'd be death? I wasn't sure who'd win this small ambush attack? One thing's for certain, my friends Dietrich and Florence were in need of my help. Hank's was also so close too; I swear I could even smell the wood fire burning at this point. I could also see the border ahead; it was at the bottom of Lay Mountain which cradled Hank's Lodge on the other side which was encased, in the confines of Draper's Mountain. I was close! Dear Lord, I'm so close! But also close to me from behind were two pissed off Comanche warriors who had every right to shoot my ass down.

I beat the horse's back, telling her to "Getty up!" Every chance I got. I was frantic of course in my mind; still numb and cold in shock from my ordeal. We were now no more than five thousand feet away, however it felt more like a hundred miles. My life flashed before my eyes; at one point I even believed I saw my dear sweet Anna. I knew my fate, and I knew what could be. However, a part of my mind was in denial; numb from the waist down as I continued to push my stead forward. Arrows soar right by my ears; I even heard them make a slight *whistle* sound as they were moving so fast. I then turned around towards the first Native that had ambushed me. In quick defense of myself I quickly drew my gun, cocking it back in a *click* that gave me a slight jolt I fired! I missed of course, mainly due to the unsteady movements and chaos I was experiencing. The Native then reloaded his bow and quickly drew back firing again. This time his arrow grazed the top of my hat. "Shit!" I reacted.

Then suddenly, I heard a loud *BANG*! I jumped quickly, looking towards my right and left I heard a bullet quite literally *whistle* right past my left side. I then shot right back at the Comanche that was to my left. He had a rifle in his hand now, unlike the Native to my right who had a bow and arrow. I was of course taken off guard. More than likely the gun was taken from an unfortunate traveler who had entered and never came out. Regardless, I could care less honestly; my main objective now was to make it no more than one thousand feet. The water *splashed* violently as all three of our horses trotted in a violent game that anybody could win at this moment. The time was brewing and my nerves were shaking like a billion earthquakes. I was almost there! Now it was no more than five hundred feet. Then *BANG*! Again the Native to my left fired; I heard the bullet and this time it sounded only millimeters away from my head.

Dear God! These Natives were aiming to kill and they were killing without showing any ounce of mercy! I was frantic still; then I heard them then *YELP*! It was a battle cry of the Comanche, and it was brewed of course by the adrenaline rush that was indeed this moment. It was now a three man war; however it was two of them versus just one of me. I was for certain I might die, but then again I still clang to that horse with high, high hopes. I was now one hundred feet away from the border! I turned around again and fired back another shot. This time I shot the Native to my left side. Although I didn't actually shoot the Native; I shot his horse instead. I shot the stead directly in the front. I saw blood spray out as the horse instantly reacted in pain, falling down head forward into the icy cold river. The warrior was of course flung off quickly; though merely injuring him in the process.

Though I had a quick moment of victory; I did not let my guard down for one blink. I was now fifty feet or so away. We came to this steep embankment; now panic drenched myself and my ever weary mind. I motioned the horse; beating the ever loving piss out of it, I felt myself sweating once more. My breaths got heavier and of course my heart pumped faster. I heard another arrow *whistle* right past my right ear. I turned around and fired back in mad self defense. I missed, however it didn't matter, because now I had crossed the border, finally! I was, however, still soaked within the moment. I cocked back my gun and held it regardless. But to my surprise the arrow holding Native did nothing. He simply stopped his pursuit and watched me get away in victory.

"Woah!" I shouted in joy. I was relieved obviously. The Comanche that was trailing me to my right, had now stopped dead within his tracks.

He had known the border was right before him now. The pursuit was only unless by this point on. I was back on American soil, and to my utter shock I was still alive. I made it through the bulk of trouble, but now what still lay ahead was Hank's Lodge. I was no more than about ten miles; I was coming at it from the backside of Draper's Mountain. It was the mount in which Hank's was built upon and at last I was there!

Chapter 18

I could feel all of the spaces of my mind and heart tightening. I could feel the agonush and pain; although there seemed to be no danger in sight, I started to feel it. I felt as if I had entered a whole new reality; the rotation of this world again felt off and the gravitational pull of existence was out of place. I climbed a slight elevation; over the ridges and hollers of both Lay and Draper's Mountain. The sun had started to settle over the peaks and there was a slight change in the weather. Snow had started to spit; there seemed to be a slight skiff over the ground as I approached the outer ridge of the mountain. Now I could see it! At last! Hank's Lodge, which was now nestled within view; it looked quite peaceful in the distance over this ravene.

I'd say now I was no more than a mile away; I could even smell the smoke burning from Hank's fireplace. Though much hope seemed present; there was a small wrinkle in the wardrobe. Within the ever growing faith that was excelading, there still cripply moved another problem, my horse. She was tired of course, and I knew I had run her ass ragged that day too. However, at this point, I was nothing but a desperate man. I was pushing her hard; that's when I soon found myself; quite literally a pebble's throw away from Hank's Lodge. I was almost there, Dear Lord I was almost there! That was when she finally fell down; fastly falling forward trying to capture a blink moment of rest. She *snarled* heavily of course. I fell forward with her too. I caught myself, bracing my back and waiting for her to tip over to either side of the saddle. "Woah! Girl!" I yelled.

She sighed heavily; then in a moment's notice she laid down upon her right side without even a slight bit of warning. I fell to that right side with her; though quickly trying to move my leg out of the way. Thankfully my foot was all that was caught in her collapse underneath the side of the saddle. "Shit!" I exclaimed. I felt a shock of pain move fastly up my leg. I then stumbled a bit and fell forward away from the horse like a drunken fool. My foot was still caught; I was frantic in all honesty. With all of my might though, I then pulled myself out from underneath the horse's side miraculously. Relieved and breathing heavily, I pulled myself up swiftly checking all of my surroundings. The snow had started to fall a bit harder, and the light beyond the twilight sky had now transformed into a purplish, dark orange color. It was God Awful cold though; my legs and my whole upper body were numb. I then, in a bit of angered rage, spat into the snow and grabbed my rifle. The horse was now lying half dead; it seemed right in front of me. "Alright old girl! I know I ran your ass off! But come on! We're here! Just a few more steps!" I shouted.

The horse *snarled* in pain again; then she took a few more heavy breaths and then all was still. She passed out; a look of disappointment drenched my completion. I then took my rifle and pulled the trigger. *BANG*! My gunfire pierced the air in an unsettling soundwave that sent shivers up my spine. I took the old stead out of her misery completely; I knew there'd be no way of bringing her back to health. Once again I was desperate, and I was in it for all or nothing at that moment. I was quickly then silenced; nothing but the sounds of brisk cold winds could be heard. My breath was a thick vapor and I could feel my lungs closing in from the pressure. For some reason, I then found myself in a fit of rage. I flipped the rifle around and used the wooden end of my Spencer to slam my horse's head in. I was pissed! I then kicked the poor stead trying in a last effort to get it going again, though obviously there was no point, she was dead. She didn't move, obviously; so I slammed her head in again, and then again. I was hitting her in anger trying to get her to come back to life almost. Yes, I knew it was stupid of me, but I was frantic and life it seemed was on the line here. I felt uneven in my thoughts; I think it could've just been the long haul in all honesty that made me so bat shit crazy?

Not wanting to continue in my tantrum; I simply just backed off and collected a pause. I drew a heavy sigh; then I reached into my heavy coat pocket and put on my red rounded spectacles. The snow and cold winds were punching my face now; it felt unbearable beyond anything I had ever experienced on that trip. I then lifted up my scarf and covered my mouth in an effort to receive a moment in warmth. I could feel a case of frostbite coming, but at this point I didn't lose a train of thought on it. I shrugged off all of my troubles and continued forward on foot. Though now the lodge was no more than a few hundred feet away; it felt more like a mile from this distance.

All of this was in regards to how my upper torso was feeling; everything felt disjointed and I felt nothing but my nerves being shot to hell. My feet could barely move it seemed, and my whole upper body could barely move too along with it. But I pressed forward; a stubborn jackass and fool hearted individual. It was all for my friends and it was all in an effort to stop an oncoming evil force. The winds were hitting my face fiercely; my legs moved one step at a time. I felt like I was sinking; it seemed in quicksand. The brisk cold that was whipping at my knees certainly didn't help. My God, I was a desperate man, and now no more than one hundred feet from my destination. I could smell the whiskey from out here; I could smell the perfumes from the women and the cologne from the men too.

Chapter 19

There was only one direction I was heading, and it was forward. I felt my skin under my coats; it was frostbit from the instant touch of my hand. I slipped back on my glove though and continued forward. I sighed heavily; I began to pant like a heifer with a broken leg. I was dragging my ass; though it felt like an eternity only a mere two minutes had passed. The winds seemed to grow stronger, my heart rate increased. I was just waiting to collapse, right then and there. I'd go down like my horse; pitiful and not much energy left. But I pressed forward, I never once thought of stopping, that'd be foolish by this point. Eventually I found myself up at the entrance to Hank's. I stopped and paused; taking in a few last inhales of the cold Texas night air. I then pushed the door open; I used every ounce of strength.

The doors, both of them, swung open fast. I staggered a bit upon arrival, but by God I straightened myself up quickly. I stood to attention; staring hopelessly it appeared into that lively and warmly looking place. I could feel the cold air quite literally weaken off of my shoulders. I swear I saw vapor rise instantly as the warmth of the fireplace melted what little snow and ice I had on me. "Son...of... a...Who am I kidding?" I asked, muttering to myself. "My brain's so frozen...I can't even...Finish...A full sentence," I said. I then rolled my eyes; quickly piecing together the contradiction of that statement. "Oh, whatever," I mumbled. I then whipped off my spectacles; of course all of the guests in the lower lobby of Hank's were staring at me in confusion.

I paused a bit, taking in my newfound comfort and breathing in a few impatient breaths. I brushed off my shoulder gently and proceeded forward. I could see all of the guests whispering. I knew they were somewhat shocked by my sudden entrance; there were two men seated across from each other smoking cigars and three other men seated on the other end playing some sort of card game. The room was heavy in cigar smoke and drenched in the smells of freshly burning wood. I was numb in my walk; my lips were tightly sealed and my teeth were underneath still chattering about. I finally gazed upon a sight I had long been desiring; it was both Dietrich and Florence. Both men were staring directly at me; their lips were moving however I could barely hear them. The cold had frostbitten my eardrums and all hearing was down to a train tunnel in clarity. I got right in their faces; I could see Florence speaking and I could hear him, though, there still remained a constant ringing in my ears. "Old buddy!? Old boy! Sweet Mercy! What brought you back?" I faintly made out.

"Well, not sure?" I asked; I was panting with no signs of stopping. "All I know is, my face is numb, my pecker is as well, and my eardrum is screeching to beat the band," I commented.

"Dear God man! Your ears are purple!" I heard Dietrich say.

"I kind of figured that," I responded. I then in anger plopped down my spectacles along the bar. I sat down and put my head into my arms. I was not only exhausted, but I was certain I might die from the cold, right then and there. I breathed into my arms; seeing nothing now but darkness and smelling my armpits which quite honestly killed me. I smelt like horse piss, mixed in whiskey, and then brewed in a brothel of pig shit. I needed a hot spring right now, but not as much as I needed a strong warm drink.

Though I was wanting a whiskey from Hank; at this point I could barely raise my head up to ask for it. Again I was numb, but on a brighter note, within about a minute of laying there, I then faintly heard my hearing, starting to return. The ringing began to slowly dim and all of the other chaos was starting to fade. I lifted my head slowly; then within my peripheral vision I saw a happy sight for these sore eyes. By the Lord on High, it was Hank himself! He frightened the dickens out of me. "Well, do my sore eyes see right? Is that you old Eddie!" Hank asked, joking as he did. Eddie was a nickname he had given me years ago.

"Your sore eyes see right, partner, it's me!" I replied; secretly I was relieved to see some sort of happiness for once. Though I was still frozen and somewhat numb I just continued on, keeping on. "In that regard however, my eyes are still adjusting, I'm afraid," I then added in sorrow.

"Well by the creeks running on Judgment Day! Let me fix you up, something mighty fine!" Hank exclaimed; with a pleasant attitude and insistence in his tone.

Hank then quickly shuffled towards his tall drink rack; he had a slight bit of dance it seemed within his movement. Hank was a very outgoing and happy spirited man. I never once recalled him being pissed, nor did I ever recall him feeling down in the blues. It was hard to change Hank; he was one of a kind and very down to the ground when it came to being human. For once I was starting to feel welcomed; though something began to feel out of place all within the blink of an eye. Softly my eyes observed my surroundings; the people in the study and lounging area and even some at the end of the bar. There were two older men; dressed head to toe in furs at the end, acting strangely.

Yes, I was starting to feel better and a bit back into reality, but I still felt uneven within regards to my well-being in Hank's. Something felt off; it was again that rotation and gravitational pull of the world that started to feel off balance. I was starting to tremble; then I started to feel the rhythm of my heartbeat increase. Maybe it could've been the sudden change in temperature as my body began to warm up? Though a part of me was in dread, I began to think differently. I leaned towards my side and whispered into Dietrich's ear, "Can I see you in the corner over there?" I asked; pointing my finger subtly towards the corner of the room next to the fireplace.

Dietrich, confused, nodded, "Sure."

I then cleared my throat and spoke to Hank with much fear in my voice, "Um...Hank, I hope you don't mind but me and Dietrich have to set aside for a few seconds, in the corner," I said.

"Why certainly, but I might have to charge you for it!" Hank with dry humor replied.

"Very funny old boy," I tipped my hat towards him, smiling. "Just not too much, I've only got a few pebbles on me," I jokingly added.

"We'll be here all season waiting, Eddie!" Hank laughed.

I then carefully grabbed Dietrich by the shoulders and led him over into the corner. As soon as we reached it; I then whipped out a crucifix from my pocket and placed it upon Dietrich's hand without him expecting it. I did it as precaution; hoping that Julius and his gang hadn't reached the lodge before me and had infected Dietrich and Florence. Thankfully, nothing happened; I suspected that nothing would've happened to Florence either. "What in God's name did you get that out for?" Dietrich asked. "Also, why did you leave us?" He then inquired in frustration.

"Well...You see," I was struggling to respond; trying to find a good reason for my departure.

"Furthermore, we faintly heard gunfire outside a few minutes ago, was that you? Is everything alright?" He asked; shock was covering his face entirely.

"It's a long ass story, and I'd like to tell you later, but I've got a question for you doc," I stated.

"What is that?" Dietrich asked.

"When did you all arrive here?" I inquired; I began to show a bit of dread and panic in my dialogue.

"No more than thirty minutes ago, why?" Dietrich asked.

"So, right around sundown?" I asked.

"Yes," Dietrich replied; this time I started to notice his eyes starting to dodge in every direction. "Something is out of place? Isn't it?" Dietrich then curiously inquired.

"Yes, I believe so... Their cold, cold eyes when I walked in through that door, we're colder than the winds upon my back," I said; I was still keeping my talk to a whisper. I then sniffed upon Dietrich's collar and breath; I noticed a strong stench of whiskey and what was smelling of sarsaparilla. "How much has he given you to drink now?" I wondered.

"I have had two shots, and just started on some sarsaparilla, why?" Dietrich asked; I then noticed a bit of slight slur in his speech. "Hey over there," Dietrich then alarmingly caught my attention; he was nodding forward behind me towards the study.

"What is it?" I asked.

"More like who is it? I just noticed him...It's Peter our last of the town's folk," Dietrich frighteningly stated.

I turned and gazed across the lounge at a tall and skinny man; wearing a pair of glasses and drenched in wool coats. "Oh, Lord," I hopelessly muttered.

Though Dietrich was nowhere near drunk yet, I started to pick up on it and my mind was now in a panic. Now we had a major problem, but quite honestly, I didn't know how big it was. I looked over Dietrich's shoulder; where I then observed Florence throwing back a huge shot of whiskey. However, what intrigued me was the sight of five more empty glasses layed disorganized now around Florence's arm. I then motioned for Dietrich to follow me back over towards the bar. As I approached; I began to then again feel an uneven presence in the room. I could feel everything starting to slightly spin. However, I pressed forward, trying to keep upright and headstrong as I approached Hank who was now pouring my glass of not just one shot, but three shots? It was odd for Hank to do this. He normally loved talking up a storm and he never had intentions in the past of getting his customers or guests for that matter, heavily intoxicated.

It was very odd indeed, but I sat there and stared Hank down a bit. Closely observing his features, though nothing seemed out of place with him. He appeared as a husky man, wearing his fine black vest and button up cotton shirt. As he slid all three shots forward, I then strangely observed the most daring view. He winked at me? It was odd, and very out of character. "Remember Eddie, those first two are on me as usual, and after that you're on your own, friend," He commented; a chilling grin covered his face.

"Oh, I remember Hank, but I usually like to stop after two," I said.

"I know, I know, but why not one extra, hell, why not one more after that one?" He inquired. "You all have had a long journey out here, and I think it's necessary for sure," He added.

"It has been a long trip," I commented; I then grabbed my shot glass and tipped back my shot. As usual it burnt hard, and the taste was strong. I didn't cough though, due to years of experience with Florence. As I swallowed, I then slowly cleared my throat, and continued, "On that though," I started; I then cleared my throat once more. "On that, it does taste good, and son of a bitch it brings back so much," I said.

"Yes sir, really wish my dear Louise was here," Hank then somberly added; he tilted his head forward in sorrow and poured another shot.

"Oh mercy, she was taken from you?" I asked.

"Yes, last autumn, the typhoid got her," Hank replied; I noticed a couple of tears starting to well in his eyes. Hank quickly reached up and wiped them away, continuing he poured another shot for Florence and Dietrich. "But, I guess gentlemen, we must accept these changes and move along with each and every season, no matter how much of a pain in the rear it may be," Hank commented.

"You could say that again," I responded; I adjusted my positioning in my seat. I remained still and steady. I was calm; though I could still feel something was out of place with Hank. I could feel it too within all of the guests in the lounge area as well. "Um, Hank, got a question?" I asked.

"Why yes, Eddie, shoot the inquiry at me! Let me pour you another shot while I'm at it too!" Hank replied; Florence then motioned his hand up.

"I'll have another one...One!" Florence yelled out, he then hiccuped. I could tell he was starting to slur in his speech and struggle over his words.

"Yes siree! I love seeing my boys well taken care of!" Hank exclaimed. He was starting to pour another drink; that was when I gently reached forward and tapped Hank on the arm.

"Hank, I think he's had enough, and that goes for all of us too by the way," I said.

"What in the dickens of rosa, and her petals is that supposed to mean son?!" Hank with shock asked in a hasty tone.

"Well, you normally don't get us wasted like this, we usually do that ourselves," I replied. I then winked at Hank; I then saw the dead look in his eyes. I saw the look of suspicions. I think he was catching on to my question, even before I had the chance to ask him. It almost felt as if he were in my mind, I swear! For once, I didn't see Hank within those few seconds; I saw somebody dead. Or in this case, undead. Yes, I suspected Hank wasn't what he was saying he was. Nor did I believe Hank was the same person as he used to be. Just within those three minutes, I could tell Hank was no longer that jolly and full of spirit man I had remembered. Shit, Hank was honestly like a father to me at times, but tonight he felt like somebody trying to get us wasted. Wasted for what? Well from what I had gathered in my mind, he was trying to get us so wasted and drunk, that it'd give him the chance to quite possibly suck us dry to the bone. Yes, I believed Hank, and everyone else there that night, besides Florence and Dietrich, were all vampires!

The horror of that thought engulfed me, and for nearly five seconds I couldn't help but gaze in disgust at Hank's completion. Something was seriously wrong. I then steadied myself back and took in a couple of deep breaths. Everything in that room then got awkwardly silent. I could even faintly hear the whispers of other patrons in the lounge area. They were plotting, and planning on closing in on us for the kill. Rather they'd eat us or suck us dry, and make us one of them, I wasn't sure? I leaned in though, and calmly took Hank's arm. "Listen, I'm not meaning no disrespect, in you providing us some of your finest drinks, but we are busier than piss right now, and we need your help, pal," I said.

"Sure, sure, anything for you Eddie! Just found myself a little taken off guard, that's all!" Hank exclaimed; a smile then plastered his face. He then poured me another drink, "But before you ask, I was just having a chat with Florence, and um…What was your funny name again?" Hank then asked Dietrich embarrassingly.

"Dietrich Von Branson," Dietrich responded; he then began to rear back another drink. To which I gently caught Dietrich from continuing; trying to keep at least a few of us sober.

"Yeah, that, anyways, old Dietericah, was just spewing out a great well of stories from y'all's journey out here, boy those were quite the tales! Boy I loved hearing those stories! Especially about you and your bare ass in the cold, being chased by a boar! Lordy! Lordy!" Hank laughed; however I felt myself cringing upon his delivery. He was talking yes, similar to how Hank would, but he felt a million miles away too.

"Hank, I have something really important here to ask you though," I said.

"Well, come on shoot me gold, old boy! What is it?" Hank asked.

I then leaned forward and whispered in Hank's ear, "Julius? Fredrick? Thomas? Old Julie? Fred? Tommy? Either way you put it, those names mean anything to you?" I asked.

Within no time at all; Hank's face went cold, "You sure you don't want a couple more drinks tonight?" Hank asked. I started to notice Hank's nose beginning to raise.

"I honestly don't think I'm feeling it tonight, Hank," I said; I then stared at him forward. Though I was angered somewhat, I began to feel my poor old pitiful heart shatter for Hank's sake. Not just for him, but for all of the other unaware guests in his lodge. I knew things were about to get ugly, but who knew when it would? I was just sitting there, planning and piecing together, in my head, the next move to make.

That's when Hank spoke up, "Before I truly answer your question in that regard Eddie, let me just say a few recounts on those three men that you speak of," Hank explained.

Nervously I replied, "Go ahead then, did you see them come by?" I asked.

"Oh my friend, I saw them," He replied; my heart skipped a few beats. "The funny thing was, I wasn't afraid of them though," Hank said.

"What the hell is that supposed to mean?" Dietrich asked.

"Well, you see I was at first, but then they showed me a new light, if you would," Hank explained. I began to reach under the bar for my colt; I was ready for anything. I was frantic though; reaching as well for my bowie knife. "Did your momma or daddy ever tell you the old fable of the spider and the fly?" Hank then creepily asked in a smile.

"Maybe at one point in my life? Why?" I inquired.

"Well, I know that poem deals with the notion of flattering words, that can, however, get your rear end in trouble, but it also has a deeper perception hiden too and that's beautiful, but deadly…In this case towards those naive enough to believe anything they've heard or seen…Anyways, you see, when they came, it got me thinking, old Eddie, about this past summer… I had this here spider above the doorway there," Hank pointed towards the door in which I had entered. "Right up there… In that upper left hand corner, it had built the most beautiful web!… My oh my, it'd make any hardened man cry, just from the sheer beauty of it," Hank then lit himself a cigar and continued. "You know Eddie, I myself was reminded last summer of that old fable, the spider and the fly, but also of a new perception I came up with myself…And it got me thinking about how I myself have my very own web, right in here!" Hank affirmatively stated; he then blew cigar smoke right into my face. "Now I have it, the beauty of this place, that can lure any unwary traveler like yourself here!... Isn't it funny how something so beautiful can be so gosh darn deadly," Hank then explained calmly. "I invited you in, and you paraded in desperation, just like I had remembered those flies did in the summer to that spider's web...Naive...But my oh my, they showed me a different light... A release into a world of immortality and a place where power is always at your fingertips! Almost like that there spider in my doorway! My oh my, it was truly a beautiful vision, but I'm not sure if you all would like to join us in that web as the spider? Or, become the unwary fly? So, with that rambling done, which one will it be? The spider? Or the naive fly?" Hank then inquired. A cold gaze stared me down; from his eyes I saw nothing but possessed evil.

For lack of a better term, I was shaking in this here predicament! I was shaking in my boots and very numb. Without much hesitation, I then leaned inward and told Hank what Florence, Dietrich, and I were that evening. I wasn't afraid either; though nervous sweat did start to ooze out I was ready to give my answer. In a way though, I was ready to fight him. "For shits old pal, I think we'll take the duties of the fly, because we're just that foolish," I said; I then winked at Hank. To my left was an unattended barstool; I grabbed it cautiously without Hank looking under the bar. "However, unlike that fly that didn't get out of the web, our outcome's a whole lot different, so sorry, old friend," I then chillingly added. Quickly, I then raised the barstool fast, and smashed it into a thousand pieces, leaving only a small wooden, stake shaped piece left in my right hand. To which I used the broken stake piece; ramming it right into Hank's chest. Hank of course reacted instantly in pain. Quickly I saw him change into what looked to be a half man, half wolf creature, much like Luke did back in the forest. Hank instantly grew sharp fangs in horror! My Lord, I was trembling!

He *snarled* and let out some of the most God Awful roars. He was howling and *yelping* in pain; he sounded exactly like a dog in agony. My head was throbbing to beat the band; that's when everything was happening in a blink of an eye. The room was quickly turning, and soon so were all three of us! In the dash of a millisecond; we heard everybody behind us growl and moan. They shapeshifted into other vampires from behind; we quickly darted forward and flung ourselves over the bar. Florence had trouble getting over, so I quickly assisted him. By the grace of God, we missed the gunfire! Dietrich was of course in silence, and Florence was shocked but also in a half-drunken daze.

In front of me, to my horror, was now dying in agony, Hank. He still had the wooden piece rammed in his chest and he was squirming about. He suddenly lashed forward at Dietrich and I; we got down quickly and I pushed Florence further away from the counter in the making. Hank's hands grew long and spindly; he had razor sharp claws like a hawk and his face transformed even further into a wolf-like creature. I no longer could recognize him to my horror. Then from nowhere, we were ambushed again; this gunfire hit the top part of the bar. Glass shattered into a million pieces; there were a million different sounds and bursts ringing all at once. *BANG! BANG! BANG!* Gunfire still hit the bar; though we were crouched down and in cover we were being closed in it seemed. "Son of a bitch!" I exclaimed.

"How many were over in the lounge area?!" Dietrich chaotically asked; he was pouring holy water on his bullets and drying them a bit too.

"Gee! I don't know?! Let me count! Oh wait! There's a shit ton of bullets being unloaded up there! It's a little hard right now, doc!" I sniped back. I then readied my colt; Florence was reaching into his pocket grabbing his gun as well. Though I wasn't scared of Florence handling a gun. Surprisingly, Florence does pretty well with a gun, regardless of his drunkenness.

"Ter! Old boy! Look out!" Florence then exclaimed.

I turned to my right; a vampire was crawling on the walls in the corner of the room directly above the bar. *BANG! BANG!* I fired two shots directly at the hellish looking creature. It *shrieked* a blood-curdling scream and flung its body all over the walls in a frenzy. The vampire then began flaming; fire shot out from its eyes and chest. It then fell forward like a dead fly; dropping to the bar area in the same disgusting manner. My jaw dropped a bit, but I had no time to react. There was blood all over the fucking place! Hank still squirmed and *shrieked* to beat the band.

"Take care of him!" Dietrich exclaimed; he was loading his gun with holy water drenched bullets.

"With what?!" I asked.

Then in a quick silence; Dietrich reached towards the top of the bar from behind him. He still remained low, below the infinite hail of gunfire. He then grabbed a tall glass, broke it, and then used a sharp long piece of it slicing the middle part of Hank's throat clean wide open! Blood squirted everywhere! I was stunned of course, but also nervous as usual! Who was I kidding, I was more frightened than anything at this point! "Nevermind! I've got it!" Dierich then boldly proclaimed.

"Well, that works," I then said nervously.

The chaos all around Hank's lodge continued. The loud screaming of the now infected inhabitants of Hank's and their never ending gunfire. We stayed low, never gaining any energy or reasoning to rise up and face the countless number of vampires in that place! My Lord, it was a predicament, in which I had no clue as to what the outcome would be? There were only two ways out though, and that was either dead, or alive. At the moment, everything seemed like the worst of the worst, but all of us, including myself, were all holding onto a little ounce of optimism. However, judging by the ever growing chaotic nature, none of that seemed likely at that moment.

Chapter 20

The carnage in Hank's, was one I would never wish on my own worst enemy to experience. At this point, all three of us were lucky to be alive. Quickly, we loaded our bullets and soaked them in holy water. I peered over towards Dietrich; who in panic essentially threw holy water in my direction. My eyes winced, "Dagnabbit!" I exclaimed. "On the bullets! Not me!" I shouted.

"Sorry," Dietrich embarrassingly responded.

"No worries doc! When I give the nod, we stand and run like hell over towards the!" Suddenly two shots rang out from above; glasses shattered into a billion fragments. *BANG*! *BANG*! *BANG*! We of course were startled, but still at the ready. We dried off the holy water a bit on the bullets and remained still as cold waters in our place. Crouched down, we gave one last look over at poor old Hank; he had now caught fire from the impact of our initial attack. Add to that the alcohol all over the place; his entire place was starting to go up in flames! Dear Lord, it was a Godforsaken mess, that whole doggone place.

Regardless, we still stayed down, at the ready, but somewhat still nervous to rise and face the crazy evil of that place. "Where were you taking that sentence, good old buddy?!" Florence shouted in the noise. He then reached up for a drink; to which I quickly stopped him. His drunkenness had got the best of Florence.

"We're gonna make our way through the lounge area! Take out those crazy blood-sucking bastards!" I exclaimed. Then, another rain of gunfire rang out from above; the vampires were making sure we wouldn't have the wiggle room to rise up at this point and dodge a few of their bullets. I was sweating and breathing heavily of course. "We're going to take the dogs out! All of them! The best thing to do is to split apart and confuse the hell out of them!" I shouted.

"All of us! Rise up at once?!" Dietrich inquired.

"Yes, and no! I'll quickly stand up when my balls have fully grown! At that point, you and Florence head to the left and right side of the bar! Florence to your right and Doc to your left! Got it!" I exclaimed.

"Pretty simple! Well you at least make it sound that way!" Dietrich commented.

"Good as gold! Now, when I give the nod! Run like hell!" I exclaimed. However, not thinking, I nodded, which somehow confused Florence, and in doing so he took off quickly to my right shoulder. "Not yet! Son of a bitch! Flor!" I shouted.

"I'm alright old bud!" He acknowledged. Then suddenly! *BANG! BANG!* Out of nowhere; a series of gunshots barely grazed the top of his hat. He got down below a small end of the counter barely missing the hail of bullets. He of course was quite jumpy and dumbfounded. "If you can't tell!" Florence started slurring under his delivery and stuttering. "The pints ain't doing me a bit of good right now!" He exclaimed.

"No shit! Stay down!" I screamed. "Alright! Go!" I then nodded in Dietrich's vicinity; to which he jolted up and ran like hell firing rapidly without any ounce of quitting. I too jolted up, only my aim was head first forward into the lounge area. I unleashed a few shots into the lounge hitting one of the vampires directly in the chest. The one I hit was directing his gun toward Dietrich. The vampire I had shot, within his completion, I saw it to be Peter! However, I stopped him dead in his tracks! I may have hit one, but the other vampire to my left *snarled* demonically and unleashed back. I got down quickly behind the bar area again. An endless parade of gunfire rang out again; shattering more glasses. Shit was flying everywhere! Blood and whatever the hell else that was in our path, exploded!

On the floor I trembled a bit; I then looked over towards Dietrich who was now hiding beneath a table awaiting his next move. Florence was still scared, but he had his defenses at the ready. Then suddenly from above, crashing through in a thunderous *roar* came another torn and damned soul through the window. It landed right upon Dietrich who reacted quickly; he flung a clove of garlic at the ugly fiend. It was a bat-like creature walking on its tiptoes and it had the claws of a hawk. "Dear Lord!" I yelled out.

"Son of a!" Dietrich exclaimed; he was struggling with the creature and using all of his strength to hold it back. The creature *shrieked* and *groaned* God awfully. It held Dietrich down in a choke hold, carefully moving itself forward towards Dietrich's face.

"What the shit?!" Florence exclaimed.

"Flor! Stay where you are!" I yelled.

"What the hell made you think I'd even dare to move?!" Florence sarcastically sniped.

"Just stay back!" I exclaimed. Suddenly a large flame ignited right in front of my view. I quickly sprang toward my left; I was nearly inches from being caught in it. There was alcohol spilt all over the place and this only made the inferno far worse. I was now merely inches away from the creature and Dietrich's struggle. I quickly reached in my coat pocket for my bowie; however to my unfortunate surprise it was not present. Looking back towards where I had sprang from I found it nestled within a small pile of smoldering ash. "Shit!" I exclaimed, knowing I had to reach into the hot ash and retrieve my knife. However, it was for the sake of saving Dietrich's life, so without much hesitation I leaned forward and grabbed it. At first, it burnt my hand and made a small *sizzling* sound. Instantly I could feel my flesh start to roast, to which I then backed off. "Mother of holy!" I shouted in pain. I winced a bit, then I leaned forward and grabbed the knife again.

Though this time, I didn't give a rat's ass how hot it'd be.

I retrieved it, and though it burnt like hell I shook it off. I then turned and sprang forward towards the hideous creature; stabbing it directly into the neck area. It backed away from Dietrich, who was now on the floor choking still and trembling in fear. "You saved me again!" Dietrich exclaimed; he coughed a bit and then caught his wind. "Here!" Dietrich then yelled. He threw the garlic clove; to which I then stuffed it into the hellish vampire's throat. He died immediately, Dietrich and I then stood to attention. "Very good! How's your hand?!" Suddenly a gunshot was fired; barely missing the top of Dietrich's head. We got down again; this time we were shuffling along, waist length in height off the floor.

"Ain't none of that important!" I responded. "I think getting our asses out of here with no more than a burnt hand is more crucial! Don't you think?!" I exclaimed sarcastically. I then checked my chamber; I had six bullets. To which I reloaded quickly, the chamber again at full capacity. I then cocked it back and nodded toward Dietrich. "Alright! Go!" I screamed. Dietrich and I both rose up and I shot off shots like maniacs. I hit the lamp in the lounge which exploded and the top portion of the couch. The vampire left standing from my ambush quickly got down. Flames began engulfing the place faster, and the wooden beams from above began falling. Both sets of our feet shuffled like jack rabbits and our hands shook like a dead leaf on a tree. Suddenly, some wooden beams from above came crashing down, but to our luck it had crushed a majority of the other vampires that were present in that room, in the act of doing so.

We reached the other side of the bar area where Florence was still cowering. Our ears were ringing out and the lodge was still crumbling. With no time at all we then decided to all three sprang up and move forward. I jolted quickly with Dietrich and Florence staying closely behind me. We noticed another individual in the lounge area; a woman it appeared to be who shapeshifted into a pale skinned and gray haired beast. In fear we all three reacted; I then pointed my finger towards the stairs. Within the flames we then noticed what appeared to be two more vampires descending the stairs. "There's some upstairs old buddy!" Florence exclaimed.

Now we were being surrounded, and our options for escape were becoming more and more questionable. Not only that, I wasn't certain that all three of us would even make it pass the first flight of steps. Much less, I didn't believe we'd stand a chance in the downstairs lounge. Without much hesitation Dietrich and I sprang forward towards the female and male vampires in the lower study. I stabbed the female in the arm, unfortunately missing her chest which would've only weakened her and possibly would've killed her. I didn't even have time to pull the knife from her wound in her arm. To which she then unleashed in wrath and pushed me back about ten feet from behind. I came crashing down on my back; slamming my body right through a small wooden table. Instantly the breath was kicked right out of me. From the corner of my eye I caught sight of Dietrich who had now taken on the male vampire. He had flung holy water in his face, it instantly began to *sizzle*, weakening that vampire. "Hey doc!" My stiff voice then asked. I slowly pulled myself up in grueling pain. "You mind for a second?!" I chaotically asked.

"Oh, yes!" Dietrich exclaimed. He then quickly threw holy water at the back of the female. She *snarled* like a wild animal and then charged Dietrich. "Shit!" Dietirch reacted. However, Dietrich thought fast; quickly leaning in he pulled my bowie knife out of her arm and then jabbed it aggressively into her chest. He then took the bowie knife and slowly sliced open her chest from the same point of impact. A shit ton of blood spewed all over the place. "My God!" Dietrich exclaimed, reacting to the sight of the dead female vampire.

"I was about to say the same!" I shouted in the noise of the fire. Dietrich ran over to pull me up to my feet; I was still sore and somewhat deadwinded. As soon as I found myself back on all twos, I was then greeted fastly by the male vampire from behind Dietrich. Thinking fast as lightning was splitting the sky, I yanked the bowie knife from Dietrich. "Duck!" I shouted.

Dietrich then got down, and within the blink of no more than a half a second I found myself penetrating the chest of another vampire. It was indeed a close one, but we took out another, doggone it! My heart was racing so fast; I felt as if any second could be my last. The sweat was constantly spilling down my back. I quickly turned; shielding Dietrich behind me we found ourselves staring at Florence battling another demon. He was at the bottom step; a piece of wood then fell right in front of us obstructing and blocking our way. "That's gonna make things complicated," Dietrich whispered in my ear.

"Indeed! Come on! Around here!" I commanded.

I slowly led Dierich to the side of the sofa in the study; flames were licking every inch of that lodge. I could start to feel my lungs start to close; that's when I got down on my knees and released a nasty coughing fit. For about ten seconds; it felt like a million hands were gripping tightly in my windpipe. My eyes grew foggy and my voice grew weaker. I was certainly at the lowest of all lows in this portion of our fight, but this small escapade didn't stop me. Determined I then shrugged and rose confidently. Staring forward we still found ourselves glancing at the brawl between Florence and another vampire. We walked carefully over the burning bodies of the vampires we had once slayed and readied ourselves for an ambush upon the devilish fiend. "You catch your wind back there?!" Dietrich inquired; he then began coughing heavily.

"I think?" I responded; turning I quickly gave Dietrich an old handkerchief from my left breast pocket. "Here partner! Give your lungs a break!" I exclaimed.

"Look! Hurry!" Dietrich shouted, covering his mouth and pointing his finger towards Florence who was now in a choke hold with the vampire. Then suddenly, I felt nothing but this fast and jolting wind from my back. I was hit hard in the back of my left leg as I was extending forward toward Florence. I felt flames shoot down my back; it was an agonizing burn as I realized a large piece of lumber had fallen. "Ow!" Dietrich exclaimed from behind. Then suddenly he was silenced.

"Ah, shit nips!" I shouted. Turning I found myself staring in somewhat disbelief. Dietrich was now caught beneath the hold of a large two by four inch piece of wooden trestle from the ceiling. It appeared the doctor had been hit hard in the back part of his neck! Horrified, I sprung forward; a few flames danced around our vicinity. Reaching forward I tapped Dietrich's shoulder in the chaos, "Hey, doc! Get up, partner!" I yelled. Dietrich did not respond, he had been knocked out cold turkey! Not wanting to leave him, obviously, I reached forward and pulled him out from under his armpits. Sitting him up hopelessly, I again tried to bring him back to a conscious state, "Hey, doc! Dang rabbit! No!" I shouted.

"Hey! Ter!" Florence exclaimed; he was still struggling with his fiend.

"I'm a little held up at the moment, old buddy!" I shouted back at Florence. I then with all my might, picked Dietrich up and heaved him over my shoulders. He hopelessly laid on my top like a dead boar I had just shot. Frantically, I then darted towards the fighting pair; to which again I attacked and slayed another creature within the blink of a second. I pierced the chest of the vampire in ease; miraculously keeping my balance with one hand holding my bowie knife and the other propping up an unconscious Dietrich. "There!" I then sarcastically boasted.

"That ain't all of them though! Upstairs!" Florence exclaimed, pointing up the flight of steps before us. Then we heard a *creak* beneath the stairs; it sounded like the framework beneath was starting to weaken. "Move! Old boy! Move!" Florence shouted.

As we glanced upward through the heavy smoke, we then noticed an ominous bunch. The group of men you could say were the 'Fang Gang.' Fredrick my bounty, Thomas, and the mysteriously presented Julius Verna. We froze in the heat, ironically we found ourselves not wanting to proceed onward. We were in shock, I guess you could say. Though we were also angered, and somewhat at odds with our emotions. "That's them I suppose?!" I nervously asked within the fire; coughing heavily and heaving to beat the band.

"It would appear so," Florence softly spoke in my ear. "Old slick back hair, that's Julius!" Florence quickly snickered.

Not hesitating, we both drew our guns and fired away. Unfortunately our shots missed every inch of them; it was honestly too hard to see at that vantage point. We then started up; to which then suddenly all three men reappeared back at the top of the stairs. We got back, stumbling our way around the posts at the bottom. Ducking down from every free range shooting bullet and praying to God that all of this madness would soon end. The whole lodge was burning, but we still had a bit of hope going up with it. The three men we were pursuing and our main objective were merely inches away. It felt like a final duel really, but we weren't for sure if it'd be the final destination for us all, yet?

Chapter 21

We were now cowering at the bottom of Hank's stairs. I must admit, I was still heartbroken by the way Hank had to die, but our mission was plain and simple now. It was us, taking on a legion of vampires; with more power than any other living being had ever had. It was frightening of course, but we had no time to be big babies, we had a burning lodge before us, and we had to think logically about our next motives. More importantly we had to think fast. Dietrich was still out cold, and unfortunately I didn't know the extent of his damage? Though even worse, I noticed a troubling sight within his completion. His face was starting to turn pale white. I then noticed blood on my collar, though it wasn't my blood, it was his blood.

Thinking fast, I buttoned down the inside of his shirt. I then noticed a gunshot wound around his collar bone. It was oozing with blood; I then quickly took my handkerchief and pressed it down trying to stop further bleeding of the wound.

Dietrich remained silent with his eyes sealed shut. I was hoping that this wouldn't be the end for him. "Is he alright?!" Florence frantically inquired.

"God I hope so!" I yelled. "Come on doc! No!" I shouted. Suddenly another gunshot rang out from over top of us. Turning around I saw another vampire behind the bar aiming a rifle right at us. "Move! Behind there!" I shouted. Moving quickly and dragging Dietrich's body along the way trying to protect it from further damage. We found ourselves on the other side, at the bottom of the staircase now. There we readied our guns and shot bullets right back at the bar area. *BANG! BANG!* Our shots ran out frequently! "I am!" I started; I then found myself ducking quickly as a bullet barely missed me at the top of my head. "I am…Really SICK and TIRED of this shit!" I shouted in wrath.

"Nah, really!" Florence sarcastically barked back.

With no hesitation from our furious claims; I then pointed the rifle directly at the chest of the vampire behind the bar. I hit that son of bitch directly on the mark; instantly flames shot up from the wound of impact as the vampire spasmed and fell backward into the vast array of glass bottles from behind. Needless to say, he or she was dead. The fire then grew angerer; we were now scrambling. Staying at the ready, we then bravely took our attention towards the top of the staircase. Though this time, the trio of men were nowhere to be found. "Julius! You ain't got nowhere to run now, old boy!" Florence shouted; he was trying to provoke the men I could tell.

"Careful what you say, old boy!" I shouted. I then picked up Dietrich's unconscious body and gently heaved him over my shoulders. I still miraculously held my bowie knife in hand. Florence grabbed my rifle and I motioned towards him, "Stay ahead of me! I'll try to keep up!" I shouted. I then coughed; the smoke was getting thicker. Though the upstairs didn't look as bad as the downstairs.

Once we reached the second floor; we found ourselves staring in fear at nothing more than a dimly lit hallway, three closed doors, and one opened door to our left at the very end. However, we knew the men were close by, and furthermore we could sense the presence of more vampires, of course being them. We were on high alert; our minds were constantly brewing our next motives. As we wandered the hallway; I could feel my lungs tighten and my nerves start to tingle. I was in dread, though my eyes had to remain affixed to every single movement regardless. Dietrich was still draped over my back unconscious; my legs were starting to tremble from the weight of carrying him. Though he was a small man, the constant time strain was certainly taking its toll on my back. Florence remained close to me and I prayed every inch of the Lord's prayer as we walked step by step through that mysterious corridor. There were a couple of lamps lit at the end of the hallway, and a beautiful chandelier dangled from the ceiling.

We walked past two rooms and found ourselves in somewhat of a slight daze I could tell. Florence looked just as jumpy as me, and I was no better. We still remained ready on our feet; that was when suddenly I felt a breath at the very nape of my neck. I quickly turned, expecting to see someone there. There was nobody. Florence stopped as I did, but he didn't speak a word. We pressed forward a few more steps; this time I heard what sounded like a million different voices and distortion. At the ready, I jumped and turned. I subtly dropped Dietrich down holding him in the strength of both Florence's right arm and my left arm. I fired my gun. *BANG*! Nobody came out of the dark room at the end in which I aimed at. The suite at the end of the hall was eerily quiet. I felt a slight bit of drafty air come from it, but no one exited the room, nobody. I gulped in fear; that was when a hideous *shriek* came from my left! I turned and saw the ugliest fiend I had ever gazed at in our expedition. It must've been over eight feet high; it had a million razor sharp teeth and had piercing red eyes. It cleanly knocked all three of us into the walls.

I flew back so fast, it felt like every ounce of oxygen had been released from me. Dietrich fell to the floor; though miraculously it actually woke him up. I slowly pulled myself up, all in an effort to help Dietrich, but more importantly Florence who was now in another struggle. I slowly stood to my feet; my will at this moment was quite strong. I then shot at the creature; hitting him directly in the right arm as blood shot everywhere. Carefully aiming again, without intending to hit Florence, I shot once more; this time directly in the chest. Blood squirted out everywhere; then flames began to build around the point of impact. "Guess there's still a bit of blessing in that one," I mumbled to myself in the chaos.

"Dear Lord!" Florence shouted in wrath.

The creature *shrieked* and *groaned* constantly; I then readied my aim again. This time I was still, though my eyes were closed in, and locked fully on the beast. I then realized in the faint completion, it was my bounty, Mister Boothe himself. Though I wasn't killing him for financial reward, no. I was just simply killing him for the sake of saving us and possibly the rest of humanity. I shot at his head as determination was written all over my face. *BANG*! *BANG*! My shots fired, penetrating the very depths of my hearing. I could feel the fury within every shot and I could feel the anger flow. Though it was bitter cold outside; Hank's lodge felt like the very bottom of hell now.

In one blink of no more than a second; the creature, or in this case Fredrick; slumped backward through a door. He crashed his way through and broke every ounce of wood in it. Debris was flying everywhere and blood splatter was everywhere. The weight of that upstairs fight was starting to grow unbearable. I motioned my head forward; Florence followed me into the room where Fredrick was weakly retreating to. I pulled Dietrich from behind; still hoping in my mind he'd still be alive by the time this all had ended. My furious anger was only intensifying, and my eyes were growing stronger in enraged emotion. I fired at Fredrick again, *BANG*! I was getting closer towards his shapeshifted body now, I again fired, *BANG*! Blood was shooting all over that suite; a few oil lamps inside were starting to violently flickering within a rustling wind.

This violent breeze was caused in part by the powers of this being, I had no doubt. With no hesitation; I was getting even closer towards Fredrick. *BANG*! I fired once more and then without any chance of changing my intention, I then retrieved my bowie knife and stabbed Fredrick directly in his abdomen. Then vigorously; I took the knife and ran it swiftly up his front cutting him wide open. Blood then shot out of his stomach and esophagus like a warm spring geyser. Quickly Florence, Dietrich, and I all got down. I covered my face and shielded Dietrich's half awake body. Florence was crouched behind a table; then all of the oil lamps in that room began to shatter into a million pieces.

It was absolute madness, but not as maddening as I knew it'd soon get. "Alright! Move! Come on! Let's get the hell out of here!" I shouted. I then propped up Dietrich and carried him outward back into the hall looking desperately for an escape.

"How the hell are we supposed to do that?!" Florence asked in a snipe.

I then opened a door to a room right directly in front of my ever hazing vision. It was growing much dimmer in that hall as the fire was starting to spread into the upstairs. I coughed a bit, Florence was coughing as well. The room ahead was filled with smoke; though fortunately we did not see one ounce of blaze in it. We pushed forward, all three of us, and then without much waiting I turned and slammed the door shut from behind. I saw a window to the outside ahead of us, and what appeared to be a long draping curtain made from strong materials, it appeared to be both satin and lenin. Regardless, I sprang forward and cut up the curtain into what looked to be a strong fortified rope. I then smashed the window in with my colt and discarded many other parts of the glass remaining in it. I motioned for Florence, "Tie this around the frame! I'm gonna throw it outward over the roof and onto the ground below! I'm taking the doc too!" I instructed.

"Whatever you need to do! Old buddy!" Florence responded; he then gave me the thumbs up as he quickly tied the curtain around the frame of the window.

I then backed myself outward, crawling carefully through the shattered out frame. Dietrich was now flopped over my back and I was carefully waltzing my way backward hanging on tightly to the curtain. The roof was quite slick; I could feel my balance become extremely unsteady as I made my way towards the very edges of the roof. Florence was holding on to the frame; cautiously he was watching the curtain that he had tied into place. As I reached the edge, I could feel every ounce of my back start to tighten slowly. It was the most unbearable pain, but it wasn't the worst I had felt in our journey so far, believe me. I then carefully sprung out on the curtain; using it geniusly as a rope as I dangled helplessly along the front of the lodge. My neck was tightening, I then started to wince in pain, and within seconds I began to hear a slight tear. The curtain was slowly ripping. "Shit!" I muttered. I then quickly slid down, with no time remaining, and fell backward letting go of Dietrich. I fell instantly to the cold hard ground; though fortunately I didn't have very far to fall. I may have fallen no more than six feet, and I was still alive regardless. The wind had been knocked out of me, and every nerve in my body had been shot. However, I was alive, by the grace of God I was alive. I then tugged the curtain; as I did I then saw Florence carefully stumbling his way forward as he swung down and crashed into my arms. I caught him, but I fell backward in a maddening motion.

"Son of!" Florence exclaimed. Suddenly the curtain then hopelessly tore. However, we had all made it! Thank God! We stood carefully to our feet; we were now trying to catch our breaths. "Well!" Florence started. He was breathing hard, heaving in and out, in and out. Then he caught his breath and continued. "Well! We got one of them!" Florence exclaimed.

"Yeah! But it ain't all of them!" I exclaimed back. I then cocked my gun and sheathed back in my knife.

    In front of us now remains a burning lodge. Every bit of mordor, stone, and wood was starting to disintegrate. Hopelessly Hank's lodge was going up, but thankfully, every damned soul within was burning alive. Everyone, every vampire, from what we had gathered, was dead inside, and if there were any alive, they'd suffocate instantly regardless. We watched for a moment as the lodge burnt to a crisp; then both of us turned our attention to Dietrich who was now laying upon the snow still knocked out. "Hey, doc!" Florence shouted.

Miraculously, Dietrich's eyes were starting to open. "Mister Hill...Sheriff," He slowly said. Then he closed his eyes once more. He then went right back to sleep.

"Oh no! Doc!" I exclaimed.

"We need to get him checked out by fire light!" Florence exclaimed.

"Well, we clearly got some here!" I sarcastically stated.

"We need to set up camp! That's what I mean," Florence angrily sniped back.

"I know, I know…We ain't got much time though! You've got the remedies on you, right?!" I hastily asked.

"Yes sir!" Florence responded.

I then nodded and picked Dietrich up. We hauled him carefully away from the burning lodge; soon finding ourselves in a peaceful spot about two hundred yards away from the inferno. The carriage that Dietrich had rode upon had been destroyed; though miracuously not every piece of defense, water, or food supply was destroyed. We sat up a makeshift camp for the night, placing various items around the site like crucifixes, garlic cloves, and other Christian relics. We propped up Dietrich, as we fastly began nursing him back into health. Though we weren't sure if our actions of tending care would be substantial, or if they'd be too late by now? We were frantic, but we all had one ounce of hope left in our souls, and our prayers were only ever growing, no questions asked. We rounded up two horses that we had remaining on the grounds; as the others had either run off or were stolen. I gathered up my saddle bags from my dead horse; it was loaded with a few other remedies and some gunpowder. From there, Florence and I both were blinded by what would be. But we kept watch over the doctor, and we kept our prayers alive and well the whole night forward.

Chapter 22

The night was moving fast, and the cold brisk air was getting colder. To make matters worse; Dietrich's color was starting to fade into the same color as the new fallen skiff of snow upon the ground. Hank's fire was starting to calm thanks to the precipitation, however much of it was still running wild in small parts. Florence and I kept a close watch on it, making sure the fire would not get loose and into the surrounding forest. Thankfully Hank's lodge was in the middle of a small opening, so the likelihood of it spreading was slim.

All three of us were sheltered by a small bundle of trees, and all of us were frozen stone cold. My face was going numb and Florence was huddled under a very large deer skin; he was warming his hands and breathing into them warm air. I got up to check Dietrich; by now he was starting to awaken. Again though, his colors were pale, and his completion was starting to slowly drift away. Every minute that came and went, I was hoping and praying for the doctor's sake, no doubt. "My dear man," Dietrich calmly spoke.

"Yes, doc?" I asked; I was reaching forward to check the status on the gunshot wound around Dietrich's chest.

"AH!" Dietrich winced. "Sorry," He then apologized.

"For what doctor?" I asked. I was becoming dazed in my thoughts, though knowing full good and well that Dietrich was feeling every ounce of guilt.

"I dragged you into all of this nonsense, and look what happened to the three of us," Dietrich commented. His eyes then grew sad; he coughed a bit and then caught his breath. "I guess… I guess I was just," Dietrich then paused; I could tell he was having trouble getting his words together.

"Now wait a minute," I intervened. "I drug my own ass into all of this, and then I drug my ass out of all this," I stated. I then put my hand to my chin and was puzzled. "Then I came back, but it wasn't for the sake of Fredrick, believe me," I said.

Dietrich smirked at my statement, "But you returned Mister Hill, why?" He curiously asked.

"I reckon there was this force, this power?" I pondered deeply. I was really coming to a realization for my return to the expedition. I had already concluded my intentions, but much of it was starting to sink in. "I guess if I hadn't returned, none of your asses would've been safe?" I was still; Dietrich had a somber look upon his face.

"No Mister Hill, something much deeper I believe brought you back to us, and I know it was something of great significance," Dietrich said.

"Hell, I ain't so sure honestly? But there are bigger things at play in this world... Far greater than I could've ever imagined, but I guess now, none of it matters, they're gone now, off somewhere else, and as for our hope —"

"That still remains, my good man," Dietrich then confidently interrupted. "We will not lose this, I have much faith in that bounty hunter, and I have it strongly within the aspects of both you and Florence," Dietrich then added.

"What about you old doc?" Florence then cut in; he was messing with our fire and its kindling.

"As for me gentlemen, I can feel the cold getting colder, and my breaths getting heavier... I'm afraid, my trek here... Is near its end," Dietrich spoke sadly, but he had a slight bit of faith within his own delivery.

"Nah! Nah... You ain't gonna check out doc, not now, we're so close to finishing them off, once and for all!" Florence proclaimed; he was panicking in his breath.

"Do not fear for me, I know my place after this place, and I know Vera will be there," Dietrich said; he was starting to breathe at a very slow pace now and his voice was raspy.

"Doc," I leaned inward, trying to comfort Dietrich and checking the status of his pulse. I checked his wound as well; it was still a mess and much of it was still protruding small spurts of blood.

Dietrich then slowly grabbed my hand and removed it away from the tending of his injury. "Do... not... Fear," He said. Dietrich was starting to tremble; I knew that these were going to be his final words. "Mister Hill... Florence," He said.

"Doc?" Florence asked; I heard him gulp in his inquiry as he got closer into Dietrich's vantage.

"Do not fear him… Though I also beg of you both not to… Underestimate his power… Finish your journey, please," Dietrich said.

"You ain't checking out on us doc," I said; I was becoming hasty in my delivery.

"It's not a check out Mister Hill, it's just a quick stop, this place," Dietrich said; a slight smirk plastered his completion.

"Doc, it's been my pleasure," I said; I titled my head downward in remorse.

Suddenly I then felt this cold wind hit my back like a million different bees stinging me all at once. It hurt, but I had become oblivious to my surroundings, and within no time at all I could feel it in the air. Dietrich then slowly handed me his crucifixion.; gently tucking it into the cradle of my hardened hand. I heard slowly the *wheezing* of Dietrich's breath and then instantly following that I heard no more breaths. Dietrich slowly died; all I could hear was the fire *crack* and the cold winds hit my face. It was cold, and the death of Dietrich certainly reflected our circumstances. It was hell, and much of it I knew would only further prolong our suffering. Strangely, though I didn't know the doctor that well, the death of Dietrich there by that fire side, felt like losing a father. Though too I also felt a sense of peace within the madness of his death. I knew he had found peace, but his final words felt like a bit of persevering drive. A slight push to finally take out our enemy; destroy the very evil that had been prolonging our expedition. A threat that may destroy our world, vampirism. The threat was now Julius and Thomas and our objective was to kill them in the name of all that was Holy. Though also, it was for the sake and push from the final moments of Dietrich's time here.

Chapter 23

That night, in the dying smoke of Hank's fire, it had become the longest and most grueling minutes I had ever felt. Florence and I could not get one blink of sleep it seemed. The fact of losing Dietrich, was one fact, I wasn't able to buy for the first two hours I had rested my head upon the cold hard ground. My eyes opened and closed about a hundred different times, and each time I was about to drift off I'd always find myself jolting back awake. At one point even; I jolted up out of my bearskin and walked about our blessed campsite. The crosses and cloves of garlic were still spread throughout the grounds and the fire was now slowly dying.

As I paced back and forth, I lit one last cigar I had left in my saddle back. I used what little fire was remaining to light it and sat back easy upon a lone rock about four feet from my skin blanket. It was cold, but quite honestly none of it bothered me until about three minutes after I had jolted awake. In feeling that cold night's air; I slowly then leaned forward and grabbed my bearskin and wrapped myself up tightly as I sat there in remorse. Of course I was sad and depressed, and quite honestly I didn't know where our journey and hunt would lead us from here? Though still I had a bit of faith left in my soul and a bit of wisdom in my mind. Mostly it was wisdom in the final words that Dietrich had spoken before he left this world.

The notion of not fearing, to not be afraid, but to also not underestimate. Pretty simple advice, but advice that went way beyond the hunt at hand. It felt like advice towards my own predicament in life right now. Leaning back and slowly falling asleep in that dying fire, I soon realized my own faults and fears within regards to how I handled my own shitty situations. Yes, life had been hard since my dear Anna and my newborn had died. No father, no husband, would ever want this fate, I have no doubt. Though a part of me was facing this fear right now, and in a shorter word it was the fear and dread of facing death itself, quite literally.

The death was of course my own fear, but more importantly it was an embodiment of all the regret I still had, up unto that point. I felt like the death of my newborn baby, should've been me, and the death of my wife too for that matter. I was feeling guilty for being here, but then again if I hadn't been here, God only knows what would've happened if this evil wasn't quite contained like it had been? For that matter, I wouldn't have been here for Dietrich or Florence. Though then again, Dietrich was dead now, and that part was certainly prolonging my anxiety further.

Then again, I kept tracing backward to what Dietrich said in his dying breath, which was again quite simple. We will not give up now, no chance in hell. As I soon dozed off, I then found myself staring into the immense beauty of another dream in time, thinking fondly of that simple advice. I saw Anna again, this time we were back at our home in Austin, and again it was another beautiful summer's day. This time though, I didn't see her in pain. Instead she was smiling and holding our newborn child in her arms. She was beautiful, and the sunshine radiated off of her glowingly. My eyes went somewhat blind, and my mind went somewhat crazy as to figuring out the circumstances of what was occurring.

To be quite honest, I wasn't sure as to what all of this meant at this time? Though I think it was that simple nod of peace. Something wonderful was coming for me, but I knew sadly it wouldn't be a life back with Anna. It may be a life to myself in Austin when I get back? A life and moment of break in peace? Maybe I needed to stop killing and hunting bounties? Maybe I needed a rest for a while? Maybe that's what Anna was telling me with her smile? To be honest, I wasn't sure? That's when I jolted awake again; this time I was staring at a slow rising sun towards the east.

My breath was still very thick and my face was still bitter cold. My feet and thighs were numb to touch and I couldn't stand to exhale. I pulled myself out of my skin and took a good look around at the birth of another day. It certainly felt different without the presence of Dietrich, but God willing Florence and I were going to finish this hunt no questions asked. I gazed upon the smoldering dead matter of Hank's; now resting in a dead cold air that felt tightening upon first glance. It was depressing, all around me, everything seemed very unclear. I was for certain, it could be because of all the mayhem from last evening? But to be honest, it was an unclear journey that shared its unorganized and unorthodox roots all the way back to when I had first intersected Dietrich and Florence.

From the start of my hunt with Dietrich and Florence; everything seemed like an unending blur of events. As I peered around in the new morning; my ears caught a faint sound of what rang out like a shovel. It sounded like the shovel had hit a rock, and in some ways it had startled me. I looked over at Dietrich's bed; it was now vacant and no longer in use. Florence was also missing; leading to my assumption that Florence had ventured out to bury Dietrich. I quickly then ran away from the site; the snow was kicking up violently from my feet. I ran about a hundred yards to the edge of Hank's property, to where my wandering self found Florence digging up a grave in the stone cold ground. "Flor!" I yelled.

Florence looked my way; peering over the hole he had dug. He then signaled for me to lower my voice. "Keep it down," I read in his lips.

"What! The hell are you doing?" I then exclaimed; soon changing my response to a mouthing one.

I then stomped over towards Florence, who continued to dig in the dirt in the making of

Dietrich's grave. He was sinking downward into a bitter cold grave; he was around four feet down at this point. I noticed he was working diligently; while also keeping his guards up and keeping well aware of his surroundings. "Old buddy, it ain't light yet! And they might be waiting for us in the shadows!" I then exclaimed in a whisper.

"What the hell does it matter anyways?" Florence inquired.

"The doctor, that's what matters! Now get back into the holy circle of our site! Before them bastards come back! Get out of there!" I continued to keep my exclamations in a whisper.

"I'm almost done! I've got this too by the way!" Florence then showed me his cross.

"Who cares at this point! He told us not to underestimate them!" I shouted.

"LET ME FINISH THIS FIRST!" Florence bursted out in wrath; his outburst actually silenced me a bit.

I warmed my hands in my mouth; I then rubbed them together for warmth as I had become quite hasty in my response. I collected myself for a bit, because in much honesty I was somewhat taken off guard by Florence's reply. However, even though there was a slight heat in our exchange, Florence continued on digging and going about his business. He was now about five feet into the ground and he was starting to hit stone at this point. He then backed up away from his progress and turned towards me. He stared at me, but did not say one word. He then reached over, and without any effort at all he pulled Dietrich's dead body, now wrapped in cloth, down into the hole hopelessly. He then smoothed out the wrapping and threw a few pieces of dirt on it. "I figured this would be deep enough," He then said calmly.

"You should've waited on me to help you, old buddy," I said in impatience. I then extended my arm outward to help Florence out of his newly dug trench.

Florence firmly grabbed my hand as I pulled him upwards. "Lord have mercy... I ain't cut out for this, you know," Florence commented.

"Ain't none of us are," I responded.

Florence then bent forward and dusted off his pants. He then turned around and looked downward at Dietrich's newly rested body. I stared at the body with him and began remorsing a bit in a moment of remembrance and silence. The cold winds hit our faces gently, as our mouths began to tremble a bit. We were shocked, but somewhat scared and confused. The heat was starting to build between the two of us, I could feel it too in regards to Florence's heated exchange back at me. "Sorry I was a burning flame on you earlier," Florence said.

"Don't even bother apologizing, old buddy," I replied.

"It's just, he's gone… I don't know what to do now?" Florence questioned. He then reached down and pulled his shovel out of the hole. Suddenly, Florence then shoved it violently into the ground in anger. "I don't know what we'll do now?" He questioned me again.

"It's two of us, versus two of them," I said.

"No, old boy, it's actually two of us, versus like forty of them… Remember, the power that Dietrich spoke of," Florence then corrected.

"I know, don't underestimate them," I then said.

Within our nervous exchange, both of us found ourselves oblivious to our newfound matter.

We were both processing the death and we were both frozen in time at that changing situation at hand. We stood there for about two minutes or so; not saying one word at all. The only noises that could be heard were a few early morning birds singing and the inhales and exhales of our breaths. We were steadily approaching some kind of end in this whole journey. For how it would end? Not one of us knew the answer. One thing was for certain; Thomas and Julius were on the loose and they were running out of space. Not only that, they were soon to be low on a significant source of life and bloodline. Despite our troubles, with heavy hearts deep within, we covered up Dietrich's grave and gave our final farewells as we soon found ourselves back out on the trail once more. We had wrapped all of our belongings and examined the full extent of the remains in Hank's rubble. The lodge was of course nothing but charred remains and small bits of smoldering infernos. However, it seemed very dead, so we just shrugged it off and continued forward into the unforgiving Texas wilderness.

The sun climbed quickly, as did the temperature outside as we descended off of the mountain. It was now around noon when we found ourselves back at a lone river, for which I did not know the name of. Personally, I was more far east than I had normally traveled; so much of this part of Texas seemed extremely unfamiliar. My thoughts bumped about, as my horse and Florence's horse carried us slowly through the graciously set treelines and groves of Northeast Texas. I still thought of Dietrich; we had left a cross at his graveside. Along with it, Florence had left a note which read: *Kiss Vera when you arrive up there we love you and miss you doc.* There wasn't much to say from that moment onward, from both of us. We moved along quietly through the rest of our journey. However, both of us kept our eyes wide open for anything out of the ordinary.

We soon found ourselves further up the river with no name; it was a half past twelve now and the sun was straight forward in the center by this point. We stopped at a river bend to get the horses some water and to give ourselves a quick bite to eat and our own refreshment of fluid. We untied both of our saddlebags and led the horses towards the water for a quick drink. The horses calmly moved onward; while Florence and I soon settled gracefully upon some rocks about a hundred yards behind them. Florence whipped out a cigar and lit it. To which I acknowledged, "Is that your last one?" I asked in a smile.

"Unfortunately yes, so I'm gonna enjoy every last second of it," Florence replied.

I smirked at Florence's comment; we then both sat there in silence for a few moments. I gazed fondly upon the beautiful landscape and river before us. I took in every ounce of beauty and stared admirably at it in amazement. Our horses remained embedded in a slow moving river as they drank, and our supplies from what we had left were now detached in bags and perched along the riverside in grace. We were at a height of peace and serenity now. "I'm sorry I left you both after Bertha," I said to Florence, finally apologizing.

"Hey, no worries old boy, ain't none of that relevant now," Florence replied.

"I don't care, I'm still feeling the regret of leaving you two," I then sorrowfully added.

"Ter, you left, but you came back... And you saved our asses," Florence said, correcting himself. He then took a huge puff of his cigar. For a moment he stared at me; then he looked away and glanced back at the beautiful surroundings. "Quite frankly, you saved us from a lot of headaches long before Hank's Lodge," He then added.

"I understand, but there's been something far more complex in my mind, and I ain't one to confess it really," I said.

"What the hell might that be?" Florence asked.

"Anna, my sweet Anna," I responded. For the first time in a long time though, I started to feel tears welling up slowly within the corners of my eyes. "She, um," I then nodded my throat; I was trying to hold back the emotion. You see, I was pretending to be tough, but in this exchange I couldn't contain it. I did the best I could in explaining Anna's death and my daughter's. "She again, passed away... Back last autumn, her and the baby," I explained once more to Florence. I then put my hand to my eyes and wiped away a few tears.

Then there was an uncomfortable silence; it lasted about fifteen seconds or so. However, within that short span of it, much of it felt like hours. I sat there in saddening regret as every single moment of good and bad between Anna and I flashed before my memory. I was growing from this traumatic event, and I could tell that Florence was picking up on my ever changing ways. "Listen old boy, I know it still hurts...I figured long before you told me the other morning about Anna, that something was off with you...Because you didn't seem like your old self when I first ran into you, on that night in the grove... I know, this type of hunt isn't what you're used to, but in a way, I think that under that damaged interior is a man, who's still the same at heart... Though much of him remains somewhat broken... Which is why he ran away from the things he couldn't face... That's you old boy," Florence commented; he was beginning to paint a very surreal picture of my life and emotions up until that moment and I could feel a closure was coming to us.

"Where were you going with that?" I asked.

"I'm just saying that sometimes the things that give us the most fear, are actually sometimes the things that build us up... I understand that pain, and I don't blame you for leaving, but we're dealing with something far greater than just evil... We have to face it, old boy, both of us... Do this for Dietrich, the town of Canden... Do it for her, Anna," Florence said.

I then felt my tears dry up a bit; I had become extremely motivated by Florence's words. "You know pal, I used to give you advice, many years ago, but now I see, you're starting to do the same for me, and I thank you," I said; I then grinned in admiration and shook my head. "Maybe it's time I stop running from the sorrows that wish to eat me alive on the inside? Maybe it's time I, and you, both of us, face those troubles together?" I then questioned Florence.

"I wholeheartedly agree, and if all else fails, in the end, we know where we're going from here," Florence then added in a smile.

I smiled upon Florence's remark; my eyes then wandered downward at a shiny object. It reflected a bit of sunlight and much of it caught my interest. I leaned forward to get a better view; buried within the top part of a few pebbles was a bullet shell casing. Though it wasn't just any old bullet casing, it looked very similar to the ones that came out of my chamber. I walked over and picked it up, carefully examining each and every imperfection on it. It was the same in diameter as the bullets I had been using, an eleven millimeter in size. It was unique in appearance and each blemish looked very familiar. I even noticed a bit of blood on it. It almost looked as if the bullet and casing had somehow been lodged in someone and had fallen out. "Hey, come look at this," I said to Florence.

He was already bewildered by my actions, "You find something odd there old pal?" Florence asked.

"Not odd, just very familiar," I replied. "Looks an awful lot like the bullet casings that come out of my colt chamber," I commented.

"Well, there's only one way to find out," Florence said. He then motioned for me to hand him the shell, to which I did. "Open your chamber," Florence sternly commanded.

I opened the colt, it *sprang* out as Florence nestled the shell casing comfortably within one of the holes. Obviously, it was just a shell casing but still, it was very odd to say the best of words. It perfectly fit, "Still though, that doesn't prove it came outta here," I commented.

"Yeah, but think about it… Why in the Lord's name is that shell casing, doing out here in the middle of nowhere?" Florence asked.

There was a small pause between us, both of our minds were constantly thinking of an answer we couldn't find. "If it did come out of what we think it came out of, then last night, we shot one of them bastards, and they're staggering around now with an open wound," I said in confidence.

"Look, you see that," Florence then pointed his finger towards the tall grass along the shore of the river.

Upon first glance, it took me a second or two, but I finally caught an eyeful of what Florence was caught by. Within the tall, dead looking grass; there appeared to be a slight disturbance in the confines of the rustling brush. The grass appeared to be weighted down and almost moved about as if a horse had possibly come through. We then quickly noticed horse hoofprints within the rocks and cold mud by our feet. It was clear that someone, or a group of individuals, had recently come through the area, and were possibly nearby. We were now back into a full hunt and investigation scenario. Florence and I quickly got our belongings together and rounded up the horses. "We'll follow that trailblaze, stay close to me," I told Florence.

"You think it's Julius and Old Tom?" Florence asked.

"Not sure old buddy, but we'll follow it regardless," I said.

I could feel Florence's nervous anxiety heightened; he gulped as I told him and as for me I did the same gesture as well. We then motioned our horses and slowly traveled along through a high plain. The grass of this plain stretched for miles and miles. We traveled away from the river with no name, with not one ounce of answer as to what we were following. We were desperate men, and we were determined to finish this reign of terror. The reign of terror, that had been unleashed through the dreaded powers of the undead, and the group we called 'The Fang Gang.'

Chapter 24

Our senses were very in tune with all of the nature that surrounded us. We were now about ten miles from our spot, where we had started at the river. We were fastly moving through the remaining course of the afternoon. It was quite warm in this part of the trek, but as soon as we crossed over a few more small creeks and hills I started to notice a slight drop in temperature. The grass was still fumbled about as we kept a close eye upon the grounds and terrain ahead. Quite literally, we were following a trail that had been blazed by a few or more horses. Whether they were Julius and Thomas' we weren't certain?

We had strutted along a flat plain for a long while; until we found ourselves in this wide open valley with four separate ridges on either side. We were low, the grass seemed dead, and we were surrounded by cedar wood pines. The sun was starting to sink over the ridge to the west; that's when my eyes started to lose sight of our mysterious travelers and their blazed trail. The grass was still fumbled about and still appeared to be disturbed. "Seems like our loss of light is starting to take its toll, old boy," Florence remarked.

"This here seems odd... The trail blaze seems to stop right here," I said.

I pointed towards the ground; as the fumbling about and matted down grass slowly receded to normal. "These winds have probably created an obstruction," Florence said.

"God only knows, this could mean many trails matted and many different types of hoofprints," I hopelessly stated.

"Regardless, are we heading back up on that ridge tonight?" Florence asked.

"No old buddy, we're setting up fire right here," I replied.

"In the middle of this Godforsaken opening?!" Florence inquired in exclamation.

"Well, I figured hiding out wouldn't attract them," I confidently responded.

"You do make sense there, old boy," A look of realization came over Florence's face as he responded.

With that I nodded and hopped quickly off of my horse. We sat up a small makeshift fire and rounded up a few other supplies to have on us for our first part of the evening. This included small quantities of food, water, whatever remaining alcohol we had left, and of course Chirstian relics to ward off any oncoming vampires. By this, I of course meant Julius and Thomas, the only remaining undead fiends we had left. I perched back a few small dry sticks and built a small warm fire while Florence leaned back and relaxed his head upon a small rock behind him. We were positioned in the middle of a wide open prairie; with again a dense and overly abundant pine and cedar drenched forest on either side.

The ridges of this forest surrounded us; every single inch of it felt undisturbed and unexplored. None of this wilderness looked to be tamed. For a lighter word, we were in the middle of the wild, and in the midst of God's country and His country only. Before time had even crossed my mind; I bent my head downward to check on my pocket watch. It was now a few minutes past five. By now the sun was beginning to set, and if there were to be any enemies nearby, of course sundown would be the time to attack. Though we remained aware, we remained surefooted and very faithful to the protection of the Lord's Holy gifts placed around our campsite.

The only food we had left were a few slices of stale bread and a few jarred up apples that Florence had brought along. I cracked open the jar of apples; I was in the mood for something quite sweet, yet very filling. The jar made a loud *pop* sound as it echoed slightly throughout the dead dusk filled prairie. It was quiet, too quiet. The jar popping even caught the horses attention; to which they whimpered a bit. "Hopefully those still taste like they did when we were kids," Florence smiled.

"I have no doubt they will," I commented. I then took a small glob of apples and put them slowly into my mouth. "Not bad," I complimented. The apples were quite tender yet very soluble. "Here, old boy," I said; extending the jar outward for Florence to take a few.

"Don't mind if I do," Florence said; he got up from his position and gently took the jar from me. He took a huge glob out too and took a big bite. "Stored these," He started; however, halting his speech as he continued to break down his food. "I stored…these bad boys back…wanna say, last July," He said.

"Well, it tastes like yesterday, and it tastes like childhood," I warmly commented.

"It sure does," Florence agreed. "To be quite honest, old boy, boar shit in the middle of this field tastes good right about now," Florence said; he then turned around and went back to his resting place at the rock he had been sitting at. He leaned back confidently; taking in a huge inhale, "You know though, I feel very stressed though, more than anything," He said.

Looking around at that exact moment; I then noticed a small remedy and that was English Lavender. "You know what you need," I commented.

"What's that?" Florence asked.

I then got up and retrieved a few pieces of lavender. "This right here…when it burns, my oh my, you talk about a stress reliever," I commented.

"English Lavender?" Florence inquired.

"Indeed brother, and it grows wild pretty much all year round," I said; I then began to burn it in the fire. The aroma of it blew in the cold breeze toward the vicinity of Florence. His nose snarled a bit as he began to breathe it in. "Already in good use, isn't it?" I asked.

Florence smiled, "Hell yeah, it's actually not too bad," He then reached inward and gently took the burning piece of lavender from my hand. "Though, it ain't that there peyote," Florence laughed.

I laughed subtly; I then sat down slowly in front of Florence. "Since when did you try that there stuff?" I asked.

"What? Peyote?" Florence asked.

"Yeah," I replied.

"Oh, it was Dietrich," Florence laughed. "We actually ran into some growing wild last week, it was way before we found our way towards that grove where we met you," Florence explained.

"Oh I see," I smiled; then I reflected upon a sweet memory and moment of laughter I had with Anna back last summer. "Well, personally I'm not one to speak of, but Anna and I actually got some from a local Comanche Native back home, last June... and let me just say, I don't have any memory of that night," I said. "You wanna talk about seeing some crazy shit," I then chuckled a bit.

"We didn't use it for that purpose, but we used it for our joint pain," Florence said; he smiled at my story. "Doc said it was a good remedy," Florence then went into a deep train of thought, he looked dazed.

"Really miss that man," I commented. "Really could use him right about now," I then solemnly added.

"Yep, me too, but you know something Ter?" Florence asked me.

"Yes, old pal," I replied.

"You've really come into your own on this here expedition," Florence then grinned. "You might have to change your status of hunting when we get back home, because you might be good at bounty hunting, but I think you ain't too bad at vampire hunting, if I'm honest," Florence then tipped his hat forward.

"Yeah, well, I just felt like I needed to do what I needed to do, because honestly, it ain't about the money no more," I said.

"I believe you came back to Hank's for a greater reason too, old buddy," Florence commented. "To me, you've got these layers, and under that confused mess that you've said, you are, I still see a true spirited individual, no doubt," Florence smirked some; he then went back to inhaling the aroma of our lavender.

"Woo wee," I said. "That's some strong smelling stuff," I commented on the strength of the smell.

"Very relaxing, thanks old buddy," Florence said.

Then suddenly, from a far off distance we heard a horse cry. It wasn't our horses of course; so it only meant a mirror of many different sources. It could be a Commache? Though both of us were in doubt of this. It could be a couple of desperados wandering about in the trees? Though I had not one ounce of belief in that. Only one source or two could produce this, and both of us were initially believing it. It was more than likely Julius and Thomas. They were either approaching us or they were staying at bay watching us closely. Either way, both Florence and I stopped dead within our moment of peace, and quickly turned our attention into making a final plan.

Chapter 25

Again, our senses were well in tune. We were in a state of shock; yet not one of us had one moment to stay right where we were. The enemy was approaching; it was sundown, and now it had become their time to come out and play again. Though, this time, Florence and I were prepared for anything. We may have just the two of us, but we've got the faith of the most faithful. A vast number of crosses and other holy items were spread about along the plain. It created a safeguard between us and them. We had firmly made crucifixes hanging from our necks and we had loads of goods ready to face them. No matter the outcome of this final showdown, we were prepared. It was a showdown at sundown, and it was only us and the holy Love of the Lord before us.

It was the strength of forty or so men; versus the mere weakness of us two men. Only again, we had that faith, more powerful than other weapons we had ever held. Florence and I gathered ourselves together and quickly grabbed our defenses. Within the eerie dread that was that late winter's dusk; we stared hopelessly as two riders came approaching us. Our eyes were locked upon a ridge towards the west. More than likely they had seen our fire, which was the plan all along. However, was it a trap that I set? Furthemore did I fully understand the outcome from here? To be honest, I had no clue at this point. It was either spring the trap, or have them spring another trap upon us.

Our anxieties had started to build as the surrounding air we breathed got thicker and the pressure of that atmosphere got more unbearable. I swear to you, every time we came in the presence of one of these crazed fiends; it felt as if the world was off of its rotation. The environment of us seemed elusive and the ever growing evening felt more like an eternity of pain coming. I *clicked* my gun and then cocked it back. Florence did the same; though he remained steady as I had wanted him to. Then they were no more than five hundred feet away, maybe it wasn't Julius and Thomas? I questioned this in my mind, though within seconds I soon realized it was more of a hope than anything else.

I was honest to God hoping it wouldn't be them, but for better or worse we had an enemy to face, and we both had made a promise to Dietrich to finish them off. Though I remembered to not underestimate their power, nor did I not forget to use my heart instead of the instincts within my mind. I was a rattling brain though, nervous as I bumped about violently from one bad thought to the other. "Maybe it ain't them?" Florence inquired.

"No, wait old boy," I replied; I motioned my hand for Florence to stay calm.

Within the fast trotting of one hundred feet, we soon recognized our evening travelers. To our unfortunate dread, it was Julius and Thomas. Thomas was dressed like a Texan, much like Florence and myself. He was wearing a thick buffalo hide upon his pants, he had on a thick fur coat, and he was wearing an oddly made cap. It looked to be made from a badger, but also interwoven with a raccoon. It was odd looking, but not as odd as what Julius was wearing. He had on a large fur scarf that draped all the way down his body. He was wearing a black long peacoat, and he had perfectly combed and slicked back hair. His hair was darker than ink though somewhat faded, and his eyes were just the same. "Lordy on high! Lordy! Woo Wee!" Thomas exclaimed.

"Your hair still looks as nice as ever Julius, but I'm afraid it's starting to show a touch of grey," Florence commented; he was cheap talking.

Julius grinned, "Really? That's how you start our exchange? A cheap insult? Only shows true weakness, really," Julius angrily commented.

"This ain't no exchange here pal," I started; I then regurgitated up some phlegm and spat hastily upon the stone cold ground. "You know why we're here," I said; I could feel my skin start to burn and my blood start to boil with rage.

"What happened to the rest of your possy?" Thomas impatiently asked.

"You oughta know Tom… You both started that shit show back at Hank's… That's what killed the poor soul!" Florence stated in anger.

"We?" Julius inquired; a look of shock drenched his completion. "No, you think this, but in a harsh reality, it was both of you that killed him," Julius pointed at us, saying his words in an innocence that felt very unappealing to me. "Have you ever thought of this? Both of you?" Julius inquired.

"Nah, because there's no reason to!" Florence angrily replied.

"Well, let it sink in, and for the record, let me open your minds for a moment," Julius said; however the tone of his voice was starting to shift to a very welcoming one. Though Florence and I knew deep down not to buy it.

"And what the hell should our minds be open to?" I asked; I was readying myself for anything.

"Think about these defenses you've placed before you, bounty hunter, sheriff," Julius stated; he was frantically thinking upon every word. Thomas was standing by; though under his breath I started to hear *hissing* and animal noises being made. Almost as if he was mocking Julius. "Quiet friend," Julius calmly stopped Thomas. "As I was stating my friends, you have these defenses, but are they enough? Have you ever thought of the fact that what you're fighting for is no different from what you're fighting against?" Julius firmly inquired.

"What do you mean?" I asked.

"The real monsters, the real demons, are humans really," Julius replied. "That crucifix you hold dearly, is mostly just used as a false weapon... It is a weapon, a means to protect, but just remember how much blood was drenched all over it... How many tears of innocence were cried over it when your country, your homeland, your place you call free found its way out here and KILLED EVERY last one of them, those Native to this place... You stole it from them, this land, and you'll continue to steal it for many generations to come," I could read fury in Julius' face.

"And don't forget about the women we've raped... The waters we've poisoned, the villages we've wiped clean either, bounty hunter!" Thomas intervened in rage.

"Yes friend, all of that too," Julius commented on Thomas' point. "Furthermore, in the long run of these trials though, through that disgrace you've called faith and ransom paid sin, I see a man before me who's quite honestly, just as lost as the country and state he serves... A man running from something, yes bounty hunter I can read the confusion and despair within those eyes, you can't hide it from me," Julius then turned completely motionless within his face.

I gazed upon Julius and Thomas within a creepy silence; the only sound heard was the heavy breathing of all four of us. I started to feel my head throb violently and I could feel slight droplets of sweat pour down my backside. The moment had become more tense than I had ever anticipated. The air was growing thicker and much colder now. I could feel my heartbeat increase and I could feel every inch of my fingers start to tremble beneath my gloves. I knew that any moment now, somebody was going to snap like a twig. Somebody was going to unleash in wrath; whether it'd be the undead before us or Florence or I, I was for certain? Somebody's nerve was about to get plucked, but we all stood on our grounds, all of us. "You paint a very surreal picture in your head Julius," I commented. "You've got unmatched perception, and you've certainly brought up your points," I said. Though I was agreeing, I was veering in a new direction of reasoning. "Though, some of it," I started; Julius then raised his hand in a polite interruption.

"No, hunter, all of it! Is true! All those words I've said about humanity! You are monsters beneath your churches, your crosses, and all of the other good faithful objects you've knelt before!" Julius exclaimed; he was growing impatient I could tell. "You see, you and your sheriff have only witnessed these atrocities for a mere fraction of a lifetime… Whereas I have seen your downfall for many lifetimes… I have seen many wars, I have seen the savagery you've all unleashed, and mercy upon the souls of those damned… All that was committed is a nasty blood stain… You can't hide it either, the stain… That mark drenched upon the fallen snows of time," Julius deeply spewed.

I then pondered a bit, but quickly found my voice. "That may be, but you've never seen the love of brothership," I turned my head towards Florence and nodded. He immediately acknowledged my statement and slightly grinned. "You've never seen the values of friends, nor have you ever looked into a woman's eyes and told her you loved her… Even though that woman had died a horrible death… Dear Lord, even though she did, I still loved her, and I still love her" I said; I could feel my emotions start to brew as I thought deeply about my dear sweet Anna and our deceased baby.

"You're in fear though, bounty hunter! You can't hide that!" Julius hopelessly snarled.

"Maybe I am? Maybe I'm not? But the arguments made here are not quite valid on either side, and by this point we're just wasting time really," I sarcastically said. "Only one will ride out of here alive tonight, and it sure as hell ain't gonna be y'all!" I angrily stated.

"You better watch your choice of words, bounty hunter!" Thomas shouted; he then motioned his horse to ride.

"Then if fear isn't holding you both back! Come forward and slay us then! But I warn you! Both of you are gonna wish you hadn't messed with us!" Julius exclaimed.

"Oh trust me partner, it ain't gonna be the dumbest thing I've ever said or done," I said with a smile.

Then without hesitation I leaned backward and grabbed a pouch of highly explosive gunpowder from my horse's saddle bag and threw it promptly in the air. It dustied the fallen ground around the wooden crosses that blocked us from Thomas and Julius. Florence and I stared in admiration. Thomas and Julius were drawing guns; that's when I quickly lit a match and threw it towards the ground. Fire shot up fast and a massive explosion interrupted the firing of Julius and Thomas' gunfire. Fast and without much waiting; Florence and I both ducked the hail of bullets from the two. It was chaos again! Though this time, it was a blazing inferno in the middle of a wide open field at sundown.

It was crazier than hell as some might perceive, but it was either kill or be killed. Sure my motive may have been outlandish or fool hearted, but I had that faith within, and I wasn't about to let this evil get away and continue in its undead and unholy terror. All of the noise was quite simply drowning though, our horses refused to move. Mainly because of the gunpowder explosion, but we were headstrong and without much caution as we trotted forward. All of the crosses and other holy objects were burning; quite literally I was facing demons and in many ways I was facing my fears. Florence didn't hesitate either; he had his gun drawn and he was firing away. We moved fast around the outer edges of the fire; shooting our bullets straight through the dancing and violently scattered flames. My heart was a non stop drum and my legs were a non stop spasm as I continued to motion the horse in every single direction.

Sporadically we were missing every single gunshot, and miraculously we were still alive. Our faiths again were strong and our intentions were bravery at the most dense measure. I ain't a man to be fearful, but in many ways it had manifested. Now, I was fighting it, Florence and I both were fighting it, or in this case them. Julius and Thomas moved around like rabid dogs. In many ways, their faces started to shapeshift into a being that looked like a sickened dog, if I'm honest. The cold air of that night strangely felt foreign to me, and at that moment I could care less if the fire and cold harmed me. Florence was giving off hip shots; we were down to our last blessed bullets. He fired one shot right in my left ear *BANG!* I jolted a bit from the sound; somewhat startled by his approach. "Ter! They're over yonder!" Florence shouted.

He pointed his finger towards the left side of the prairie. "Head this way!" I exclaimed; nodding my head into the right side of the outer edge of the vastly expanding fire.

We quickly trotted around the flames and made our way towards the other side. We were now on the other playing field; we were in the angry lion's den. The den though was a peacefully laid prairie and before us were two angry lions who were immortal. Julius and Thomas stared us down; we both stared right into the eyes with furious intentions. I cocked my gun back and checked my ammunition; I was down to a few more bullets. However, I still had another rifle locked and loaded on the right side of my saddle bag. I *clicked* the gun back and twirled it easily within my index finger. Florence's gun also *clicked* and within the blink of a fragment we charged them. They also charged us, and within no time we were running head on towards each other.

The burning crucifixes and other holy objects were still violently in flames towards our left. We didn't care though, we were locked within the moment, and we were frantically firing towards them hoping for a shot to send them out. I heard a few bullets *whistle* past my ear; I ducked of course and jolted forward everytime. *BANG! BANG!* Our guns rang out like the devil's chore and our horses cried like there was doomsday in sight. The plain and prairie we were stampeding upon was firm and stone cold, but not as stone cold as those eyes that watched us to our core.

Julius and Thomas had these stone cold, hardened eyes. I swear their looks made my skin crawl.

Florence and I were both brushing with death, but life had a whole other card to play. Miraculously, we all passed each other. Our horses were colliding so fast; nobody had not one moment to get off a close hip shot when the timing was right. Dear Lord, we were inches away, but not one bullet hit either one of us. My heart raced like the horses we were riding, and my head throbbed like the stomping of our steads hitting the winter's ground. Just as I believed the notion of coming out completely unharmed; a shot fired from behind to my right. *BANG*! Before I even had time to react; my horse's head exploded and toppled quickly towards the ground. I had blood and brain matter all over my torso and I had not one word to react with. I was paralyzed and petrified all the same. Everything moved so quickly; in no time I was falling towards my left side. I braced myself for impact, and within no second I was crushed by a now dead horse. It was truly a grim sight, but now I was to face a dilemma more scarce than the situation at hand.

I was now caught beneath the stead; my right leg of course was squashed instantly. I tried to move myself out but I was stuck solid. The stone cold ground felt very uneven where I was pinned. "Son of a bitch!" I exclaimed. The pain was excruciating, Dear Lord I thought this would be the fateful end. However, faith returned, and it wasn't too long until I heard another *BANG*! This time from my left side; it was Florence providing cover over me. Julius and Thomas had circled around and were coming for another attack. The fire *cracked* and *popped* as it continued to burn frantically among the crosses. Terrified wasn't enough to describe us, we were both speechless and in a somewhat trance-like state.

"I got you old buddy!" Florence exclaimed. He was firing off several shots towards an oncoming stampede. Julius and Thomas were approaching at a storm wind's speed. *BANG*! *BANG*! Florence was shooting off like a madman. His right hand was then hit; only Julius' shot hit Florence's gun directly, knocking it clearly out of his grasp. He dropped it towards his right, but this gave him a quick opportunity. He drew, and within one shot his bullet hit Thomas and his horse. They fell face first into the ground; landing a mere ten feet from my body. I was trying to pull myself out.

"DANG IT!" I cried out.

Florence exclaimed, "Don't worry! Old boy! I got—!" Before Florence could finish his exclamation; he was shot in the arm without any warning. His horse was then shot directly in the lower body; to which it instantly fell over on its left side. Florence though acted quick and landed clearly out of the way. He was free from being pinned, but he was now injured and being ambushed by Julius.

Julius rode past my position; I was still pinned beneath my stead and I was still trying to wiggle my way out. I was surprised that Julius didn't try to finish me. More than likely he was hell bent on finishing Florence, I wasn't quite sure? Regardless I was frantic, so I tried with more might to pull myself out, but nothing would give. Then over the horse's body, which now obstructed my view; I heard another series of gunshots. *BANG! BANG!* Then I heard a horse cry; almost as if another one had been shot in our massive parade of gunfire rain!

I then froze, not moving one muscle. I waited for the inevitable to attack me. However, nothing came for me, miraculously. Then with one more try up my sleeve, I wiggle once more; to which the horse's side finally gave in and I painfully moved my pinned self out. I then stood quickly; turning around I was though not out of the clearing! Oh Lord! I was ambushed from behind as I turned; I didn't even have one second to breathe. It was Thomas; who had now shapeshifted into a dog-like creature. He had these massive claws as he *shrieked* and *moaned,* dragging me violently across the grass. "Ah! Ah!" I shouted.

I was now truly paralyzed; though this time I knew it was for real! It was painful, and honestly I wanted the pain to stop. I could feel every bone in my body get tossed about and wrecked like a sack of pig's feed. It was brutal, and it felt like my whole body was being torn apart. Then Thomas picked me up and flung me over his head like I was no more than a small child. I flew through the air hopelessly; hitting the ground hard I felt every ounce of air get pushed out of my lungs. "Son! Of! A!" I exclaimed; though in my agony I couldn't even finish my swearing it hurt so bad.

Then out of nowhere; Florence came to the backside of Thomas. He attacked him with a long limb that had been broken in half from a nearby tree. He stabbed him in the arm and upper shoulder; barely missing the heart. This of course enraged Thomas; to which he then grabbed Florence by the throat and choked him with all of his might. I pulled myself up; I was trying to find my feet again as I was hoping to find the energy once again. I swear though; the pain was unlike anything I had ever felt. But I wanted to help Florence; so I started to drag my ass in the most grueling way possible. I crawled upon my knees; without any means to quit I was determined to kill Thomas. My ears rang, my mouth trembled, and my knees were starting to buckle again. Dear Lord though I kept on moving, I never stopped.

Florence was still in a choke hold; he was holding back this horrid demon's claw. Pondering a bit, with what little action I had, I then reached into my pocket and grabbed my trusty bowie. Then I looked down; I could feel the blood and sweat start to pour. Then in my mind; infinite noises of over a million voices were ringing! They were telling me to get up! Keep moving! To which I did; I sprang up and attacked Thomas with everything I had in me. In doing so I pushed Florence out of the way and stabbed Thomas right directly in the chest. Flames then shot up and within seconds I flung back once more. The bowie was still in my hand; Florence though was unfortunately in its line of path.

Landing backward, as Thomas slowly decayed into a million fragments; I found myself settled upon the grounds again only this time I held the knife directly into the chest of Florence! Dear Lord! Somehow by accident; I had landed on him and stabbed him in the chaotic predicament! Lord have Mercy, guilt immediately drenched my well-being! The knife was lodged deeply too; there was no way that Florence would survive this. "OH NO! NO! Old buddy!" I cried. I then rotated around and perked up Florence's half dead body in a sitting-like position.

I then got up and drug his body over towards a small perched boulder in the middle of the grass. There was no sign of Julius, but I didn't care at the moment as I was more concerned for the status of Florence and if he'd be okay or not. As I perched him upward, I examined the deeply lodged bowie knife. My breathing was getting heavier and I could feel every nerve in my body begin to shake erratically. Then Florence raised his hand and stopped my caring to his wound. "It's alright old boy," He calmly stated; his color was beginning to turn to a whiter shade. Blood was oozing out and I knew there was no way of stopping this madness. "Don't you feel bad… Don't feel bad about this," Florence said in a struggle.

"But I will!" I screamed aloud. "I'm the dumb son of bitch!" I then trembled upon my words; I couldn't finish my chaotic ramble.

"No old boy, you ain't dumb… You're only human… You make mistakes, so don't bother with it," Florence said; I could tell he was dying now. "Old slick back hair ran up in the trees… I think," Florence painfully spoke with every word. Then he coughed; a massive glob of blood shot out of his mouth. "Old boy, go finish him… Go finish his ass off… Remember I'll be watching from above," He then smiled slightly and gave me a noble nod.

"No you ain't watching from nowhere! Because you ain't dying on me!" I exclaimed; at this point I was begging for him to hang on. However, these were soon to become Florence's final moments; unfortunately deep down I knew this but I was in sheer denial.

"It's alright, again, you're human old boy… Now, get him…Go—" Florence didn't finish his sentence though. He then slumped his head over and took his final breaths as he died hopelessly in my eyes.

I of course cried; though my tears welled like a violently dug spring. I then lowered my head and firmly held Florence's shoulder tightly. Losing him was more hard than losing Dietrich. Obviously, Florence was like a brother to me, and it was harder than any other loss besides of course Anna and my baby girl. I was saddened, but then that sadness slowly brewed and stirred into a feeling of enraged revenge. I was now hell bent on one person, Julius! The bastard had scurried off like the coward he was into the nearby forest, and I was now determined to slay him no matter if my own life would be in jeopardy or not.

Chapter 26

There was no perception of time now; it was now man versus man. In this case, the living versus the dead. I sprung to my feet and ran like a rabid dog into the surrounding wooded area. I was trucking along a ridge to my west; the sun was setting and now it was half past dusk. The sky was beautiful in some way; neatly painted with a deep orange and faded purple. Though in that scenario I could care less honestly. Not one thing looked inspiring to me; I was headed to kill Julius, and there wasn't anything along my path to stop me now.

I had become the very thing I was uncertain about becoming from the beginning, and that of course was this vampire hunter. I started out on this journey not believing, and now here I was. I was the final man too, the last one standing. I didn't deserve to survive that scuffle back in the plains moments ago, but I guess the Dear Lord has Mercy indeed upon my soul. One certainty that never left my side, was this brisk air that suffocated me as I pushed my half beaten and battered body through the trees and over many fallen branches. Limbs *cracked* and *snapped* as I made my way hopelessly through the forest. I was keeping my eyes peeled closely; watching every single tree and gap and keeping a close watch upon every single odd movement that seemed off center to me. As I made my way through the shrubby; I soon found myself half dazed in the middle of this opening in the cedars and oaks.

The area started to spin and I began to black out a bit. In a furious moment I then slapped myself across the jawline. I was doing anything in my power to keep my well-being on high alert and on great observation. I staggered more, but eventually I came back. I found myself, however, at one point, nearly vomiting. Regardless I was back into life again and I was now more driven than ever. I heaved a bit and caught my breath back. I then stood to attention and looked forward once more; to which I noticed a bit of uneven movement ahead. About one hundred yards ahead I saw an outline move from left then to right. It then darted quickly; it was him! It was that no good son of a bitch! I drew and fired *BANG*!

Unfortunately, my shot only hit the tree in which Julius was hiding behind. It shattered into a billion fragments as I then fired again. *BANG!* Another tree was hit again by my shot. However, this time I nicked the side of Julius' right arm. He then began to catch fire as he ran fast down the side of this ridge "Ah!" I screamed aloud. "YOU CAN'T RUN JUL!" I then shouted in wrath.

My voice echoed throughout the cold dead forest as I then followed Julius. Yes I was a fool, but it was all for nothing. Now those who had hunted, were now being hunted. I was the predator I had always been as a bounty hunter, and I was for sure carrying that notion into the realm of hunting vampires. Yes, all of this seems crazy, but then again so was this long and perilous journey. I was keeping every step upon the ground well footed, and I was keeping my half dazed vision at the utmost focus. I drew my gun again; Julius was now right in front of me, or so I thought. As I pulled the trigger; I was then attacked from my right side. It was actually Julius this time; not the illusion he had created in front of my vision.

I was fooled, but I had no time to think now. I gave everything I could in that moment of distress. Julius and I then fought each other upon the cold hard ground. I threw the last pieces of mustard into his eyes. "AH! AH!" Julius reacted in pain.

I frantically reached towards my right; I was grabbing a sharply broken limb. However, Julius thought quickly and grabbed my right hand and snapped it backwards. "AH! OH MY GOD!" I exclaimed. It was the most excruciating pain imaginable. My bone quite literally popped out of my skin and poked a small hole through my glove! Blood shot out! "DEAR MIGHTY!" I shouted. I couldn't even cry. It hurt so bad. I just laid back and slowly took it all in. I closed my eyes for a second and then quickly opened them up. I was hoping to find that strength again, however, I was too weak! It was too late! Julius had grabbed a long sharp limb and was now holding it over his head. He then with all of his power, rammed it into the left side of my chest. I was shoved back a bit and was now breathing in the final bits of air I had left.

I was dying now, and hopelessly I stared at the fiend with much regret. Though I was still clinging to life a bit, because despite the wound, I wasn't fully dead yet. Julius had stabbed me in my left side, though this wasn't where my heart was. As Dietrich had stated before, my heart was oddly on my right side. Julius certainly was not aware of this defect. In doing so, he now believed he had the upper hand in this situation. However, of course this wasn't the case. In my cold death of silence; I quickly fell backward and played dead. It was hard to not cry, and it was hard not to make some sort of groan. The blood was trickling down through my upper torso; I could feel the cold chill of death now coming to take me. Though again, I was still alive, and Julius was now at his most naive state.

As he turned, he sat himself down on the ground and examined his small injuries. I could hear him subtly grumble and chuckle under his breath. I held my breath, for what seemed like four months, and then within a blink of no more than one second I sprang up. The wind hit me; it quite literally threw my back out, but I wasn't at the least in any concern. I was damned and determined; I had that final bit of life and air in me! My mind raced like the strongest wind imaginable. I grabbed Julius from the back; quickly he was in shock of course. I instantly put my worn down bowie to his throat, and with no time at all I put a crucifix around his neck. It was the same one that Dietrich had given before he passed away. Julius started *sizzling* as the cross burnt him from its touch. "AHHHH!" He shouted.

"One thing I've learned Jul, as a bounty hunter... Never turn your back!" I exclaimed in a soft tone; I was directly in his ear now. I then sliced his throat wide open.

His arms went wild; I backed up a bit and put my bowie down. Blood was flying everywhere and turning the ground from a white snow dusted floor, into a horrid mess of crimson and black shaded junk. I was somewhat mortified; I was now backed into a tree. Julius then turned around in my direction; though now his efforts were not a threat as his body began to slowly decay. In horror I watched him as every single heartbeat got faster and faster. He crawled hopelessly, as he began to melt. His skin became candle wax to much disbelief; his flesh fell off of him with much ease. He then rotted into a skeleton as his hand came merely inches away from grabbing me. However, to much relief, he never did reach me.

Julius and all of his remains then fell apart and subtly turned to dust. He was vanquished, and at long last he was destroyed. His power went into hell with him, this I was for certain. As for me though; I could still feel that slight brush of cold air and I knew it was death itself coming for me. It was painful, and it was a shameful way to end a journey. Two men, one completely disintegrated, and now one covered in blood. To be honest, I knew it'd probably end this way. Someone would die, but I didn't think it'd be all of us. However, they were killed off and the terror they had unleashed was destroyed, and so came my final thoughts in this thing called 'life.'

I rested back on that tree, reflecting back on all of the good times I had, and all of the bad too. Though mostly, I saw the good, and that's when I saw her again! Anna. My sweet wife. Though now she was appearing before me for real; beautiful as I had remembered, and now holding our healthy looking baby girl Isabella. I had died, yes, we all had died. Though this was the cost; this was a raging fire that had to be tamed. In doing so, I must say, I was rather relieved now. Nothing brought more comfort to my soul; for I was now complete. I was now reunited with Anna and the baby. I was away from this cold and damned world. I repented my sins, and now I have myself back to where I belong, and that place is with Anna, the baby, and a peaceful realm I now realize as Heaven itself.

This book again is dedicated to those who loved adventure growing up, the westerns of old, and the horror suspense of days gone by…

- Kevin s. Hendrick